W9-DIB-202

SELLING AMERICA

stories by

Tom Tolnay

Silk Label Books

Unionville, New York

Acknowledgments

The author gratefully acknowledges the periodicals in which nine of eighteen stories from Selling America have appeared or were acquired for publication. Some appear here in slightly edited versions:

"Fun & Games at the Carousel Mall," "The Stealing Progression," and "Train to Nowhere"— *Ellery Queen's Mystery Magazine*

"The Great American Appetite"—*Twilight Zone*

"Herman Burger's Tragic Flaw"—*North Dakota Quarterly*

"Universal Book of Knowledge"—*Dark Starr Magazine*

"Roots of Evil," "A Short Business Trip," and "To Each His Own"—*Pulpsmith Magazine*

Library of Congress Cataloging-in-Publication Data

Tolnay, Thomas
Selling America : a selection of stories starring a different purveyor or consumer of different products & services / by Tom Tolnay.
    p.cm.
ISBN 1-928767-38-9 (alk. paper)
1. United States--Social life and customs--Fiction. 2. Sales personnel--Fiction.
3. Purchasing--Fiction. 4. Selling--Fiction. I. Title.

PS3570.O4285S45 2005
813'.54--dc22

Copyright © 2005, Silk Label Publishing Co., Inc.
All Rights Reserved

Silk Label Books
First Ave, PO Box 700
Unionville NY 10988
845 726 3434; fax 845 726 3824
email: slb@rfwp.com; website: rfwp.com

ISBN: 1-98767-38-9

Printed and bound in the United States of America using recycled paper, vegetable-based inks and environmentally-friendly cover coatings by the Royal Fireworks Printing Co., of Unionville, New York.

Contents

About the Author

Tom Tolnay is the founder of Birch Brook Press, a publisher/printer of letterpress books of popular culture and literature. He is the former editor of *Back Stage* newspaper and former managing editor of The Smith Publishers. His fiction and poetry have appeared in a diverse mix of periodicals, including *Saturday Evening Post, Family Circle, Ellery Queen's Mystery Magazine, Woman's Day, Twilight Zone, The Literary Review, North Dakota Quarterly, Gallery, Alfred Hitchcock's Mystery Magazine, Southwest Review, Fly Rod & Reel, Woman's World, The Flyfisher, Colorado Quarterly, Chelsea Review.* Two of his novels, *Celluloid Gangs* and *The Big House,* were published by Walker & Company. His short story, "The Ghost of F. Scott Fitzgerald," was produced as a short film by Sea Lions Productions.

About SELLING AMERICA

The short stories in this book involve selling and buying in one guise or another, the mix of characters, prose styles and plots reflecting a spectrum of personalities and perspectives in sales, products, and services peddled, as well as in the techniques and motives that go into such transactions. While each has a separate story to tell—sometimes dark, sometimes light—each is part of a cumulative overview of a society in which the great majority of us have been channeled in one way or another into selling, marketing, promoting.

As in the typical sales pitch, sometimes the spiel in these stories is realistic, sometimes fantastic. The "bottom line," however, is that all of these accounts, directly or indirectly, incorporate one or more of the ways in which our personal, family, and social lives are altered, often—though not always—adversely, by the powerful, pervasive commercial circumstances of our time and culture. This is hardly news to you, and is by no means an appeal for the impossible—to roll back our lives to another time, another way of thinking, behaving, and functioning. Rather the intention is to remind myself (and others who might be interested), of what has happened to us through the individual stories of those who act out this compulsion on both sides of the counter: from sales person to customer and, in the case of one story, even when acquisitions are made without actually handing over cash, credit card, or check.

In America we are bought and sold at every twist of the dial, every click of the remote, every flip of the page, every opening of e-mail or tearing of an envelope, every lift of the receiver, every turn of the head on the highway—even in our dreams, as recorded in another story herein. With every dollar bill that changes hands, it seems, we spend a few more cents of our limited reserves of humanity.

Under such exhaustively planned and cynically focused indoctrination—such a consistent and intensive siege, how can we not think of ourselves primarily as conveyors and consumers, and only secondarily as wives and husbands and lovers, parents and teachers and students, artists and philosophers and poets, scientists and inventors and mathematicians?

And now a word from our sponsor: Can I interest you in buying a copy of this book?

**Who buys a minute's mirth
to wail a week?
Or sells eternity to get a toy?**

—William Shakespeare

A SHORT BUSINESS TRIP

Seventh Avenue Fasteners is the third largest button maker in New York—fifty million annually in more than one hundred styles. My job is to sell SAF Buttons to garment manufacturers, and my telephone style is considered classy, and relatively unsoiled by our boss' lectures on the boiler-room, hit-and-run approach to sales. I believe in service. If a customer (large or small) has a problem, I do my best to solve it—over the phone or, if absolutely necessary, in person. Recently a situation arose that required this kind of personal attention and, despite my credo, I was none too happy about it.

Bruno Styles, Inc. in Toledo, Ohio had a problem with our new line—a featherweight "miracle" plastic in a triangle. If our design department had asked me, I could've told them they'd have trouble with that item. Triangular buttons, like square balloons, just weren't meant for the real world. In buttons, round is still the standard, though you can sometimes get away with oval.

Sharply changing temperatures at our warehouse in Jersey city (in one evening we went from Indian summer to Eskimo winter), followed next morning by a severe jolting during shipment, apparently ganged up to nullify the miracle. The truck pulled up at Bruno Styles, not with a cargo of triangles, but with five-hundred boxes of blue, green, red, and white plastic crumbs. Only the Toledo people didn't find out until two weeks later, when they were ready to complete production on their new line of winter coats.

With unfulfilled orders mounting, Bruno Bleshensky stammered at me hysterically over the phone, "Your buttons have... exploded!"

I

A cold-pitch salesman would've turned his back and said, in essence, "tough shit." Not me. I reassured Bleshensky that some kind of adjustment could be made—assuming his story checked out.

"Adjustment?" he roared. "If you don't get your ass over here, consider this account *dead*." Then the phone went dead.

Even assuming he had good reason to hang up on me, I was miffed, and I sat there staring at the dead receiver, trying to be objective. The Bruno Styles account was not large enough to make an important dent in my annual sales tally, except in one respect: Ultimately it could've meant the difference in meeting my bonus quota, good for an extra fifteen hundred—off the books. That's worth nearly two thousand over the counter. Besides, with competition growing more cut-throat daily, I couldn't afford to be cavalier about *any* client—especially one who's been with me four years. Repeat business is the name of the button game.

After giving him a half hour to cool off, I dialed Bleshensky. "No reason we can't straighten this out," I told him. "I'll catch a plane for Toledo on Monday."

"Monday's no good, Hillman," Bruno squealed. "Modern Modes is hot for my business; they can have it the way I feel now."

The very sound of "Modern Modes" on the lips of one of my clients was like pouring molten lead into my heart. Following a silence during which the logistics of such a trip dashed through my mind, I said calmly, "I'll try to book onto a flight late this morning. *"If* I can make a connection, I hope to be out your way by mid-afternoon."

"I'm expecting you, Hillman," were the words he used, but his tone said: *You'd better be here.*

Partly it was that threat, and partly pride in my salesmanship that got me back on the horn, dialing American Airlines. Nevertheless I was disturbed I had to alter my plans for the day. I had prepared a list of twenty customers I was going to check in with—routine phone calls that mixed a little kabitzing with a little business. All part of my technique—a gimmick that almost always pays off somewhere along the line. But sometimes you've got to give your all to one client, and not just a little to twenty.

After hastily explaining the situation to my fast-talking, fast-walking boss—following him around the office, I smile-nodded through his story of how he would have handled such a "trouble-maker" in the old days. Then I placed myself in the hands of the Gods of Transportation. They were reasonably benevolent to me. I stopped a cab only one block from the office—by jumping in front of it after it had dropped off a passenger, and the cabbie made the mistake of letting me get seated before asking, "Where to?" When I said "La Guardia Airport," his eyes pinched and his nose dilated, but I served him that unblinking New York stare which means: *You'd better take me out to Queens if you don't want to explain it to a cop.*

For some uncanny reason, we breezed through the Midtown Tunnel. All the way to Flushing we had only one important delay—an overturned Macy's van. Thousands of dollars of mer-chandise—white cotton sweaters—were strewn across the Brook-lyn-Queens Expressway, their pearly buttons glinting in the cold sunlight. Yet I arrived at the terminal fourteen minutes in the black.

The take-off was delayed anyway. And by the time I had roared out of La Guardia and touched down at Toledo Airport, and had out-raced those newly weds to the only waiting cab, and had pulled myself out of the back on a dismal street at a forgotten end of a forgotten city, I was reassessing whether a day's ag-gravation was worth a new set of braces on the kids' teeth. Es-pecially since I didn't get to the plant until 4:36, which meant Bleshensky was going to be even more foul-minded than he'd been over the phone. Especially since I had to face that rapid-fire trip all over again in another couple of hours. The thought that I might even have to dine with Bleshensky, in Toledo, shot a chill through my flesh as if I had scratched my nails across a blackboard.

Stepping through the narrow doorway into the plant, I found it remarkably quiet—no roar of heavy, unoiled, outdated machinery. And clean! Usually the scraps of cloth and thread are ankle-deep. But they work differently outside New York, much too tidy for real output, real profit. Only five workers were visible, shutting down for the day. I approached one of them, a woman of about sixty, with a blast of white hair. "Where's Mr. Bleshensky's office?" I inquired. Without looking up from her workbench—wiping down the black industrial sewing machine with a care that bordered on affection, she pointed toward a steel door at the rear of the cinderblock building.

A well-timed cigarette has helped me through many tense situations, so I set down my briefcase and pulled out a box of Marlboros. But the woman in the print dress grunted and pointed to a sign: NO SMOKING. Pocketing the cigarettes, I moved toward his office, passing rows of metal-tube hanger racks: hundreds of ladies' coats were helplessly crushed against each other, buttonless, like people on a soup line during the Depression.

At Bleshensky's door I made sure my corduroy sport jacket was buttoned before knocking. Immediately a voice responded, heavily: "Come in."

Though I had spoken to Bruno Bleshensky many times, we had never met face to face, and I was surprised to find he was even taller than I—I am nearly six feet. Because of the Eastern European traces in his voice, I had always thought of him as a gracefully ripening contemporary of about forty. Bleshensky was deep into his fifties, ungracefully bulky, and had taken up combing his hair forward to coat the thinning spots.

Bleshensky apparently had sized me up better than I had him. "Good of you to come, Hillman," he said with only the barest edge of sarcasm. And I wondered if he knew my first name.

"Glad to meet you in person after all these years," I replied brightly, trying to remind him of our long association, extending my hand.

When Bleshensky pointed to a black chair alongside his desk, my hand fell back to my side as if a big deal had just fallen through.

Sitting down on the flat metal seat, I produced a reasonable facsimile of a mid-western smile. The stooped, square-shaped man got up and, with a rock-bottom weariness, said, "Must take care of something first." Stomping past me, he left the room and closed the door quietly behind him.

I looked around. The room was small and amazingly well organized for the office of a coat manufacturer, almost as if it had been straightened up for my visit. On his desk I saw the orders he had referred to over the phone—a wad of pink slips impaled by a pointed prong. Two pens and three pencils, sharpened, stuck out of a lucite cylinder. On the far wall was a framed industry proclamation, maybe on behalf of the National Garment Manufacturers Association, with the customary gold seal. Three olive green filing cabinets stood in the corner, all drawers fully closed.

It wasn't until I straightened my knitted tie for the third time that I admitted he had been gone far too long. Checking my watch—it was already past five, I was becoming concerned I might miss my return connections, that I might be forced to spend the night in a motel in Toledo. And I was upset that there hadn't even been enough time to call my wife before I left New York. Just when I was preparing to stand up and find out what had happened to him, Bleshensky entered the room. Without a word he closed the door, passed by me, and sat down behind the squat metal desk.

Glancing at my watch for his benefit, I said: "I'm sure we can straighten this matter out quickly, to our mutual satisfaction."

But Bleshensky's mind was in the past, not the future. "1970 I started this business," his accent suddenly thick, as if talking about those times required that earlier voice. "I was young man then—in this country only three years."

"You've really built it up," I replied, looking around the cramped office as if impressed.

Bleshensky slipped the batch of orders off the prong, leaned back in a wooden chair that seemed as old as he, and proceeded to leaf through them, one at a time. Checking my watch again, I managed to refrain from commenting directly on the 6:00 flight out of Toledo. *Business,* I reminded myself, *is business.* But I couldn't help thinking: *God knows when there'll be another taking off for New York from this outpost.*

At last he spoke. "How are these orders going to be filled?"

"That is exactly why I am here," I countered in my best business English. "To help solve your problem."

His furry eyebrows slid up his forehead.

"Our problem," I corrected.

"Buyers couldn't care *less* about my problems," he said, unleashing a traditional industrial gripe.

The familiar tone cleared a potential path of communication between us, for there is a measure of love we all share for this business, and which is manifested in our complaints about it. "Yeah, it's getting tougher every day to make a living in this field."

Bleshensky looked at me as if I had called him a fool. "Your buttons are no damn good!"

6

His head-on declaration caught me by surprise, and when I don't have time to prepare a reply, I have a tendency to lie. "Well, I have to tell you the truth—you're the first customer to experience trouble with our new line. The triangles are very popular."

"Do you know what I did when I left you here awhile ago?" he said.

It sounded rhetorical enough to keep my mouth shut.

"I visited with people who have been with me twenty-five years."

My eyes must've gone blank—at least that's how they felt inside: two tiny panes of glass out of which I was trying to peer at this stranger, someone who had suddenly acquired a physical outline like a caricature.

"Our customers have fallen behind in their payments," he stated, staring deeply into my eyes. "I figured if we could build up Christmas orders for our winter line, we'd pick up the slack."

I wanted to get up and leave, but it occurred to me I was bound to listen to his story because Bleshensky helped sustain the Hillman family, even if only in a small way. Precisely which way it was impossible to say. Commissions on sales to Bruno Styles might've taken care of snowtires on the Buick, Sheila's cavities, a bike for Bruce, and perhaps half a dozen trips to the beauty parlor for Joan. Beyond that, I had no reason to be sitting on that hard chair in Toledo, Ohio on a chilly autumn evening.

"Because I ordered 50,000 buttons from you," said Bleshensky, as if reciting from an annual report to stockholders, "my customers won't be getting their garments—never."

Suddenly I understood everything. *Bruno Styles Inc. was out of business, and nothing could be done to save the company.* The realization injected me with anger, and I momentarily lost sight of my duty: "You made me come *all the way* from New York to tell me you're shutting down?"

With crimped, dry eyes, Bleshensky said: "This business was my life."

Too long I sat there staring at the orders in his hand, and when it finally dawned on me that Bleshensky was no longer a client of mine, I reached for my shiny leather briefcase and stood up. That's when I spotted the framed photograph, lying flat, next to a coffee pot on a utility table: two small girls, one boy, and Bleshensky himself—with a full head of hair, his arm wrapped around a frail, dark-haired woman....

Out of his office I stepped with long, rapid, heavy strides, through rows of sewing machines, past rolls of cloth, toward the fireproof door.

THE GREAT AMERICAN APPETITE

A thin but sturdy figure entered a restaurant which had already stuffed and sent home the few patrons it had received on this chilly, drizzly evening. Sitting down at a round table in the center of the square space, the customer inserted his narrow face into the menu.

At a table in the corner, the waitress stopped counting her tips, pushed herself up off the chair, and moved to the occupied table. "Late snack, sir?"

The customer did not look at the waitress. (With her coils of greasy hair and eyes of no particular color, she was not much to look at.) "Sirloin steak—medium rare," he said. "Mashed potatoes, string beans. And coffee—regular."

The waitress had figured the miserable weather would make the manager send her home early again, and that her boyfriend might drop by her place for an hour or two of TV, or whatever. Hadn't the cashier left already, picked up by her husband in their Chevy? But now she had a customer, and if others should straggle in, she'd be there till eleven. Carrying a menu between her thin arm and bony ribs, on skinny legs the waitress marched glumly to the kitchen, and placed the order. The cook was a fleshy black man with two temperaments at his disposal—agitated or tranquil, very little in between. And the news that he had to stop reading the sports pages and throw a steak dinner together agitated him. Not only was he anxious to escape the hot stove, the heavy odors of mixed foods, but he had planned on getting home earlier than usual to butter a bowl of popcorn, pop a can or two of beer, and watch the late ballgame on TV. But he had mouths to feed at his apartment as well as at his job, so the cook folded the newspaper with a snap and cursed under his breath as he went about broiling the steak, and shoveling the potatoes and green beans: Since they bathed eternally in steam, the vegetables looked more gray than white and green.

After the waitress had served the beef, filled the mug with coffee—"milk and sugar's on the table,"—she sat down at the back table and, because it was a pleasant pastime, started counting her tips from scratch. As the coins clinked into the water glass, she hummed a tune that could be heard on the radio several times an hour, in between hamburger/french fries commercials. But when she had totaled her "take," she stopped humming: It was a rotten night for tips, worse even than the rest of the week. The bone-scraping dampness had forced people to sit at their own tables at home, eating leftover meat loaf or their household specialty in quickie, cheap meals—macaroni and cheese, Spanish rice, franks and beans, sour cream blintzes.

In a short time, the customer called the waitress. Quickly scribbling a bill, she stepped to his table, the pencil notched over her ear. "Check, sir?" she said, setting it face down between the salt and pepper shakers.

"Chocolate layer cake with whipped cream topping, please. Another regular coffee."

Taking a full breath, the waitress waxed philosophical as she collected the dishes, telling herself that if no one else came into the joint in the next half hour, the manager might still close up a little early. Into the kitchen she disappeared, and in a few minutes returned with the Pyrex pot of coffee and the slice of cake with a puff of cream on top. As she poured, the customer stared out the window into the night. His look was so determined it discouraged her from making small talk by commenting on the long stretch of awful weather. She retrieved the bill and headed back to her table.

After she had added the dessert and coffee to the tally, and had counted the coins and dollars in the glass again—arriving at the same total, the customer called out, "Waitress." Slowly she got up and went to his table, this time placing the bill on the napkin holder, where he could see it better.

"I'd like the shrimp creole," said the customer, "with a side order of broccoli."

The waitress looked into the intense, oily eyes of the customer a moment before saying, "Sorry, we don't do outgoing orders."

"What makes you think I'd have a picnic on a night like this?"

His tone was not unpleasant, so the waitress pursued another thought. But it was only *after* she had asked if something was wrong with the steak that she realized he had finished every scrap of fat, every lump of potato, every cut of bean. All that remained on his plate was the well-trimmed bone.

"Could you please bring me the creole?"

The waitress gathered the dishes, if hesitantly, and backed into the kitchen. "This guy must *really* be starved," she said to the cook. "He's ordered a second dinner."

The cook looked at the waitress as if to say 'I've got my own problems,' and he began dishing out the shrimp creole and broccoli: It took only a few minutes since both items were simmering in the stainless steel pans on the steam table.

When the food had been served, the customer asked, "Doesn't this come with bread?"

"If you want," said the waitress, turning away somewhat curtly. By the time she had returned with a basket of slightly stale light and dark slices, and a saucer of butter pats, the customer had already finished the broccoli and was scooping the creole into his mouth with the coffee spoon. With his other hand, he reached into the bread basket.

The waitress crinkled her nose at this spectacle, then went back to the corner table without bothering to consider why the customer was so famished. She added the new items onto the bill.

Three minutes later she drifted to the front window. The drizzle had turned to rain again ... a steady wringing of the clouds. But the rain pleased her: This customer would surely be her last of the evening. While she gazed out at the little raindrop explosions on the shiny black pavement and the water rushing along the gutters, she thought about her boyfriend, wondering what he was doing at that very moment: probably reading a horror novel, munching on potato chips. Then she heard a voice: "Oh, Miss. May I have some service?"

The waitress managed to hold onto her cheap smile as she tripped toward his table with the bill in her hand.

"I'll try the ham with pineapple rings," said the customer, his long finger pinpointing the entrée on the menu he had taken from a nearby table.

The waitress stared stupidly at the customer.

"Which vegetables come with the ham?"

After a few moments the customer had to repeat himself, and the waitress, stiff as a flounder in the freezer, finally loosened. "Oh, ham?—that's with sweet potatoes and corn."

"Creamed or kernel?"

"Either way."

"Creamed, please."

The waitress did not move. "Are you expecting someone else?"

"Where do you get these peculiar ideas?"

Abruptly the waitress collected the menu and dishes, and in the kitchen she dropped the heavy-duty porcelain into the greasy, leaden water of the washtub. "Now he wants the ham dinner!"

"The same guy?"

"He must have a hollow leg."

"And weigh three hundred pounds," added the cook who, weighing well over two hundred pounds, was beginning to get interested.

"That's the funny part—he's skinny as a hot dog."

Secretly flattered that someone wanted to eat so much of his food, the cook, tranquil again, lumbered to the round windows in the swinging doors and looked out. "Not bad for an amateur," said the cook, who had seen two or three skinny people put away plenty of chow in his time.

"Even if he could finish three dinners—which he can't," said the waitress, "he hasn't paid up on the first two."

"So that's his scam!" said the veteran cook. "Before I throw a ham steak over the heat, you better go tell the manager."

Respecting the cook's food-service savvy, the waitress tugged on her black-and-white uniform, then pushed through the swinging doors. She trod softly between the tables (the customer had the coffee mug to his mouth, bottoms-up) and entered the tiny office next to the rest rooms.

The manager sat at the tiny desk, receipts spread out before him, a calculator in the palm of a hand as meaty as a center-cut chop. "All this rain," he complained, jabbing the numbered keys hard, as if they were responsible for the poor business all week. "The owner's going to have a fit when he sees these figures."

"Looks like we got another problem besides," said the waitress, her hand on her hip, and she concluded her sad tale like this: "His check is over twenty-five bucks already—with the ham it'll be around thirty-five. Not counting tax and tip."

The manager, his body as hefty as a side of beef on a hook, hauled himself up from the desk, squeezed past the waitress, opened the door slightly, and peeked out. The customer was tapping his fingers on the plastic-coated tablecloth, making the sound of rain. "How can a man that thin eat three dinners?" the manager whispered.

"That's what I'm telling you. I think he's up to something."

It had been such a terrible week that the manager was afraid of scaring off any customer—especially one who was running up a big bill. At the same time he didn't want to get beat out of thirty-five dollars. "I'll go up front and take down today's list of specials and put up tomorrow's," he said. "You go to the customer and try to collect on the first two dinners. Don't insult him; speak nice. But if he makes a run for it, I'll lock the door."

"Supposing he gripes about paying before he's finished."

"Just tell him it's restaurant policy."

The waitress looked doubtful as she watched the manager roll up his shirt sleeves, snatch the typed sheet and cellophane tape off the desk, and sneak out the door.

As the manager moved to the front the customer called to him, "I certainly hope your waitress is okay."

"What do you mean?" said the manager.

"I was afraid she might have died on the way to the kitchen."

"Sorry, Sir. She'll be right with you."

And she was—bill in hand, and still looking doubtful.

"Where's my order?" said the customer with more than a trace of annoyance.

"It'll be ready...in a minute," stammered the waitress. "But could you please...pay this check now?"

"I haven't finished," the customer protested.

"Yeah, I realize, but it's restaurant policy."

The customer aimed a line-up of sharp teeth at her. "Afraid I'm going to take off without paying?" he asked, licking the creole sauce off the tips of his fingers.

14

Not knowing what to say, the waitress merely blinked at the customer, who finally reached into his jacket pocket and pulled out a leather wallet as fat as a double-burger.

With plenty of white showing in his eyes, the manager, taping the list of specials to the glass door, watched the customer slip three greenbacks from a wad that must've been an inch thick and toss them into the empty bread basket.

"Thank you, sir," said the waitress, grabbing the basket with a trembling hand.

"Now how's about hurrying up that ham and sweet potatoes."

As she scooted to the kitchen, the waitress inspected the greenbacks closely. The cook, who had also watched the customer flash the overstuffed wallet, was already chucking a thick slab of ham into the microwave oven. In a few minutes, the cook piled the food on a large white platter and said, "This'll shut him up." There was enough for two meals.

The manager was gone when the waitress popped out of the kitchen. As she set the platter on the table, the customer gazed wistfully at the mountain of food and said, "My cup is empty."

The waitress scurried to the kitchen, grabbed the coffee pot, scurried to the table, filled the white mug, scurried back to the kitchen, and set the coffee pot down on the electric hot plate. The cook and the waitress exchanged grave glances. Then she scurried to the tiny office and handed the money over to the manager, who gave her change. The manager and the waitress exchanged grave glances. Then she scurried to the table and deposited the change near the salt and pepper shakers, realizing she'd have to wait until he was finished before she could get her tip—if she got a tip!

About to explain that she would make a separate bill for the ham, the waitress noticed, to her horror, that the meat and potatoes were gone. And the customer had taken still another menu from still another table and was studying it with great interest.

As she started to flee—leaving the soiled dishes behind, he stopped her with these words: "Boiled chicken in sour-cream sauce."

Shaking her head in disbelief, the waitress balanced the dishes and hustled to the kitchen, the cook holding the door open for her and using the opportunity to shake his head toward the dining room in disbelief. The manager, who had also witnessed the transaction, stomped out of his office and bulled his way into the kitchen, shaking his head in disbelief. While the cook, the waitress and the manager stood there exchanging grave glances, they heard the customer call out: "Oh, Miss, may I have some crackers while I'm waiting? With something to spread on them?"

All three seemed stricken suddenly by ptomaine poisoning, each folding slightly at the middle—the white faces growing darker, the black face growing whiter. But the manager told the waitress to dump a batch of saltines in a basket, and she brought them to the customer...along with a block of cream cheese on a board. As the waitress plucked the scattered, crumpled napkins off the table, the customer, as if late for an appointment, quickly smeared the white paste on a dry square and stuffed it into his mouth. Flecks of crackers and cheese sprinkled over his lap. The sight made her queasy, especially since she had avoided eating more than a slice of whole wheat toast (without butter), an apple, and a cup of clear tea all day: She was going to look like one of those models in the magazines if it killed her.

When the waitress returned to the kitchen, she had a funny look on her face. "Have you noticed anything weird about the customer?" she said.

"Are you *serious*?" cried the cook.

"Besides all that food. From the time he came into this joint, I think he's gotten...fatter."

"In one hour?" thundered the manager, who was becoming increasingly vexed. Immediately he thumped to the round windows, followed closely by the cook. Sure enough, the customer had developed a very round belly, as though he had swallowed a cantaloupe whole. He seemed bulkier all around. When the customer happened to glance their way, the two ducked.

By the time the waitress arrived with the chicken and noodles drowned in sour cream sauce, plus a lettuce and tomato salad with Russian dressing, the customer's fingers and feet were drumming simultaneously. "Phew!" was all he said, raising his eyes to the ceiling. But the drumming stopped the moment the food landed on the table. The change from his bill, she noticed, still lay where she had set it, but she didn't dare presume it was a tip.

Back to the kitchen went the waitress, where she, the manager, and the cook avoided each other's eyes by peering at the dull, battered pots hanging from hooks overhead; each was wondering not merely how the customer could put away so much food, but how it could show on him so much, so quickly. Soon they heard that plaintive voice again, "Waitress. Oh, waitress."

The waitress took the pencil stub from her ear and threw it on the floor, while the other two looked at her as if to wish her safe passage through a storm. Shouldering the swinging doors, she was gone. Shortly the manager and the cook heard her say, out there in the sea of tables, quite snappily: "I'll have to speak to the manager." In a moment she reappeared in the kitchen, looking weary, years older.

"He refuses to pay for the ham and chicken?" said the manager, his voice rising.

"The customer wants the roast beef—the full dinner." Then the bottom of her voice dropped out. "With apple pie and melted cheddar."

The manager looked at the cook helplessly, and the cook looked at the waitress helplessly, and the waitress looked at the manager helplessly, and the hefty man in shirt sleeves said weakly: "Give him what he wants. He's got the money, and we've got the food." When the employees did not budge, the manager added, "The customer is always right."

"The customer is always crazy!" the cook shouted angrily, yanking out the roast beef rack and burying the long, two-pronged carving fork into the bloody rump.

"Not so loud," cautioned the manager, his face acquiring dark-ish lines, as if it had been grilled. "And what are *you* doing?" the manager demanded of the waitress, who had just yanked open the giant industrial refrigerator.

With a tongue that felt thick as pudding she sputtered, "The customer wants to start with a dish of antipasto."

"Oh my God."

Though the manager was a dedicated businessman, a career restaurateur, he had not lost all human feelings. After the waitress had served the dish of celery and olives and pickles with grim precision, followed by the roast beef—complete with diced carrots and peas, Yorkshire pudding, not to mention apple pie topped by a ball of vanilla ice cream, the manager felt an urge to visit with the customer. As he moved toward the table, however, he couldn't take his eyes off the enlarged arms and legs that pressed against the customer's jacket and trousers, the belly that was now preventing him from getting close to the table.

"What are you looking at?"

"Nothing at all, sir! Only came over to find out if you've enjoyed your dinner." Though greatly tempted, the manager managed to avoid pluralizing the last word.

"The food is edible," said the customer, "but the service is much too slow."

"Must be the damp weather," the manager said, trying to smile, but failing. "Damp air slows everything down."

Cold-eyed, the customer forked the last piece of pie, poked it into the opening in his face, and swallowed with a grunt.

The mere thought of all that food consumed by the customer made the manager feel nauseous, so it was only natural he should ask, "Are you...feeling okay?"

"Tolerably well," said the customer. "I'll feel much better, however, once I get my knife and fork into those pork chops."

The manager gasped. "Am I to understand you're ordering *another dinner?"*

"Chops, with creamed onions. Curried rice. And apple sauce to aid the digestion. The pork must be well done, of course."

"But sir..." the manager muttered with a bewildered look.

"See?" said the customer, pointing, "it's right here in your menu."

"I don't understand."

"Is there anything wrong with my diction?" the customer wanted to know. *"Pork* chops—two of them, *on*ions, *rice, apple* sauce."

The customer was irritated, so the manager decided not to press him. He dragged his body back into the kitchen and found the waitress and the cook sitting on the wooden chairs, elbows on knees, chins in hands, staring sullenly at the concrete floor. The manager felt embarrassed, but he knew his duty: "The pork chop special."

"It's inhuman!" screeched the waitress, pointing her red eyes at the manager accusingly.

"Hurry," the manager pleaded with the cook, who was still staring at the floor.

Leaping to his feet the cook yelped, "I can't take it anymore! I never want to see another chop or fillet or cutlet in my life. Never! I want to go home!"

"I want to go home, too!" the waitress complained loudly.

Though the manager also longed to get home to his wife and teenage boys, he reminded them: "It's not quite closing time, yet."

"It'll never be closing time for *that*," moaned the cook, jerking a thumb toward the dining room.

"Beginning to seem that way," mumbled the manager.

Seeing the manager was on their side, the waitress fought off the desire to screech at him again, and she said stiffly, "Couldn't we just refuse to serve him?"

"No law sez we got to serve him," spat the cook.

"Yes there is. But that's not my main worry," the manager admitted. "This kind of customer would run to the owner at the drop of a spoon."

Even the waitress had been working around the public long enough to know the manager was right. But that didn't make her, or the cook, feel any less upset. "It's too *late* to start serving another dinner," they insisted.

"Look at it this way," said the manager, his eyes blank as a pair of hard-boiled eggs. "This is the first decent stretch of business we've had all week. And if the restaurant doesn't take in any money, the owner's going to shut down this place. And then all of us will be out of a job."

The cook peered at the manager is if he had played a dirty trick on them. Heavily he moved to the work counter, got hold of a spatula and whacked the jar of powered oregano out of his way. The crash against the concrete made the manager and the waitress flinch, and they squinted at the sharp, shiny particles of glass on the floor. In a silence as lumpy as bad gravy, the cook began knuckling the chops into the bread crumbs in the pan.

"All I know is I'd better get a big fat tip out of this fiend," the waitress threatened, "or he's going to get a big fat lip."

Afraid to ask either of them to do it, the manager began sweeping up the broken glass, the flakes of oregano. "What gets me," he said, kneeling down unsteadily to position the dust pan, "is that his body keeps getting bigger and bigger right before my eyes, and I think it's happening faster and faster. In all my years in the business, I've never seen anything like it."

The manager and the waitress and the cook had the same thought: *Maybe the customer's trying to gorge himself to death.* Yet none of them could figure out why he would want to do such a thing. A gun would've been much faster, easier. Poison would certainly have been more humane. Whatever the reason, it was a cruel way to go. But by then, none of them was feeling particularly sympathetic. They hoped the customer would choke on a sharp bone. Or at very least end up with a tapeworm. The pork was not cooked as long as it should have been.

When the food had been slung out, the manager helped the waitress carry the plates; the odors of burnt grease and curry and mashed potatoes made both of them want to dash to the rest rooms and throw up. But they stopped at the table, holding their breath. Before the meat and rice were set down, the manager inquired, humanely: "Are you quite sure you want this, sir? It would be no trouble for us to refrigerate it. No trouble at all. And no charge."

"You've kept me waiting long enough already. Kindly serve the food."

"But—"

"Please!"

The plates were dropped before him, and the manager and the waitress rushed to the kitchen.

"Did you see it?" asked the waitress.

"How could I miss it!" exclaimed the manager.

"See what?" said the cook, trotting to the round windows. He saw immediately what they meant: The customer's arms and legs and belly had not merely grown enormously fat, swelling out of his sleeves and pant legs, bulging out of his belt, but his head had puffed out like a large pink balloon that had been fed too much air.

It was not long before the customer called out again, "Waitress! Waitress! Where are you, waitress?"

This time the waitress, the manager and the cook (who anticipated a complaint over the not-fully cooked meat) ran out and stood in a row, looking small and insignificant before the huge customer.

"Spaghetti and meatballs."

Savagely the cook wiped his hands across the stained apron, as if sharpening a pair of cleavers. "Why? Why do you want *spaghetti and meatballs* after you've already had *steak* and *chops* and *chicken* and *ham* and *shrimp* and *roast beef* and all the *rest? Why? Why? Why!*"

It was less the cook's hostile outburst than his question that stamped the customer's bright red, stretched-out face with surprise. "Why do you *suppose* one orders food?" the customer gurgled. "I'm hungry."

The three of them raced to the kitchen and, as they bumped through the doors, over their shoulders they heard, "And don't forget the Italian bread."

It was only when the spaghetti was nothing more than a smear of tomato sauce on the plate, and the lamb stew was a smudge of gravy in a bowl, and the salmon salad was a few pink shreds on the tablecloth; it was only after the waitress and the cook had declared several times they would not stay *one minute longer*— already two hours past closing; only after the customer had seemed to fill half the dining room with his ballooning body... while the cook was crying over a cheeseburger sizzling on the grill, and the waitress was crying in the rest room into her glass of tips, and the manager was crying, face down, over his ledger book...that the three of them realized the steady, sharp hissing was not the tea kettle after all, for a powerful, ghastly odor had filled the premises.

Then it happened: The mass of fat gave off a high-pitched squeal and blasted off, shooting straight up and taking part of the restaurant's ceiling and roof with it. The waitress, the cook, and the manager were thrown against the walls, but no one was seriously hurt. Stunned, they stood up on shaky legs, brushed the debris off their bodies, then staggered into the dining room. The wallpaper was scorched, a radiator had toppled, and the floor was cluttered with broken plaster, shards of porcelain dishes, legs of chairs. But they could find no sign of the customer. The manager took a stepladder out of the cleaning closet, set it up under the open ceiling, climbed up, and looked out over the rain-soaked shingles. No trace of the customer could be seen anywhere.

It wasn't long before the police emergency squad arrived, and the first thing they wanted to know was if anyone was hurt. All three restaurant workers shook their head, *No.* The next thing they wanted to know was how it had happened. When the cook and the waitress started to explain, the manager interrupted and pointed to a broken pipe: "A gas leak caused the explosion." The employees glanced at each other but did not contradict the manager.

As soon as the two policemen went to make sure more of the ceiling wasn't about to cave in, the waitress turned to the manager and whispered: "Why didn't you tell them what really happened?"

"Who would believe such a story?"

"But we saw the whole thing—we know *exactly* how it happened," the cook insisted.

The manager's face assumed an expression of world-weary wisdom: "Trust me, the less said about what we saw here tonight, the better."

"Even if we don't like it," the waitress muttered to herself, "the truth is the truth."

Keeping an eye on the policemen, who were poking the loose edges of the ceiling with a table leg, the manager said quietly, "If by some miracle they *did* believe us, they'd want to know what'd become of the customer, and they might wonder if negligence on our part was involved in his disappearance."

The waitress and the cook glanced at the policemen in their dark blue uniforms, revolvers in holsters at their sides.

"Even if they didn't come to that conclusion, the owner would lose everything, and we'd be out on the street looking for work."

"Why?" the cook and waitress said in unison.

"Because there's no way the insurance company would pay up on such a claim. This way the owner might be able to sue the gas company and end up with a little profit after he overhauls the place."

The cook peered through the blown-open kitchen door at the stained, dented cooking range. "Owner damn well needs to buy a new stove."

The waitress sighed half-heartedly at the manager. "Maybe you're right."

But the cook still looked troubled. "What about fatso?"

"Near as we can tell, that customer doesn't exist anymore."

"Maybe he's lost in space," mused the waitress, an avid fan of old-time TV.

"Let's be honest, do we *really* care what became of that blob of saturated fat?"

Neither the waitress nor the cook responded, eyeing the policemen who were entering the kitchen.

"Far as I'm concerned," the manager said in a low voice, "it's good riddance to bad rubbish."

The waitress shrugged. "But why did it happen in the first place?"

"What does it mean?" added the cook.

"Why does it have to mean anything?"

"*Every*thing means *some*thing," the cook declared.

While the manager thought this over, the waitress and the cook gazed at him expectantly. He was, after all, their leader. Wisps of smoke were rising around them, and the rain was coming in steadily through the open roof, raising a musty smell of destruction. At last the manager faced them, and said in a soothing, philosophical tone: "It's just how things are these days, and there's nothing we can do about it."

HERMAN BURGER'S TRAGIC FLAW

The older I get, the less I feel....

By now my condition is quite advanced. Years ago I stopped grinning with pride when my daughter presented me with drawings of cats perched—stranded, really, on rooftops or, more recently, when she pounded out scales with a fury that was closer to calling for help than making music. Nor do I rant at my wife over the liquor bills for her parties; or dispute Accounting's tally of my commissions; or feel my stomach clench into a fist when I see a woman's smooth thighs flexing up the stairs. The roses I planted have died, and I don't care. Reading Keats and listening to Mozart don't move me any longer. I'm beginning to think my hand could be punctured by a stapler—two deep holes like a snake bite, and I couldn't cry out.

Sometimes I imagined I was losing my feelings simply because that is our nature: I imagined that as a person ages, a desensitizing hormone is released into the bloodstream (from a tiny gland at the base of the brain) in increasingly larger doses, making one's total being less and less responsive to stimuli, mental and physical. More often I accounted for this phenomenon in the obvious way, telling myself that the more a person goes through, the deeper he withdraws, gradually sealing himself off to the disappointments, the hurts which are the unavoidable by-products of sustaining a life. Another idea I had was that functioning as a salesman for nearly twenty years had affected me; that trying to get people to buy something as ethereal as life insurance, nothing at all really, something they didn't necessarily need, or want, was thinning my emotional capacity. Since other human beings in my approximate state of affairs continued to display anger and flashes of joy, however, I had no choice but to discount all those theories. I was losing the ability to feel, I surmised, because of the particular individual I happened to be, a person squeezed between a predetermined set of genes and an unpredictable set of experiences.

My father and mother had bequeathed me brown hair, brown eyes, and a brownish mind—good enough for most everyday purposes, but nothing especially flashy. As a thin, frail child, their only child (they had gotten together late), I was looked upon with a certain awe, though never as a precious toy. No, I'm sure I was real to them. In high school I played bassoon in the band (second chair); and majored in economics (plus a few pages of literature) at college, registering slightly better than average grades at both levels. I went to basketball games with the boys and movies with the girls, fell in and out of love more or less weekly and, in the end, hung around a petite poli-sci graduate long enough to wake up beside her, married, with a kid. Like of lot of other people in sales, I started out in another direction entirely—International Economics, and ended up where a job (that is, the money) was less theoretical. Which means my life was made out of nothing extraordinary, neither genetically nor experientially. So I was just as much in the shadows as ever about the deterioration of my feelings. Certainly I used to feel things all the time. In any case, this is why I came to think of my condition, simply, as Herman Burger's tragic flaw.

Remarkably my sales staff continued to look at me, the department manager, as if I were exactly the same as I had always been. The only person who realized I was changing was my wife. Sadly, Jocelyn didn't know in what way I was changing. She grew increasingly uneasy around me, as if she suspected I was breathing *tubercle bacillus* into the house. While Jocelyn used to criticize her friends for constantly complaining about their husbands getting in the way of their careers, their vacuuming or their candle-making, she began to sound just like them, nagging me on weekends to get out and "*do* something."

"Why?" I inquired.

"You make me nervous!"

Some time ago I decided to tell Jocelyn what I was going through so she wouldn't feel confused about her attitude toward me. A television report on a fire at an old-age home gave me the opportunity, the push I needed. "The firemen are breaking down the doors," I said, reaching into the walnut cabinet for a cluster of martini glasses, making them clatter.

"Been a lot of fires this month," said Jocelyn in the adjoining dining room, her mind on the celery stalks she was cutting into three-inch logs.

"They're trying to reach the people who are trapped," I reported in the tone of a newscaster.

"Trapped?" she said, instinctively glancing at the 25-inch Zenith in the living room.

"The fire's sweeping to the upper floors," I said.

"It's too awful to watch," she murmured, moving out of my sight to smear wads of cream cheese specked with chives into the dugouts of the celery.

"Look, Jocelyn, they're bringing out the bodies! Look."

"Don't make me look at them," she cried, a dash of passion sprinkling her voice like paprika on the sour cream dip.

"Then look at me," I said.

"Did you set all those glasses out yet?"

"Look at the expression on my face," I said. "What do you see?"

I could hear her tearing open a new box of Ritz crackers, which she would spread like a deck of cards around the outside of the teak platter, the center of which would be covered with pie-slices of Gouda. There would be a slab of pate—genuine French goose liver, and a bowl of cocktail meatballs.

"I don't feel a thing toward those bodies," I said.

"Herman, *please* put the glasses on the bar cart. And throw the garbage out! They'll start showing up in less than an hour."

"I don't feel a thing," I said.

When the McDonald's jingle replaced the news report, I began setting the glasses on the bottom shelf of the cart. Jocelyn was humming "You deserve a break today." Humming was something she tended to do when possessed by some pleasant expectation. In this instance, it also saved her from thinking about burning old-age homes and ice cubes that were freezing too slowly. My wife slipped away from surfaces of feeling with more facility than most, but that was because she felt *too* strongly, which was the only real trouble she had. *Her* tragic flaw, or so it seemed to me.

If that's not her only trouble, certainly her blessings are many. With her blondish coils rewound weekly by Max, stylist extraordinaire, and a size six figure, she looks as young as the day we married (well, almost); she gave birth to a blue-eyed, smart, healthy, possibly talented daughter; we put ten thousand down on this split-level half a dozen years ago, and it has a 75 by 80 foot yard out back with a brick barbecue pit, plus a resilient lawn in front—not as spirited as the Ashtons', but without the brown patches of the Preaks'; on our 10th anniversary I bought her a yellow Honda (which I'm still paying off) so she could scoot around to meetings, craft exhibits, shopping malls, and her assorted projects.

Jocelyn is involved in I don't know how many local, state and national projects—canvassing for the Republicans; hiking with the Girl Scouts; fund-raising for diabetes (her father died of diabetes); organizing rummage sales at one of the local churches; and of course her women's consciousness-raising chapter. I never interfere with her interests, for I believe the secret to a successful marriage is for each to stay out of the way of those things that keep them from thinking about the other things they wish they had done in life.

Unlike some husbands at the office, I don't run around with women, and I have difficulty finding a good reason for drinking myself into a stupor. (Well, I can think of a good reason, but it still doesn't make much sense to me.) At worst, at best I take a good look, and satisfy my thirst with a mug of cold beer. Nor does a percentage of my income belong to gamblers. (The most I bet is a dollar or two in the World Series or Super Bowl pools.) The family is insured against every danger known to humankind through American Assurance, my employer, the company which "Stands Behind Every Clause" of its life, home, automobile and property policies and which, ultimately, keeps the Burgers' mortgage paid and refrigerator stocked. I've even managed to bank a few dollars. True, I'm not Robert Redford in face or body, but then I'm not Peter Lorre either.

Despite all this, Jocelyn Burger continued to grow restless in my presence: couldn't sit still before the TV, or lie in the same position in bed very long. In my opinion she was getting fidgety because, unlike me, she lacked the proper philosophical underpinnings. Good salesmen are philosophers, at very least psychologists. While I may not have understood why I was losing touch, I was saved from mental anguish by an agent's flair for accepting one's situation in the scheme of things. Too bad Jocelyn had to learn this lesson the hard way.

For most practical purposes, Jocelyn's education began at that party, the last she ever gave. Guests arrived during a period of one hour, 8 to 9, averaging out conveniently around the announced 8:30 starting time. As Jocelyn was hopping back and forth between the bathroom and the kitchen, for a last-minute thickening of her eyebrows and raising of the shrimp salad, I answered the chimes with a solid yank of the door, an extended hand or cheek, and teeth flashing: "Hi, you old hot rod! Say, where'd you pick up that gorgeous gal with you?" "You've lost some weight, Bruce. No? Sure looks like you did." "New dress, Carol. Very, very sexy...."

It was all as insincere as Jocelyn Burger's eyelashes and Peg Preak's hair and John Tompkin's airs and Herman Burger's suit ...a stretchable synthetic in middle-of-the-road beige. I received their smiles and handshakes because they were indigenous to the local culture, gestures to be tolerated in the interest of social order. Though I tried, I could not take them into my mind as friends, as neighbors any longer. To me they were merely creatures that shared the same faculties and facilities.

By the time Jocelyn made her first official sweep into the living room, her Arpeged neck rising out of spaghetti-thin, silvery shoulder straps, the drama was wasted—our guests were already half numb, having started drinking before they arrived, and having reinforced that headstart the moment they reached our bar cart. In bad need of merriment on several counts, I suppose, Jocelyn poured a deep glass of Johnny Walker Red and downed it like iced tea on a sultry summer day. She caught up fast.

Without aspirations of my own in the way of celebration, or inebriation, I occupied myself by sipping beer from the bottle, and changing CDs on the player, and refilling the ice bucket, and muttering an occasional platitude to suit the moment: "Love is blind, but I'm not!" when I spotted Jim slide a hand over Dolores' ass. Curiously, they happened to be married to each other. Good thing our Judi was staying with her grandmother for the night—it got pretty loud, pretty gamey. Later, slinging my body onto the reclining chair like a soiled shirt, I listened to the alcohol making fools of our guests, and watched Bix Cummings as he felt up my wife.

It was not your pinch-a-behind-in-the-kitchen, brush-a-breast-in-the-hallway kind of feeling up. These were serious probes. Their backs were turned away from everyone, in the love seat, and the lights had dimmed—the way they mysteriously do at suburban parties. Concentrating on each other, or at least on what their bodies were feeling next to each other, they didn't seem to notice I was set back in the darkest corner, accidentally yet strategically positioned to see his hand moving under her dress like a kitten under a blanket. Jocelyn's hips, just about all I could see of her, had arched slightly forward with the curiosity, apprehension, delight of puberty, as if she had just discovered how sensitive that area was between her legs.

I watched this exhibition with the oddest detachment. Not even a repressed anger trembled within me; not even a crushed pride; not even a perverted excitement. Just a remotely physical sense of separation, as though I'd lost the lower half of my body a long time ago in the war. After watching them awhile longer, I stumbled upon this question: *Why such a dumpy specimen, such an invertebrate like Cummings?* It was not cattiness or vanity, just wonderment at human nature.

What finally got me up out of my chair was not indignation but a remarkable crash in our bedroom. Two of the more ambitious frolickers, I discovered, had knocked or thrown over a lamp. Pieces of pimpled milk glass lay near the threshold, and I realized the household policy would not cover the loss. Well, one or two would look upon it as a loss. In one sense it had been a good lamp. It was given to us by Jocelyn's mother, a widow, who valued things according to their age. The older, the more valuable—regardless of its condition or its lack of taste. Suddenly the lamp had reached its ultimate age, however, and disproved her theory by becoming utterly valueless.

The perpetrators, John and Eva Tompkins, looked concerned even in their tipsiness. I winked and tried to pass by them, saying, "Did you happen to see a packet of King Edwards on the night table?" The bed covers, I noticed, were disturbed.

"Look, Old Man, awfully sorry about the lamp," John slurped guiltily, grabbing my arm to keep from falling over.

I freed myself.

Shaking the hair off her shoulders, Eva qualified: "It was an accident."

"Have either of you seen my cigars?"

John's attempt to straighten his tie failed. "I'll be glad to pay for the lamp."

"What's it worth?" Eva asked, her smoky eyes narrowing as she glanced at the broken pieces on the floor.

The Tompkins couldn't hear a word I was saying. They wanted to settle the matter of that peculiar lamp right away so they could attend to their bodies without policy-riders attached to their minds. But why re-examine their sensations in someone else's bedroom, I wondered, when they had their own? When they had already gotten to the bottom of each other a long time ago? That's the way it is with feelings, I suppose—without reasons, the way it used to be with me. By that point in my life, however, all I wanted was to be left alone with a cigar, plus a match to set it afire.

I had to find the packet myself, and when I re-entered the living room, Jocelyn and Bix were gone. The others were conversing, drifting, chuckling, drinking. Straight to the recliner I went, lit up, and took several long, bitter-sweet puffs before sighing out loud, "Man, that's a good smoke." That was strictly publicity: I didn't want anyone to think I knew about Jocelyn and Bix, for I wouldn't have been able to react the way they would have expected.

Some party—I fell asleep! And when I awakened only a few souls were still around, hanging onto the ropes and, like their host, feeling nothing at all, though for a different reason. In fifteen minutes I was able to flush them out of the den and living room, into the misty night. And after gulping down a frigid glass of milk, I crawled into the big, empty bed.

Jocelyn got back to the house at 4:18 AM. I know because the eyes of the clock were glaring at me from the night table when she slammed her four cylinders into the back wall of the garage, startling me out of a calm, dreamless sleep.

Mrs. Burger was undressed before she got to the bedroom, and slipped onto the mattress without stirring the sheets, the air. Lying there in silence a minute, smelling Bix on her, I said, very pleasantly: "It was a great party, Jocelyn."

Even though I had not said it sarcastically, she flinched, stopped breathing, remained motionless several moments, apparently trying to dematerialize. At last she whispered: "I'm... I'm sorry, Herman."

"That's okay," I replied. "The garage'll be fixed like new." Then I turned over and fell asleep.

Blessedly it was Saturday. Jocelyn could stay in bed and pretend she was sleeping, and I could sip my coffee in peace. Past noon she staggered into the kitchen, weak and weary, groping for a white cup in the white cabinet. "I've got one out for you already," I said, pouring from the electric percolator, the muddy, pungent fluid whirlpooling within the circumference of porcelain.

Jocelyn sat down at the table, her hands pink and tremulous. Judging from the skin around her eyes, which shrivels when she's tired, she hadn't slept more than an hour or two. She was awful to look at in her dreariness, like a cold, drizzly day.

Once my wife recovered the power of speech, she threatened to confess. Immediately I deflected her attempt. "The rose bushes are starting to show buds already," I said. For awhile Jocelyn allowed me to keep the conversation in the garden, at the office; she was in too fragile a position morally, physically, mentally to do otherwise. Probably she figured I was avoiding that other subject because it was too painful for me. The truth is that I avoided it because I couldn't work up any interest in it, and feeling nothing seemed inconsiderate, like losing an erection at the port of entry.

Later she tried again to unload her heart on me: "Herman, I just want to say—"

"Judi's waiting for me to pick her up at Grandma's," I said. "I'll be back in a jiffy."

"But honey…"

"No butts in your ashtray," I laughed over my shoulder. That's one of our little household jokes which means, more or less: What does it matter?

It was this attitude which distressed my wife increasingly in the days that followed. At first she acquiesced, ruled by an overpowering guilt that turned her into a virtual slave, though I did not request or want this from her. When I arrived home from the office and asked, "What's for dinner?" she replied, "Anything you want," and proved it one night by stirring up an awful racket and mess, emerging from the kitchen two hours later with a flushed face and a household rendition of Moo Goo Gui Pan, one of my favorites. As I'd said at the time, a hamburger would've been fine. If I searched for a cigar, she brought me several, along with matches—I think she carried them with her. If I complained about being tired, she seemed ready to carry me to bed on her back.

As the weeks died off, however, Jocelyn became frustrated by my lack of response to her, to anything. It must've seemed I was trying to punish her by denying her existence. Although this was untrue, she quit trying to make it up to me—to my relief, and soon allowed herself the luxury of anger and then, at last, began a crusade calculated to arouse a reaction in me. But I didn't so much as blink when she "accidentally" snipped (down to the soil) the five-foot American Beauty Rose bush I'd raised from a leafless stub. Or when she spent three hundred dollars on a dress that made her look dowdy. "It does wonders for you,"

I said. Not even when she invited the nervous-jowled Bix Cummings over to dinner. Hell, I mixed him a Scotch and soda. Two or three. Turned out we had a lot more in common than I'd realized—he's a salesman, too: wholesale lingerie.

"Stop it! Stop it!" Jocelyn cried out one evening after I'd welcomed her call for a hiatus to our love-making. After all, we hadn't been connecting in that way very much anyway. Plus it would help us get more sleep so I could perk up at the office (my sales staff had been getting sluggish, and I felt unable to rev them up), and she could add a pottery class to her busy evening schedule.

Throwing her lumpy leather purse at me, she shouted: "I can't take it any more!"

"You can't take it with you," I said, handing the purse back to her.

Jocelyn and I are over that difficult period. If not forgotten, those incidents have dimmed in our minds. And we're plotting for the future. With Judi outgrowing her allotted space in the house, and my wife outgrowing her clothes—she's four months gone, we decided to pull out some of our savings and break down the northern wall, to add a nursery. It's going to be very charming, or so the contractor assures us, especially the diaper hamper (in the shape of a frog) built into the wall. Jocelyn already has her eye on a set of curtains with blue clowns. And I would like the kid to have one of those cribs with an abacus at one end awaiting him (or her) in this world. Can't teach them to count any too soon.

Jocelyn has given up Bix, Judi has given up piano, Herman has given up roses. I accept the shape my future is taking, and how it got that way; Judi accepts my silences; Jocelyn accepts what has become of me. Lately, in fact, my wife has been demonstrating how diligently she has learned the lessons which the passage of time teaches so well: not allowing her mother to get her riled up over my cigar ashes on the rug; displaying no concern over Judi's persistent cough; or the way she lies with her legs spread out, as rigid as the crotch of a tree, as I intrude on her body every now and then, as a kind of reminder.

Now we mostly wait, the hammers and saws making sounds of tomorrow, a fine dust settling over everything in the house. Jocelyn's condition has just about run out of time, her mid-section large enough, it seems, to blossom like an atomic explosion. As for my condition, I am finding it increasingly difficult to look upon it as a flaw. While many work hard at dulling their senses with liquor and sex and drugs and store-bought distractions—to shield themselves from the events of their lives, I have achieved that numbness naturally, without conscious effort, without gimmicks. For this reason I have come to the conclusion that my loss of feeling is a gift, a special power akin to Cezanne's uncanny eye for light and Mozart's ear for harmonies and Keats' grasp of the sensuality of death. But with one important difference. In a sense they have misused their gifts, arousing in the world a belief that the electric impulses which pass through the nervous system are more than momentary tremors of life; that they are intimations of immortality, as if feeling something sublime is an eternal experience. I at least deal in truth. By following the drift of days and nights, one after another, without reacting outwardly or inwardly, I become a personification of what actually lies in store for all of us.

SALES RESISTANCE

Selling door-to-door is like hand-to-hand combat: at each house I climb out of my fox hole (a decades-old hatchback) and engage the enemy at the front lines of their respective doorsteps, keeping my head low as bullets of resistance begin ricocheting off my sample case. Every so often there's a brief let up in hostilities, and I walk away with a sale—only to have the bombs of rejection bursting all around me at my next confrontation. But yesterday was truly one for the sales history books. As if a treaty had been signed in secret at battlefront headquarters, the siege by campaign-toughened consumers lifted abruptly, and an uneasy peace settled over the trenches of New Jersey. After I was blown away by a crone with a spidery shawl over her shoulders—"Go peddle your soap someplace else, Sonny!"—the people in the next nine houses in Mahwah bought one or more bottles of Miraclean from me; at my last call a corporate exec, who didn't know one end of a mop from the other, ordered a full case!

Marching from house to house teaches you to protect yourself against sales-prospect shrapnel, but you also learn to retreat while you're ahead. Two hours earlier than usual I started for home, driving 35 MPH in a 50 MPH zone to my half-a-house (the up-stairs) in Sloatsburg, New York. I didn't change lanes all the way, and made sure I signaled at every turn. One way or another, fate was going to pay me back for that streak of commercial amity, and I didn't want it to happen while I was driving a car.

"You're home early, Ernie," said my wife, her bony behind stationed on a stool in a kitchen the size of an elevator, poking a rubber nipple into the baby's mouth. "Guess it didn't go too well today."

Still keeping a wary eye on fate, I answered guardedly, "Not bad, Bea, not bad at all."

Something in my voice caused Bea to glance at me, but I kept my mouth shut. If I strutted around our three rooms bragging, I would only have to pay my dues sooner—and with interest. For starters the check for the case of Miraclean would bounce all the way back from First National Bank, and some hysterical housewife, whose hair was falling out in clumps, would be waiting for me at the warehouse with a bayonet. (Maybe I shouldn't have told her that Miraclean was "strong enough to cut kitchen grease and gentle enough to use as shampoo.")

Next morning I continued to keep that bizarre selling spree to myself. After patting the baby's head and pecking the bride's cheek, I drove—still maintaining yesterday's defensive position—to Waldwick and rolled to a stop at an ordinary ranch house on an ordinary street, the kind you can find in any suburban town in America. The battleship gray plastic garbage pails, big enough to hide the body of a man, reeked of middle-income. I walked up to the colonial-blue door and thumbed the buzzer. It was cooler than the weatherman had promised, but at least it wasn't raining. I hit the button again. At last an outdated beauty queen under a nest of brassy blonde hair, her meaty body wound up in a quilted satin robe, appeared. Before I could finish my pitch—"the miracle liquid cleaner formulated for your toughest household chores and available only in your own home"—she plucked three neatly folded singles out of her sagging bra, as if she'd been warming up the bills especially for me.

This would've made a great yarn back at American Household Products. But those battle-hardened pitchmen wouldn't have bought a word of it, especially the part about making ten straight sales. Even *I* was having trouble swallowing *that* one. And yet, the cease-fire continued. Next door took three economy-sized bottles, our largest. I stood there peering at the schoolmarm-type behind the thick lenses, her fifteen bucks balled-up in my fist.

I was tempted to ask if she could actually see what she had bought. In a moment she closed the door with a pensive expression, as if wondering who had rung her doorbell.

Pleased with the sale yet vaguely uneasy, I hauled my sample case to the next house humming "The Battle Hymn of the Republic." In a way, I was glad to find no one home, and I stomped across the lawn—a no-no in door-to-door peddling—to the flanking house. The couple in identical field-green sweats, who had witnessed my every footstep on their grass from their bay window, welcomed me like a nephew who'd just hit the lottery. Despite my firm refusal of their invitation, they ushered me into the living room, sat me down in a fake leather recliner, poured me a cup of coffee (I prefer my caffeine in the form of Coke), and confessed their basement was moldy. Had been for years. Every light in the house was turned on in broad daylight. Before releasing me from captivity they bought four bottles, 24-ouncers.

"Has the entire state of New Jersey been stricken by an obsession for cleanliness?" I asked myself out loud as the couple waved goodbye to my back from their doorway.

Although my sense of these things told me there would be no sale at the next house—the shades were drawn, for one thing—I went up the slate path anyway. In four minutes flat I came down the slate path with three more bucks in my pocket. At the next house, where the automatic sprinkler was watering more of the gutter than the autumn-seeded lawn, I passed off two bottles. And the next victim took five—also ordering a Miraclean Sponge Mop and Miraclean Plastic Bucket from our catalog via American Express. Down the concrete steps I moved, both pockets stuffed with greenbacks and checks, and feeling more superstitious with every sale.

What in god damn hell *is going on?* I asked myself, looking both ways as I stepped ever so cautiously into the street.

By the time I had locked myself into my hatchback, I was having spooky thoughts. Maybe that crone in Mahwah—the last one to turn me down—had cast a spell that made my sales pitch irresistible in Jersey. Or maybe my customers had gotten a sniff of some potent new ingredient in the product that made it impossible for them to say *no*. Or maybe everyone had gotten lucky at the races or in the stock market and had some extra dough to throw around. Or maybe ... that's the kind of shape I was in—trying to make myself believe in spells, potions, and universal good luck. It was bad enough being a fatalist.

I drove a mile south to the low-income fringes of town, parked, and moved up the spongy steps of a two-family house with a sagging porch, a buckled roof, and a couple of missing window panes. The front yard was decorated with a stack of bald tires, a crankshaft, splintered railroad timbers, lengths of twisted drainpipe, assorted hubcaps, a punctured oil drum, and an armchair that was surrounded by its own stuffing. Looked as though the place had taken a direct hit from a mortar shell. At the time I didn't consider why I had made such an unlikely stop.

A white-haired black man (buttoned up in a washed-out khaki shirt) shuffled out of the screen door.

"Good morning, Pop. Don't suppose you'd have any use for one of those so-called miracle cleaners." I held up a bottle of the purple fluid, my hand covering its label.

"Well, now, that looks like mighty powerful juice. But I'm kinda short on cash right now."

"I can understand that," I said, pleased to have been turned down at last. Somehow it seemed to help even the score a little bit, and maybe I could start being less cautious in my car and out on the sidewalks.

"Tell me, Son, could I owe you for one?"

"Owe me? What in God's name would you want any of this gunk for?"

The old man aimed a thumb over his shoulder. "My place needs fixing up."

I looked over the rotten floor boards, the crumbling putty at the windows, the broken hand-rail; the cracked, bell-shaped light fixture. It was going to take a social revolution to recover that sad old shanty. "Save your money, Pop."

"Couldn't you let me have one bottle on account? I'm good for it, Son. Honest."

A column of anger rose in my throat. "Here, you can have it," I snapped. "No charge!"

"Say, that's mighty white of you," he said without apparent sarcasm. If anything, he was confused by my outburst. "But I'll pay up soon's my check comes in." Though his hands were shaking with palsy, he managed to relieve me of the bottle. My heart, I noticed, was pounding hard as I backed off, watching him read the label on the bottle intently.

I started up the hatchback and drove steadily and, forgetting my date with fate, a little too fast—until the flashing red light on a dark blue vehicle appeared in my rearview mirror. Curiously comforted by the sight of fate to my rear, I pulled over, and so did the patrol car. A policeman popped out and came up to my window, which I rolled down immediately.

"License and registration."

Instantly the comfort disappeared and reality took its place: My license was my livelihood, and I couldn't afford to get another ticket—one more and they might take away my license. Picking through my wallet like an overloaded waste basket at the office, I found the official stubs and handed them over. I was preparing to play innocent about the speed limit on that stretch of road when the policeman's eye was caught by something in the back of my car.

"What's in the boxes?" he asked suspiciously.

"Bottles of Miraclean. I'm a salesman."

"Oh, yeah. Heard about that stuff on TV."

"Actually, Household Products doesn't advertise too much. We sell door-to-door."

"I ought to pick some up for the Mrs."

Sensing an opportunity I reached back and pulled a large economy-sized bottle out of the open box. "Help yourself, compliments of the company."

The policeman, whose brimmed hat was pulled down too far to get a good read on his expression, handed my license and registration back to me, and said: "A police officer isn't allowed to accept gifts. How much for the bottle?"

"It's five bucks but you really don't—"

"Here, I got the money in my back pocket." In a few seconds he handed me a picture of Honest Abe Lincoln, gripped the bottle, walked off with a stupid grin on his face, and climbed back into the patrol car. He'd even forgotten to write me up for speeding. Half a minute after he made a U-turn, I cranked up the hatchback and putt-putt-putted down the road in the opposite direction. I was still shaking my head as I braked for a red light in Ridgewood.

The English-style street lamps and brick shop fronts and red-tiled roofs added up to big bucks, but that was no guarantee I'd make any sales. The well-off are funny about their money. Leaving the business district behind, cruising up one of those wide, tree-lined residential avenues that stand like a wall between the management and selling classes, I pulled over to the curb and sat with the engine idling. (The black exhaust engulfing the car finally convinced me to turn off the ignition.) For several minutes I stared straight ahead, wondering if Miraclean could remove the specks of tar from my windshield, wondering how the people who lived in the sprawling mansions around me had accumulated so much wealth, wondering if the sales streak I was going through meant Bea and I would own our own home one day, too—not one of these fortresses, but at least the downstairs along with the upstairs. But this kind of thinking got me worried again, and I checked to see if storm clouds were gathering: I had little doubt that before the day had faded into darkness, I would be struck by lightning.

Had I become a super salesman overnight? *Hardly.* I was the same bell puncher I'd been the day before, and the day before that. Had the product suddenly started living up to its claims? *Nah.* It was the same soapy purple syrup I'd been hustling for more than a year; not much better or worse than a dozen other products. (And a lot more expensive per ounce—that's how I made my commissions.) Had the rush of sales been caused by a local advertising blitz over the radio and TV last weekend, when Bea and I were away showing off the baby to her mother? *Ha!*

As I sat there trying to unscramble the mystery of why I'd been handed all those commissions without hardly trying, the family that lived where I was parked drove up into their hundred-foot driveway. Drawing themselves as carefully as antique china out of their silvery Mercedes, the man in the riding pants and polished calf-high boots spotted me. Without hesitation he left his wife and son standing before a garage that seemed big enough to house a Saber-jet fighter. Striding down the pine-edged path, he had one of those short horse-whips tucked under his arm.

Tapping my outside mirror three times with the whip like a commandant, he said through a distrustful glare, "May I help you, *sir?*"

"I'm a salesman from American Household Products. I just stopped to rest awhile. I'll be moving on in a minute."

"This is not a public parking"—he interrupted himself—"what are you selling?"

44

"One of those liquid cleaners."

"What's it called?"

"Miraclean."

"Never heard of it."

"That's because it's not available in supermarkets. It's sold only in the home."

"Good concept. Let me have two jars," he said, patting the breast pocket of his tan suede jacket to locate his wallet.

"What?"

"I want two jars of Miraclean."

"I wasn't trying to sell you anything. You asked about it, so I told you. You're under no obligation to buy."

"I'd like two jars. How much are they?"

"But you haven't even seen the product. You have no idea if it's any good. Maybe it's ninety-nine percent water and one percent detergent."

"Our maid has begun her fall cleaning, and she can use all the reinforcements she can get."

"How do you know it isn't carcinogenic?"

"What isn't these days?" the man said, his gray-brushed temples lending him a judicial air.

By this time his wife, a long-legged lady in her late thirties, strutted down the flagstone path, her son skipping after her. As she approached, bulging out of her form-fitting silk suit, I wondered why women with the biggest bank accounts also had the biggest breasts.

"What does the man want, Albert?" she said, dishing me a sidelong glance.

"He's selling Miraclean, Elizabeth," her husband replied. "I'm purchasing two jars for Bertha."

"What is Miraclean?"

"Just an all-purpose household cleaner," I said glumly.

"All-purpose? Albert, why don't you buy an extra jar for me to soak my rings?"

"Good idea, Elizabeth."

There were three rings, each with a different colored stone, on each of her hands. Sooner or later she was going to run out of fingers, or the world was going to run out of gems.

"I want a jar, too," piped the boy, a yard tall, and stuffed into a tiny tailored blazer with brass buttons.

"What do you need Miraclean for?" his mother asked.

"To shine my bicycle."

The father smiled over the boy's fair hair but did not go so far as to pat his head. "Yes, we'll have four jars of Miraclean."

With exaggerated movements I climbed out of the car, partly because I felt closed-in, partly because I was upset. "You don't seem to understand," I said too aggressively, unbuttoning my suit jacket as if preparing to break the cease-fire. "I am trying to be honest and fair. Frankly I don't think this product is any good. I sell it to make a living. I would sell *anything* to *anyone* as long as I knew it would help pay our rent. Do you see what I mean?"

"I most certainly do. You are trying to back out of selling us four jars of Miraclean." A hard edge had entered his voice, and he began rapping the black horse-whip across the palm of his hand.

"You can not offer something for sale," the man's wife stated, shaking her alligator purse at me, "creating a demand for it, and then simply withdraw it from the buying public."

"You're a creep," added the kid, sticking his purple tongue out at me.

"I never said I wouldn't sell it to you."

"In that case, how much do we owe you?" said the man, his large eyes gleaming like emeralds.

Sizing up his broad shoulders and muscular biceps—no doubt he had a lifetime membership in an athletic club, and being five foot six and weighing only one hundred forty-five pounds myself, I decided to be civilized: "Did you want the small, medium, or economy-sized bottles?"

"Let's try the medium to start off."

"That's three dollars a bottle—but there's no money-back guarantee on this product. Once you buy them, they belong to *you*."

"Quite reasonable," said Elizabeth to Albert, who tucked the whip under his arm, slipped a thin snake-skin wallet from his inside jacket pocket, removed a five and a ten dollar bill, and held them out to me.

"Sorry, I don't have any change. I'll have to come back later." As I turned to jump back into my car—to get the hell out of there, the man sprang in front of me and pushed the bills close to my face. "I might as well get my boots cleaned, too," he explained. "Give me an additional jar and you won't need change."

"What kind of consumers are you?" I nearly shouted, jerking the money out of his fingers mostly to get the bills out of my eyes. "What happened to your sales resistance?"

At first the husband and wife and kid seemed annoyed by the tone of my question, but then all three of them grinned simultaneously, their teeth perfectly even, perfectly white.

"Why bother resisting when we really want something?"

"How can you really want something you don't know anything about?" I said in a lower decibel, trying to regain my self-control.

The husband replied soberly, "All I know is that I simply must have some Miraclean."

"That is it precisely," his wife agreed.

"Me too," said the boy, who had managed to gouge a stone out of the rock garden. He was clutching it tightly enough to turn his knuckles white, and I had a pretty good idea what he intended to do with that stone. But somehow the end of the truce, and the resumption of hostilities, didn't seem like such a terrible idea.

My body trembling, I wobbled to the rear of the car, opened the hatchback, and yanked five bottles from the compartments in the cardboard box stamped MEDIUM. I was now convinced that none of the customers during the past two days intended to use the Miraclean they had bought. They were motivated by something that went much deeper than the dirty surfaces this product was supposed to clean. But what it was I didn't know. Slamming the hatchback shut, I stepped up to the customers, five bottles lodged between my forearm and my ribs. Six hands reached out, but I didn't let go of the bottles. Not yet. First I had something to say and they were going to hear me out, whether they liked it or not.

"Don't you realize I'm specially trained to break down your resistance? I went to school! You are amateurs, and I'm a pro-fessional at this game. It's an unfair advantage I have over you. Sales resistance gives you a fighting chance. You shouldn't give up just like that. Sales resistance protects you from cheats and fakes, from inferior goods and services. You mustn't buy what-ever's put in front of you. Even if you have tons of money! There has to be some resistance or the system won't work, and everything will come crashing down." As I preached I sensed my voice growing steadily more shrill, and I wondered where all these words had come from.

The three of them stared at me as if I were a crazed, babbling, homeless wino, and then the woman in the silk suit crossed her arms and said, "Young man, we insist on taking possession of what we have purchased."

Thrusting the bottles at them—my jangled nerves nearly causing me to drop one, I said, "Take them. Take them all! I hope this stuff makes you the cleanest family in the world!"

The family's eyes widened and glistened as they fingered the hour-glass-shaped bottles with the red, white, and blue labels. Already they had forgotten me, the salesman, completely. The kid pressed his bottle against his heart like a teddy bear. Glancing slyly at each other, as if they intended to apply Miraclean to each other's body in bed, the couple turned and tramped right through the cultivated flower beds, up the slope of crew-cut grass. They were followed closely by their son, who was now shaking his bottle to make suds. Through the portico, across the patio, into the massive, sandy-faced garrison they disappeared.

Searching for thunder clouds again, I noticed that the elms had already passed their peak—much too early, it seemed to me: A lifeless bronzed crispness had overcome leaves which, when young, had looked like pulsating green hearts. I considered getting behind the wheel, driving home, popping open a beer, and watching an old war movie on the VCR until I fell asleep on the couch. But what good would that have done? They would only have been waiting for me tomorrow, and the day after that, and it was my job to face them, to give them what they wanted. No matter what might become of us all. I straightened my tie, leaned into the car, and slid my sample case off the seat. Now I started moving across the avenue's browned, landscaped divide, taking aim at the large stone house with white columns, plenty of narrow windows, deep cabinets, and dark corners that needed cleaning.

ABIGAIL & THE TV COMMERCIAL

Abigail Matter was raised by Commandment-quoting folks on a cold, stony farm outside Big Bend, North Dakota—realities which led her to pursue a degree in communications law in sunny Santa Barbara. Getting by on loans, scholarships, part-time jobs (mostly as a sales clerk), and the few spare dollars her folks were able to scratch up out of that poor soil, in due time Abigail was accepted before the California Bar. Communications lawyers were in demand since the public had begun increasing their challenges against newspapers for gross inaccuracies and magazines for slander and television and radio networks for violent programming and misleading commercials. Less than a month after graduation, Abigail was hired as a new associate in a small office with a long name in another warm, unstony city, San Diego.

While Abigail's migration from North Dakota to California had altered her life-ways (for one thing, she entirely stopped going to church), more conspicuous changes resulted from having a sizable paycheck every two weeks. Some of the material wants of a person struggling to earn an education, and a secure tomorrow, could now be satisfied. Abigail moved from a furnished room-plus bath into a newly refurbished two-and-a-half room apartment. Checking ads in newspapers and shopping around, she acquired a bed and mattress, a kitchen table with two matching chairs, a bedside table and lamp, an armchair and love seat, a bookcase, and so on, until she had surrounded herself with the basic personal props of American civilization.

At the office, the partners began to notice Abigail's lucidity of speech and clarity of thought. Gradually they cut down on her research tasks and invited her increasingly to accompany them at client meetings and, later, at court. Before her first year had been completed, she got a raise, a highly unusual occurrence in this firm. Feeling flattered and slightly extravagant, that same weekend she went out and shopped for something that had been on her mind a long while. Since she was still paying off college loans and sending some money home to help her mother and father, Abigail could not spend freely—especially since there was, for her, an almost sinful aspect in buying what she looked upon as a luxury: echoes of the pastor shouting directly at her (as she sat between her parents), that the desire for earthly goods was instilled by the devil, had never entirely died away. Nevertheless, before the week was over, she settled on a 21-inch portable RCA, an upgrade from her tiny Korean-made black and white set—only to her (at five-foot-four, one hundred six pounds) it wasn't all that portable. Though Abigail ended up spending more than she had planned, the salesman had convinced her that by the time she finished with repairs and/or junking a cheaper unit, she would be laying out more.

As Abigail's income increased, her two and a half rooms seemed to shrink. To get out of those narrow walls she would occasionally go for a walk to neighborhood stores and try on shoes, attend an outdoor concert in the park, or sit in the dimness of a movie theater, peering at the silver-edged figures talking and touching across the flat surface. But lacking an outgoing personality, and not having learned to make the most of her plain face and unyielding brown hair—which was rather like the roots of trees her father had had to dig up out of the earth back home, and being somewhat single-minded about her career, most often she had just sat in her apartment, alone, trying to read but not really succeeding. Once the new color TV had been unboxed, set up on a tube-frame stand and plugged in, however, the abrupt living room assumed a new dimension...as if its screen were a window to other places and times and people. Abigail was not unaware of the dangers of watching television—of cutting herself off from real events. But she felt she had more than her share of reality in her job. Plus, she made a point of watching the news every night, a daily reality check that was also beneficial to her work.

The first thing Abigail now did upon entering her apartment each evening—no matter what hour (often she had to stay late to write a brief for the next morning), even before she shoved a heat-and-eat dinner into the toaster oven—was to click on the telly, a nickname she had picked up from an old English movie. After extracting the compartmentalized tinfoil tray from the toaster oven, she would fold her legs under her on the armchair and allow her mind to skim along with a half-hour game show, an office situation comedy, courtroom mystery, hospital drama— one after another, right on up to the news at 10 PM. Meanwhile she would consume the Swiss steak and creamed corn and mashed potatoes, scan a photocopy of a decision pertinent to her most pressing case, leaf through the newspaper and, just before bed-time, devour a bowl of upscale ice cream. While she had to admit the comedies were kind of silly, and the mysteries pre-dictable, it was those very qualities which offered her a certain relief from the precision required of her each day.

Not infrequently, Abigail had such a hectic schedule—rush, rush, rush from the office to the law library to the court house and back—that she would fall asleep right before the telly, her head dropping back against the armchair, her mouth wide open. Hours later she would awaken with a stiff neck, in a room that had filled up with darkness like a great tank of night water, as little human replicas bobbed across the shimmering rectangle in front of her, selling a new detergent or truck-driving lessons or a vegetable chopper or a subscription to *Time*. Instead of getting up and going to bed, Abigail would sit through the bunched-to-gether commercials, for though she had never thought about it particularly, way down inside the young attorney agreed with something she'd read in college, in *The National Law Journal*:

The Chairman of the Federal Communications Commission from an earlier administration was quoted as saying that many commercials were more entertaining than the programs they supported.

After the half-dozen commercials had run out of their thirty or twenty or ten seconds each, Abigail would take the remote and click off the power, dropping a silence over the room and a pall over her heart. Through the liquid shadows she roamed into the other room, moving up to the bed, dropping her slacks and blouse at her feet, and dragging her hundred and fourteen pounds between the sheets. Having awakened on the sofa in the midst of a dream of some sort, sometimes she could not fall back to sleep right away, and the commercials would continue to sing and dance and talk talk talk through the studios of her mind. Once she'd drifted off to sleep, commercials would continue to run through her mind, only they would take new form in her subconscious, and in one the shadowy figure of a pitch man, in a shiny suit, emerged momentarily. While she couldn't quite see any of his features, except for long dark sideburns, she had the feeling, in her sleep, that she knew this man.

Abigail Matter's life worked itself into a pattern: arrive at the office by 7:45 AM with a container of regular coffee; discuss pending litigation with one or more of the partners; make several phone calls; organize case materials on her computer; at 12 Noon order up a ham and cheese on a club roll (with mayonnaise), a Coke, and one huge chocolate chip cookie; hurry to the library for additional support materials; make several phone calls; if scheduled, appear in court; visit the offices of a client; at 7:30 PM catch a bus to her garden apartment; turn on the TV and the toaster oven; eat a slab of beef that was as gray as the November soil of North Dakota; watch a detective and a suspect trade snappy insults on the glass screen and, past 10 PM, witness the parents of a murdered child trying to tell a newsman's microphone how they felt about the stabbing. On weekends it was about the same, only she didn't get to the office and court, and would sometimes take in a lecture or movie. But going to public events unaccompanied seemed to accentuate her aloneness, so she preferred to stay at home. While she occasionally became concerned about the sameness of her days and nights, mostly Abigail was satisfied with her life-rhythm, for it reminded her of one thing she appreciated (though only after moving away) about farm life: knowing what to expect, and when to expect it. It was rather like the way the *TV Guide* set out every date, time and show before one, and why it would be quite upsetting to her when a listing proved incorrect.

If this routine gave her life a shape which made her feel "at home," one important element in the pattern began to discourage Abigail: the firm for which she worked. By that time it was evident there was little hope of making partner or earning a really big salary or meeting interesting men. Even uninteresting men! And when the bland, not-especially bright male associate who had been with the firm half a year less than Abigail quit to claim a much larger salary than she at a well-known firm in San Francisco, all one hundred twenty-one pounds of her felt envious. The following week she began sending resumes out in response to recommendations from headhunters and to classified ads in legal newsletters, as well as to job-sites on the internet. Since she wanted a substantial raise and upgraded title, however, there were no opportunities open to her. Despite a report she'd read in the *Times* that the demand for legal talent was growing, she knew that advocates for better children's programming and anti-violence citizens groups had been defeated by the networks in crucial court tests, weakening their public support and forcing these activists to become considerably more conservative; this was having a negative impact on jobs in communications law in California, where most of the nation's television production was done. Abigail expanded her search to companies outside the city and state.

A few months later, something opened up. Though it wasn't quite in her field of law, and though she would have to relocate to Los Angeles, she accepted the offer: to become one of a team of lawyers at a major corporation with diversified electronic interests. With a bigger salary, Abigail was able to look for a bigger apartment, with a full eat-in kitchen. Rent was higher in the larger city, however, so she had to settle for an apartment which wasn't *that* much bigger. Still it was definitely a step up. Most of her furniture she sold to the landlord in San Diego for a fraction of its value, including her RCA, for Abigail was ready to upgrade her personal belongings again, too. By now she was the holder of half a dozen major credit cards; in no time at all she was able to refurbish her life with a sleek designer sofa, black walnut end tables, a pair of bulbous Chinese lamps, and a microwave oven to speed up food preparation. But the most significant acquisition she made in that first month in Los Angeles was a 32-inch, floor model Magnavox, complete with surround sound.

As she began to assimilate the styles and smiles of a Los Angelean—as much as was possible for a farm girl from North Dakota—there came about an occasional movie date with someone from the office, or a dinner with a client that wasn't strictly business. Abigail was cautious with men, however. Her first sexual experience had been with a traveling salesman who had pressed his way into the solemn farm house when she was fifteen, and her parents were in town. Overall, her life-pattern in L.A. wasn't much changed from before. These days, for example, she could watch her comedies and talk shows and news on a screen so large the electronic figures seemed to be interacting right in her living room. Her lunch consisted of tuna (no mayo) on whole wheat, with Diet Pepsi. And she rarely picked up a book anymore, or wrote home, or thought about the salesman who had somehow managed to get her to remove her clothes.

In L.A. Abigail began to have a recurring dream: a man in a slate-colored suit, a black bow-tie (like a two-headed hatchet), is standing at attention beside a table; behind him is the broken cuckoo clock from her mother's kitchen, the immense iron stove of her youth; the man's hair, dark and oily, has receded, leaving arrow-tips of skin at his temples; but his face is featureless, and his left hand is gesturing at her sharply, as if to say, "No, no, you mustn't do that...." Probably the dream occurred just before she woke up, for she could usually see it vividly for most of the day. Abigail tried to recognize this man from the shape of his head and body, his attire. It wasn't her father, nor one of the bosses, nor the blondish man she dated occasionally; nor the preacher or traveling salesman from her youth; certainly not any of the judges—they were too old or too large to fit the image. All she knew for sure was that the man had long sideburns, and that he left her with a powerful sense of being caught doing something evil, only she didn't know what, and this disturbed her more than anything else.

One evening, after making more than one poor judgment in her presentation of a case involving the corporation's major distributor, Abigail Matter had an argument on the telephone (over an editorial in the newspaper attacking the Consumers Union—over nothing, really) with the man she'd been seeing. The exchange ended when she told him *never* to call her again, and the man slammed down the receiver. Fuming, Abigail tore open a bag of pretzels, turned up the volume on the telly, and stretched her one hundred twenty-three pounds on the sofa. Chin sticking out, she began watching a made-for-TV movie. Once she got into the story, she stopped noticing she was upset. It was about a woman, a member of a federal undercover unit, who had taken a job with a *haute couture* fashion importer to help bust up an international heroin ring. While working her way into a position of trust—this was the movie's "hook"—she fell in love with the narcotics kingpin. Not once did Abigail get up off her sofa as the plot progressed from bedroom scenes to a helicopter shoot-out, ending with the narc's lover dying at her feet on the deck of his yacht.

Once the movie was over, however, Abigail realized she hadn't enjoyed it very much; but there hadn't been much else on—repeat comedy and variety shows, and this movie had been widely and steadily advertised, not only on the station but in newspapers and on the radio. The commercials claimed the show, a pilot for a projected series, had cost thirty million dollars and took more than two years to produce. Sequences were shot in the Middle East, the Mediterranean, Central America, Europe, and all over the United States. Plus it featured a lot of big names. To compensate for her feelings of unfulfilled expectations (feelings which gave her a vague sense of guilt), she told herself the TV movie had at least given her glimpses of places she might never visit, and that the plot had at least taken her mind off that blond-haired bastard.

After the long list of movie credits finished sliding down the glass, before turning in for the night, Abigail sat watching the commercials that had sponsored two hours of escape. First there was one for Coca-Cola, "The real thing"; then, without any break, "Did anybody say McDonalds?"; next aired a commercial for Chevy truck dealers, "The heartbeat of America!" And several others. Finally there was a very short message that, after a few seconds had elapsed, made Abigail jump up off the sofa and kneel down in her robe before the receiver. It happened so quickly she couldn't be sure, but if she mentally shifted the man on the screen from the modern suburban kitchen to the country kitchen of her childhood, and blanked out his face, she had a strong sense that he was the man from her dreams: same hatchet bowtie, same gray suit, same arrow-tipped hairline, same long dark sideburns. The trouble with this notion was that Abigail was absolutely certain she had never seen this commercial or this man on TV before: How could she dream of a specific person in a commercial before she had seen it air?

Sprawled in bed she kept thinking about the man in the commercial, trying to make up her mind if he was the same one as in her dreams. At length she drifted into sleep. Later that night she dreamt of him as usual—making his gestures of admonishment, of warning, of threat, and when a shrieking siren woke her up, she lay there shivering in the slatted darkness, her body damp, struggling to draw back from the edge of her subconscious. For a time Abigail was helpless, incapable of reorienting herself to the glowing dial of the clock, the night table, the lamp, the venetian blinds, the framed print of a stretch of pasture. Objects seemed to float about her, making her feel as if she were submerged in a pond filled not with water but a syrupy remoteness. Then she remembered her latest dream, and she knew at once that the man in the commercial and the man in her dream were the same.

In the weeks that followed, Abigail kept her television playing until the early hours of the morning, sound turned up, clicking from channel to channel, but she couldn't find that commercial. Still she kept on the lookout, growing more and more uneasy, getting less and less sleep, not finishing her meals. Which wouldn't have been too bad in some ways (she'd been trying to lose weight) if it hadn't led to another critical lapse in a key legal action against her company. This convinced her to try a public rather than private approach to solve the mystery as quickly as possible. Abigail called the TV station which had aired the commercial, using her professional connection to ask for details—its length, the agency, its frequency, the product's name. (Having been so interested in the seller, she'd failed to notice what he was selling.) Though she spoke with the chief engineer for quite awhile, she was unable to give him enough information to identify it. As he pointed out (with strained patience), the station broadcast hundreds of commercials day and night, and the schedule was changing all the time, and a lot of them sounded alike any way.

It occurred to Abigail that a little professional advice might help alleviate her nervousness and bring back her appetite. (She had lost ten pounds in six weeks, and this worried her even more than looking chubby.) Nothing very intense—just someone to talk things over with. Following a few days of relative calmness, and a hearty Chinese dinner, however, she told herself she had simply been overreacting. Rather than see a "shrink," the next time her hands began to shake, she went to a drug store and bought a bottle of pills she'd seen advertised, and two of these, just before bedtime, knocked her out for the night. But Abigail would sleep six, eight, sometimes ten hours and would awaken not refreshed but with a head that felt as if it was filled with helium.

After one of these unrestful nights, Abigail Matter arose, drank two cups of artificially sweetened and lightened coffee, wandered from room to room without managing to get any of her Saturday chores done; finally she pulled on a pair of jeans, hurried out of the apartment building, and caught a cab downtown. She toured several department stores, specialty shops and boutiques, walking herself into a daze as she searched for items she'd seen advertised on television. Despite the millions of dollars spent in advertising these products, she was unable to find most of these things available for purchase. Abigail never even stopped for lunch. By the time she had returned to her apartment—the sun already closing in on the horizon, she had nothing to show for all that expended energy except a shortness of breath, two puffy feet, and one sizable skin-colored box.

Abigail lugged the box into the kitchen, using considerable effort to lift it onto the counter. Cutting the cord, she then pried the thick staples loose with a knife. Encased in glossy white plastic, and nearly half the size and shape of a fire hydrant, her new Do*It*All Kitchen Helper was fronted by a large chrome dial, with a lever at each side, and four buttons (green, orange, blue, red) at its base. A short black cord stuck out from behind like a rat's tail. At the bottom of the box Abigail found the warranty postcard, including a consumer questionnaire, along with a thirty-six page book of directions. Skimming through the booklet, she plugged in the Do*It*All and pressed the start button. A red light the size of a dime blinked on, off, on, off, and a low, soft humming came from its smooth body. By adjusting the dials and levers, and by pressing buttons in certain combinations, one could accomplish any number of household tasks quickly and easily; just what Abigail needed—she had no patience for kitchen chores. But though the young attorney followed the instructions with legal exactness, and reread the instructions, she couldn't get it to operate.

The Do*It*All was a complex piece of electronic hardware—the very latest—and Abigail knew it would take time to master, so she wasn't particularly concerned. With the entire next day free to play with her new gadget, she went into the living room and turned on the TV. It wasn't until she had settled on the sofa that she realized a football game had come on. Thinking she would have a better chance of finding that special commercial if she tuned in programming different from what she usually watched, rather than change the channel she sat and watched the game. In college the crashing of men in side-striped leotards and built-up, numbered jerseys had seemed ridiculous to her. Boiled down on TV, however, football took on an intriguing, microcosmic aspect, like a war in which no one dies because the combatants are not big enough, and are too distant, to take seriously. She stared at these miniature men, their bodies piling up on the turf, with the same fascination she stared at the commercials which followed each Time Out.

Exhausted from all that walking, and from lugging the box, Abigail dropped her one hundred four pounds on the bed early, and fell fast asleep—without the aid of pills. Once again she had that dream, only this time the man without a face was demonstrating a Do*It*All, explaining how easy it was to operate. At 7:30 AM the next morning she went straight into the kitchen and pressed the start button on the Do*It*All. The red light began blinking on and off; the humming started. She set the dial to different functions, adjusted the levers, and pressed various combinations of buttons, but was unable to make coffee, poach an egg, or make "golden brown toast"—or do anything else the Do*It*All promised to do. After half an hour, she gave up, convinced something was wrong with it. But the appliance store was closed on Sundays. The rest of the day she sat before the telly, annoyed with the Do*It*All, and reluctant to move away from the screen just in case that commercial should come on again.

At the office on Monday, armed with a paper cup of black coffee, Abigail dialed the store. In a low voice she explained her problem to the operator who, without a word, switched her to Customer Service. Again she explained the problem, this time with more urgency. When asked if the red light had come on and if the unit had hummed, Abigail answered affirmatively. Customer Service advised her to read the instructions *very* carefully, once again, and to follow them step by step. Abigail huffed that she'd read them several times, and had understood them perfectly, and had followed them precisely. But it still hadn't worked. Sounding skeptical, the Customer Service rep began to explain that the Do*It*All performed so many functions it sometimes took a while to understand the machine. Abigail interrupted, demanding: What about the warranty? Oh yes, Customer Service said with a certain condescension, the warranty covers parts and labor for ninety days. Do you have your receipt? Yes. Did you mail in your warranty card? Yes. In that case all you have to do is send the unit back to the manufacturer in Chicago. No, the store doesn't pack and ship items on warranty claims. No, the manufacturer doesn't pay for shipping. Assuming they're not too busy, you should be hearing from them in six to eight weeks. Of course the warranty is in effect, Customer Service emphasized, *only* if the unit has not been abused by the customer. Abigail was furious, and she would've threatened legal action had she been able to dream up reasonable grounds just then. But she protested loudly enough, at least, to attract the attention of one of the Vice Presidents, who happened to be passing by her cubicle. In any event, going through all that hassle was more trouble than it was worth to her. Besides, she hadn't mailed in the warranty card but had thrown it away.

That evening, in the privacy of her apartment, Abigail plugged the rat tail into the wall again. Step by step, as detailed in the instructions, she set the dial to Knife Sharpener, opened the cap marked "K," inserted a long bread knife in the slot, then pushed the green button. Nothing happened. Remaining calm, she pulled out the Can Opener lever, set the dial, locked in a can of tuna, and hit the orange button twice. The Do*It*All sat there humming, the red light blinking at her. Abigail removed the plug from the socket, went into the living room, sank down on the sofa, and stared at the huge blank screen with a frustration too powerful to be expressed with action.

Abigail was reluctant to discuss the Do*It*All with others: It made her feel stupid, as though she couldn't follow simple instructions, as though she had made an irresponsible buying decision. But the desire to get feedback, perhaps even sympathy, finally overcame these concerns; casually she mentioned the Do*It*All to a colleague at the office. To her surprise the effeminate attorney reported that he too had bought one as a birthday gift for his mother. Terrific gadget, he said. Nothing it can't do, he said. What'll they think of next, he said. Abigail didn't mention the problems she was having with hers. Instead she concurred with his assessment, claiming it had saved her lots of time and effort, too.

The operation of the Do*It*All was only part of Abigail's problem with it. Since the unit was quite large and bulky, it looked ugly and out of place in her not-very-spacious kitchen. And when her credit card statement showed up in her mailbox, she realized it was grossly overpriced as well. Unfortunately the Do*It*All was too big and cumbersome to store in a cabinet, and Abigail couldn't give it away—not without explaining why, not without admitting she had spent far too much on something ugly and useless and incomprehensible to her. In the succeeding weeks she considered throwing the Do*It*All away. But her North Dakota upbringing made this seem too wasteful. She just let it sit off to the side of the kitchen counter, unplugged, mute and bleak. This wouldn't have been all that inconvenient if she hadn't also grown increasingly uncomfortable entering her kitchen, and if she hadn't found herself eating a hamburger and french fries at Burger King more and more.

From time to time Abigail Matter would come upon other Do*It*Alls. When she visited colleagues, or had dinner at the apartment of a client, she would sometimes see one through a doorway down a hall, sitting upright on a counter, on a table, cold and white and immutable…the red light on, the red light off. But she didn't say a word about them. Nor did her hosts. Seeing them around made her feel less stupid, at least, and gradually her confidence increased. One evening, after spotting several of them lined up in a store window on her way home from work, she felt inspired. Without turning on the TV, she went straight into her kitchen. For a moment she thought the red light had just blinked off, but since the Do*It*All was unplugged, she realized she'd been mistaken. Now she plugged it in. Anything at all she wanted it to do—even open a can of Campbell's Soup! All the unit would do was hum in a slightly higher pitch, and blink slightly more brightly at her.

Yanking the cord from the wall, Abigail strutted to the hall closet and retrieved the pale box. Back in the kitchen she tilted the Do*It*All onto its side and pushed it into the corrugated cardboard, slapping the flaps closed and binding them tightly with cord. Abigail dragged the box to the front door of her apartment, looked out into the dimly lighted hallway. Certain no one was around, she lifted the box and took a dozen long steps to the refuse closet, setting the box inside on the tile floor. Then she scurried back to her apartment and double-locked the door. Feeling mildly relieved, Abigail clicked on the telly and sat down on the sofa. But she couldn't concentrate on the show, a comedy about a traveling salesman and a farmer's daughter. Her mind kept wandering back to the refuse closet, wondering if any neighbors had seen her carrying the large box into the building the day she bought the Do*It*All. Even if she hadn't been seen, since the unit looked brand new, the superintendent might ask people on the floor if it had been placed there by mistake. It occurred to her the episode could be concluded more discreetly if she deposited it in a lidded trash can, perhaps under a plastic garbage bag (like the black tarpaulin that had covered the electric milking machine repossessed from her family's farm). That way, it would be carted away at dawn by strangers.

Abigail sprang off the sofa, unlocked the door, rushed down the hall. To her relief, the Do*It*All was still there; leaving it in the closet, she pressed the elevator button. In a minute the elevator arrived—empty. Re-entering the refuse closet, she forced her hand between the cord and the flaps, carried the box to the elevator, pushed the button to reopen the door, and entered. On her way down, the elevator stopped on the third floor and a man with receding hair got in, his sunken dark eyes glancing at the large pale box. Abigail barged past him, the doors snapping shut behind her. Carting the box, she walked the rest of the way down.

The lobby was deserted. But having been seen, she no longer felt comfortable about dumping the Do*It*All into a trash can; silently she went down the hollow hallway and out the back door of the building.

Passing nervously, rapidly through a shadowy alley, Abigail came out on the next block, and started walking between the rows of irregularly lighted apartment buildings, crossing the street whenever someone came up the sidewalk toward her. Within twenty minutes she was moving between the glassy, darkened office towers; here the streets were desolate, the traffic a distant whisper. In another ten minutes she could smell the river, and soon was stepping along the concrete quay. By now a deep weariness had worked its way into her body and mind. Checking frequently to make sure no one was near enough to notice, she raised the box up onto the guard rail and let it slip from her sore fingers, causing a dull splash in the water. The box sank, its paleness consumed swiftly by the oily black waters. Feeling slightly faint, she walked slowly back in the general direction of her apartment building, taking another route, staying out of the light as much as possible.

A few nights later, watching television very late, Abigail Matter saw the commercial again. The man was cradling a Do*It*All in his arms like a baby, and a chill shot through her body. She climbed off the sofa and dialed the station, demanding details on the commercial. At first the engineer didn't want to cooperate with the loud, pushy woman, but when she told him who she represented, and that litigation might be involved, the young man on duty looked it up. In a few minutes the engineer got back on the line and said no commercial for a Do*It*All had aired. Though Abigail argued with him for several minutes, he did not alter his claim. Maybe it was another station, he suggested. No! she snapped, screeching the name of the show she'd been watching. Stung by her outburst, the engineer conceded that show had just aired, but he didn't budge on the commercial. Abigail declared she was going to initiate legal proceedings against the engineer, the station, the network, and the young man told her to go right ahead. No commercial for a Do*It*All had aired, he insisted, and invited her to inspect the schedule of commercials at the station for herself. With her TV still gabbing in the background, Abigail hung up on him.

For the first time in years—since that morning the pastor had threatened her with eternal damnation; or the afternoon the traveling salesman had talked her out of her innocence; or the night she'd seen the bloodless skin of poverty, her grandmother, spread out in their parlor at the farm—Abigail Matter felt afraid. Afraid of the telephone, afraid of the sofa, afraid of the walls, afraid to take her pills, and especially afraid of going to sleep…knowing that dream was coiled under her bed, waiting to spiral up the bedpost, over the pillow, and into her ear: sliding along her mind as it did night after night.

The only thing in the apartment that did not make her afraid was the telly. Abigail sat on the floor, crossed her legs, and stared at the glowing screen as the anchorman went through the events of the day in the order most likely to arouse the emotions of viewers, and concluding with a brief statement on the dissolution of the Citizens for Children's Television group. Abigail blinked through a series of commercials, on into a brownish, muffled movie whose characters, during the next two hours, disintegrated slowly into dots before her eyes. At last no picture came on; only a dull glare, a low humming. Over those hours there had been no sign of that commercial, but Abigail was too tired to care one way or the other. Around 3:30 AM she clicked off the remote and moved listlessly through an undulating blackness, relinquishing her ninety-six pounds to the mattress. Feeling nothing, thinking nothing, wanting nothing, Abigail toppled into her subconscious instantly. For six straight hours her body did not stir in the tangled sheets, as if she were Juliet waiting to awaken from her deathlike state to reunite with Romeo.

Next morning, Abigail's eyes clicked open and peered into the digital eyes of the clock on her night table: 9:30. *Damn! I'm going to be late for that early meeting with my boss*, she thought, forcing herself to sit up and climb out of bed, though very slowly. Even though she'd had nothing to eat or drink the previous evening, her stomach felt bloated, her head felt woozy. Rinsing her hands and face, she yanked onto her bony limbs a Laura Ashley skirt and a Gloria Vanderbilt blouse, then forced a brush through her hair. At the elevator she pressed the button repeatedly until it lifted itself to her floor. Hurrying through the lobby and out onto the street, she began waving her hand wildly. At last a cab jerked to a stop, and she climbed in, nearly screeching the address of her office building to the driver.

As they rocked down the wide avenue, cutting in and out of traffic, stopping with a jolt at street lights, Abigail noticed something odd: from behind, the cabbie—with his very pale skin, his very dark hair, his very long sideburns—reminded her of the faceless man in the TV commercial. Unable to find the driver's identification photo, which was required by law to be posted in the vehicle, she shifted her position on the back seat, but was still unable to get a good look at him. In a few minutes the cab came to a stop in front of her office building. When the driver turned to collect his payment, Abigail was struck by how ordinary, how unthreatening his forehead, eyes, mouth, and chin appeared to be. That's when she remembered her dream of early that morning: Abigail had run into the faceless man in a department store; they chatted like old friends. Only, as they talked, his face took on definition and for a moment Abigail thought he was the traveling salesman from her youth. But the scene shifted. Once more she was talking to the faceless man, seated on the sofa in her living room, and he leaned over and kissed her mouth. The young attorney arose and led him by the hand to her bed.

Since Abigail did not reach into her purse for money to pay the driver, he said: Isn't this the address you gave me?

I want you to take me downtown instead, she replied.

A quizzical look in his eyes, he turned to his steering wheel, and shifted into drive. Several minutes later the cab rolled up near the entrance to a large department store. Abigail paid the driver, adding too large a tip, causing him to thank her twice. For a moment she stood at the curb, watching as the cab pulled away and blended in with the mid-morning traffic. Now she turned and went through the revolving doors into the store, already buzzing with shoppers, and rode the escalator to a higher floor.

The moment she stepped off the moving stairs into the vast, windowless space, she saw it—the smooth white plastic body of a Do*It*All, set up on a counter in the appliance department, red eye blinking. Now the rest of the dream came to her: Long after the faceless man had left her bed, dressed, and disappeared out the door—disappeared from her life, Abigail began to feel the vibrations of life in her womb, and in due time gave birth to a boy with tiny red eyes and white, glossy skin.

As Abigail Matter moved up to the sales counter in Appliances, she fished frantically in her wallet for her American Express credit card.

A man with long, ivory teeth scurried across the busy commercial street and stepped in front of a man with wide, nervous eyes.

"How have you been?" the teeth inquired.

"Who the hell are you?" nervous eyes snapped, starting past him.

"Wait, Bill!" the teeth called. "I've got good news for you."

The eyes looked back. He wondered how this stranger had gotten hold of his name...*probably the same mysterious ways all those companies that mail me sales flyers got my name.* "You're confusing me with someone else," he said, tucking the folded newspaper under his arm.

"You attended the School of Business at the State University."

The man's shiny teeth, set in a doughy face, began to seem familiar to Bill, and he considered asking for his name. But he had to get back to his apartment and go through the classified employment ads without further delay. "No, I did not go to the School of Business," he replied, turning away.

"Majored in Public Relations, right?"

Bill stopped, and in the tone of someone who'd been caught in a lie, he muttered, "What is this news you have for me, this supposedly good news?"

"It's about a job."

Just then Bill noticed the trucks and shoppers were gone, that the two of them were no longer on a crowded street downtown but were standing outside the brownstone building in which he resided: the blunt odor of boiled potatoes, the four-letter words in chalk on the steps, the iron gates across the windows.

The teeth kept opening and closing: "Of course it may involve some repositioning on your part, learning new disciplines and new skills."

"What're you driving at?" Bill said, not moving away mostly because he wanted time to reorient himself, to figure out how he had gotten from one place to another without realizing it was happening.

"I'm talking about knowledge," the teeth explained.

As if to see him more clearly, Bill blinked several times.

"Take me, for instance. As soon as I think I have a handle on the book trade," the teeth chuckled, "my perspective is overthrown by new developments in the product and in the marketing of that product."

Though he wanted to leave the grinning man standing on the sidewalk, alone, talking to himself, instead Bill remained face to face with him and said: "Everything is constantly changing, so what's the big deal?"

"That's why knowledge has to be updated and supplemented all the time."

Eyeing the black book satchel in the man's hand, Bill realized what the man was leading up to. "I already own a set of encyclopedias," he said, stretching his legs up the steps of his building.

As Bill stepped onto the concrete landing he heard the teeth, just behind him, say in a confidential tone: "Did you know the set of encyclopedias in the American home today, on the average, is 12.7 years old. Incredible! Three hundred million people thirteen years behind the times."

"What difference does it make?"

The teeth flashed: "Every decision based on outdated information can alter one's fortune in very significant ways."

"The more you know," said Bill, "the worse off you are."

"I'm sure you don't really believe that, Bill," the salesman remarked pleasantly.

The nervous eyes faced the teeth. "Can't you see I'm not interested?" he said, searching for keys in his pockets. "Besides, we've got the Internet now, we don't need encyclopedias, at least not in book form. Books are dust collectors."

"Yes, except that the Universal Book of Knowledge never grows old," the teeth clacked. "From moment to moment you get the latest in politics, science, medicine, education, sports, transportation, commerce, the arts, religion—everything under the sun and over the moon."

"Get *lost,*" Bill hissed, twisting his key in the vestibule lock, entering, and shutting the door quietly but firmly, automatically relocking it.

The man with the ivory teeth stood outside, grinning through the window of the door. "The UBK updates itself—you don't have to do a thing," he said through the wooden door.

Bill moved weightlessly through the drab light of a bare bulb past the landlord's apartment, noiselessly unlocked his door at the end of the hall, and inserted himself into his rooms. The encyclopedia salesman was seated on the sofa before five red leatherette, gold-stamped books, which were spread like a hand of poker playing cards on the short-legged table before him.

"How did you...get in here?" Bill stammered.

The salesman's straight lip sliding up over his gums, he went on from where he'd left off downstairs: "Just imagine, within these pages is everything you'll ever need to know about any subject at every moment, and its glossy, acid-free paper will last a thousand years."

Though stunned to find the salesman in his apartment, Bill had to admit that weird things had been happening to him ever since he'd been fired from the small public relations agency. Rather than let this strangeness get the better of him, he decided to respond coolly, rationally—to get rid of this nuisance by using a strategy of unequivocal rejection:

"Even if you claim they're the most comprehensive encyclopedias on earth—even if you're practically giving them away, I don't want them. Encyclopedias in print and on computers cut everything down to a few meaningless paragraphs or pages. They oversimplify complex events, distort vital issues, and leave out too much. What can they tell us about the history of an ordinary man's life, moment to moment, day to day, year to year?—nothing. I'll never own another encyclopedia as long as I live. Never."

"How old is your set?"

"I *don't* own a set."

"May I have a look at them?"

"No!"

Seeking out—and spotting on a shelf above the television—the dusty volumes, which were oxblood-colored, the salesman shook his head gravely and clicked his tongue. "A public relations writer needs timely reference resources much more than the average citizen."

"I'm not a writer," Bill said, adding quietly, "not anymore."

"And after ten years with the same company," said the teeth, shaking his head sympathetically, still staring at the encyclopedias on the shelf.

"What gives you the idea I was with that company so long?"

"Don't be discouraged, Bill. That's why I'm here. The Universal Book of Knowledge will help you find a new job. At a higher salary. With a fine benefits program."

"How can it possibly do all that?"

"Because the UBK continually monitors the job market, so you'll always know when a company is upgrading and looking to build up its staff."

"Are you saying these books are supplemented by print-outs from central computers?"

"Oh, no, no, no, my dear friend. This information is contained entirely in printed books—you know, in the tradition of good old Gutenberg. But with a difference. These pages simply revise themselves in print on a moment-to-moment basis. You won't need to wait for updates to arrive in the mail or to insert any disks into your computer. It's the best of both worlds, print and electronics."

Bill shook his head vigorously, as if attempting to absorb and understand what he was being told.

"UBK's up-to-the-minute edition, for example, has an extensive rundown on jobs in the computer field. Have you ever considered entering the rapidly exploding field of business graphics? Or spread-sheet analysis? Or data program development? Have you ever considered traveling through cyber space for the sheer thrill of it? The UBK can make it happen, and all through printed materials."

"You'd better get out of here," Bill warned.

"If computers are not for you, what about a career in selling? Sure, that would be perfect for you, with your background in public relations. After all, one way or another, isn't everyone in this country involved in selling?"

Anger flared in Bill, and he strode to the salesman on the sofa. But instead of pulling him up off the seat and dragging him to the door, he leaned over, picked up the ballpoint pen on the table, and began scrawling his name on a black line at the bottom of a long printed form.

It wasn't until the man with the ivory teeth began tucking his samples back into the satchel that the man with the nervous eyes fully comprehended what had happened. "Give me back that contract!" Bill demanded.

"Shipping takes six to eight weeks," the teeth assured him, snapping the buckle shut and clutching the handle of the satchel. Now he stood up. "The good news is that you don't have to begin making payments until you receive your complete set."

"Payments? I haven't paid my rent in three months."

"The Universal Book of Knowledge will straighten all that out," the salesman smiled. "All you have to do is show a little patience, a little trust."

The customer shouted, "You're not leaving with that contract in your possession!"

"My business card is on your table in case you want to show the Universal Book of Knowledge to neighbors," the teeth insinuated, pivoting to go.

The customer sprang at him, grasping the doughy neck with his outstretched fingers. But the salesman did not fight back, or even struggle. All he did was stand there, grinning grotesquely. His lack of resistance angered the customer even more, and he drove his fingers deeper into the pliable white flesh. The harder he squeezed, the more distorted the grin became. Suddenly the salesman's lung exploded with a muffled clap, throwing open his ribs, long and white and sharp-edged.

Horrified, the customer peered with huge eyes into the gaping mouth of the chest and saw the salesman's heart, hanging by its tubes, pumping, pumping. It was slimy and black, the size of a clenched fist, and it bulged as if stuffed with coins. Sensing that organ was at the core of all his troubles, he plunged his bare arm into the dark cavity, yanked the heart loose from its moorings, then rushed out of the room and down the hall, splashing thick blood on the floors and walls as he fled.

Night had draped over the city, and not another person was on the street outside his building. His wild eyes searched frantically for a trash can or sewer cover. Finding no place to discard the heart, he dashed into an alley between two tenement buildings.

Through the plasmic darkness he moved as in a nightmare. Along the brick wall he found a line up of battered metal cans. As he yanked the lid off the closest one, he realized the black thing in his hand was still expanding and contracting, and he understood that it would go on beating forever.

Remembering how Native Americans acquired courage from the hearts of the beasts they would slay, with both hands he raised it to his mouth and sank his teeth into the throbbing organ, tearing off a slab of the tough, juicy muscle. The bloody meat was bitter on his tongue, but he chewed vigorously, steadily until it had been entirely consumed.

ROOTS OF EVIL

A man and his wife were living in a little apartment in a big building, and this couple went without lean meat and without new coats and without babies for five years, putting every spare buck aside for a down payment on a house all their own, where kids could be brought up surrounded by real grass, and where the music came from blue birds rather than taxi horns. Occasionally their resolve weakened—they splurged on a movie, pizza pie and a bottle of red wine, but by and large they stuck to their dream.

Once the couple had more or less reached their financial goal (maybe a little before), they began reading every line of the Sunday classifieds, sent away for free property lists, clipped coupons for Built-It-Yourself house plans, scrutinized the coiled photographs in real estate office windows, and on weekends would ride a bus—any bus—as far as it would take them, assessing dozens of houses along the route, whether they had a FOR SALE sign out front or not. Buoyed by a feeling they were closing in on their dream beams, they seemed to float rather than walk up to model homes—ranch, split-level, double-decker, triple-decker …any shape or size, as long as it had walls and a roof. This went on for months until, inevitably, their feet landed flat on the freshly paved driveways of reality.

Prices and down payments and mortgage rates were plenty higher than when they'd started saving, and while inflation had made it much more costly to get by, their income had remained about the same. The man was employed at an insurance agency in 'midtown as a part-salaried, part-commissioned salesman, and a growing number of people were putting their money into to-day's needs rather than tomorrow's security. So the couple was forced to bypass new and not-so-very-new homes, and to concentrate on houses that had been around a terribly long time, the kind that real estate ads referred to as "homes with charm." But the homes with charm they came across were either far beyond their dollar-power, or far too ripe to provide shelter *and* comfort, not to mention a reasonable basis for pride. Certainly the man and his wife were willing to put in quite a bit of work on any place they moved their pudgy couch into. But if a house had to be jacked up so that its foundation could be replaced stone by stone, or if a house shook in the laziest of southwesterlies, was it worth the expense, the energy, the aggravation that went with rehabilitation?

Just when the couple seemed ready to tear up, in despair, their photocopied lists of houses, one of the many brokers they had registered with located a stick-frame structure of about thirty years' standing which "looked like new," according to the broker, and which was only slightly higher than they could realistically afford. Seems the woman who placed it on the market had recently lost her husband—divorce or heart attack or whatever, and she was anxious to get out from under its memories. The woman was willing to sacrifice the bi-level dwelling, the broker explained, for substantially less than its market value. Though greatly discouraged by then, the couple decided to make the effort and take a look.

It was not long after the man and his wife had pulled up—heavy-faced in the back of the broker's sedan, and had walked through its six and a half rooms, and had made a few alterations to the place in their minds, that they knew they had come home. All the way back to the city the couple chattered about its sunny kitchen, broad backyard, extra closets and, most impressive of all, its setting near the end of a quiet, maple-bordered lane. Back at their cramped, sunless apartment they talked it over for hours that night, not even thinking to turn on the TV. Finally they went to bed with fluffy hearts and in total accord: This is the house for us.

First thing next morning they took all the cash they had folded in his wallet and tucked under her scarves in the bottom bureau drawer—even borrowed a few bucks from their friends across the hall, then downed one cup of tea each. Out the door they fluttered, hopped on the subway, caught a bus at the terminal, and rode for an hour. Then they stood out on the walk until the broker—astonished to see them so early—arrived and unlocked the door. "You could've just called or done this by credit card," he said. "No, no," they said. "We wanted to do this in person and in cash to make sure no one put a deposit down before we did." Surrounding him, they put a $100 binder on the house, signed something pink, and shook hands with the pleasant man in the suit. Smiling broadly, the couple immediately rode back to the city and applied for a mortgage.

Though everything was now in the works, the couple still didn't feel secure. During the ensuing weeks, they kept telephoning and barging in on the broker and the banker, trying to find out what if anything was happening. Be patient, they said. These things take time. But the couple, their hearts churning like an old deep-well pump, kept after them. At long last the banker telephoned them, and they immediately telephoned the broker. Later that week they met with the broker, banker, house owner, and attorneys at another bank. Here they signed green, yellow and mostly white papers, handed over the check, accepted the keys to their new kingdom, then nearly shook the hands off the sad-eyed ex-owner, and the happy-faced broker, banker and attorneys.

Within two weeks of that historic moment in their lives—the former owner having moved out quickly, the man and his wife had packed their life's accumulations in cardboard boxes they'd been collecting in their tiny living room, rolled and tied their rug with leather belts, and said their farewells (over punch and popcorn) to their friends on the ninth floor. Tears bloomed in their eyes. But the next day—mid-afternoon by the time the men finished loading up, they followed the moving van in a rented Ford station wagon (loaded to the roof with those items too precious and/or dainty to trust in the paws of professional haulers) out along the Expressway. As the buildings became shorter and more rectangular, the couple's excitement grew rounder and higher. Gradually the concrete gave way to cut-outs of green lawn, which were topped by cubed constructions wrapped in brown, blue, red, green, or yellow siding. By the time they pulled up in front of the next-to-last house on Peaceful Lane—to *their* house, the man and wife were on the verge of exploding like a pair of balloons that had floated too high, too fast.

The house was not in perfect condition, nor especially large, but it was certainly roomier than their apartment. And a lot more airy. The not-perfect-but-airy house had flower boxes (although somewhat rotted) at the front windows, and quaint (though loose) shutters out front. The screens that stood between them and the flies/mosquitoes had only half a dozen or so punctures each. The interior paint (the color of mold) would serve them another year or two…until they had saved up enough to repaint the place themselves. The grass had bare spots, plus legions of dandelions, and consisted of a narrow strip left and right of the house, with maybe twenty-five feet front and back—not nearly as large a yard as they remembered. But it was more or less green, and a lot softer than the concrete courtyard of their old apartment building. The broken bathroom tiles could be remortared without much expense or mess, surmised the Lord of the House, and the leaking faucets could almost be silenced by twisting the knobs with both hands, noted the Lady of the House. No, their home was not without its flaws, but that only gave it that lived-in sense of comfort, the man and his wife told each other, reveling in the incredible basement storage space, in the amazing privacy.

All in all, the new residents of Peaceful Lane felt very lucky. Except in one regard. While the man had worked all of his professional life for the Continental Insurance Company—first as a messenger between CIC headquarters and the branch offices around the city, then as a desk clerk on policy riders, and finally as a full-fledged salesman of life, home and auto protection at one of the company's bigger agencies, the man who lived next door, in the last house on the block, had worked most of his professional life for the National Insurance Company—by now he ran the local agency for NIC, offering life, home and auto protection to suburban property owners. Dating back to early in the century, when both companies were founded, Continental and National had been the most vicious of competitors, and continued that tradition to this very day. If anything, as the years dragged on, the competition had grown more and more ferocious.

To gain an advantage over the other in the marketplace, CIC and NIC tried every trick that crawled into the minds of their advertising creatives and marketing strategists. Ever since the FCC had permitted the practice, they had been making sly references to swampy spots in each other's policies via their countless coast-to-coast television commercials. The companies' competitiveness had become so famous it achieved the status of an old joke with the public. But National and Continental were so closely matched in annual grosses that their respective officers and stockholders couldn't see beyond the bottom line. The hit-and-run rivalry was most fierce at the point of sale. Partly because that is the logical battlefront of commerce, and partly because their reps were weaned (in sales training courses) on suspicion of the other company, with techniques in retaliation offered in advanced sessions to promising up-and-comers. It had gotten so bad the employees of CIC and NIC were forced to take loyalty pledges at their respective companies. Therefore, when each of the two salesmen residing at the end of Peaceful Lane found out how the other earned his living, the emotions shot up their necks automatically, turning their faces green and yellow, approximately the color of the aluminum that sealed their respective houses. These were also the banner colors of their respective companies—green for CIC, and yellow for NIC.

The natural enemies might still have managed to ignore each other sufficiently to exist peaceably on abutting properties—that is, if the man from Continental and the man from National hadn't also had very different value systems: a reflection, each was convinced, of the subversive organization for which the other worked. While Mr. and Mrs. Continental had lived all their married and unmarried lives in the clutter of kicked-over garbage cans and with the subways rattling their windows and sirens snarling all night, and had moved beyond the city limits to find contentment through the orderliness of equally spaced houses and discretely growing daffodil bulbs, Mr. and Mrs. National had lived all their married and unmarried lives in this community of trimmed hedges and hosed driveways and sluggish dogs and temple rummage sales, and after that many years in this community the peppy pair found it all as bland as bran flakes.

Since they had been drilled to expect the meanest behavior from—and to display the foulest hatred toward—one another, the sharp contrasts in their life-styles seemed quite appropriate to them...the way cats and dogs accept their hostile feelings toward each other. But habitating garbage-can-to-garbage-can made it impossible to avoid being reminded of how the other lived and, therefore, who the other worked for, and this made each all the more determined to carry on precisely the way each saw fit. Both salesmen had brought their competitive urges home, and that, in the final accounting, is what caused all the heart-burns and stomach-aches.

Though they didn't mean anything by it, Mr. and Mrs. Continental were not inclined to go around smiling without particular reason. People who did that, they felt, usually proved to be a little "off." Smiles, like parties, ought to be saved for special occasions. These ideas on smiling were only too evident as they marched, straight-lipped, milk-eyed, in and out of the greenish house, causing Mr. National to comment to Mrs. National on several occasions: "I'll bet his face would shatter if he smiled." And when most people in the eastern time zone should have been sleeping, or so the Nationals thought, somewhere between 11 AM and 1 PM, Mrs. Continental would be scrubbing and hosing the garbage cans, making it sound "like Niagara Falls" below the Nationals' window. Still another irritant was that the Continentals insisted on chasing the Nationals' terrier off their lawn. It's a free country, Mr. National firmly believed, especially as far as dogs were concerned. They could do their duty when and where they wanted. At the same time, whenever Mr. and Mrs. Continental were settling down for a Saturday evening of pleasantly numbing, barely audible television, Mr. and Mrs. National seemed hell-fired to learn the latest, loudest dance. Or if Mr. Continental stretched out in his lawn chair after church with the Sunday business section, a sticky paper plate from next door was sure to blow into his face. On any day of the week, the Nationals' car was subject to be left idling in the driveway between the houses: Fumes would sift through the screen door into the Continentals' kitchen, fouling a meatloaf that already was none too tasty, lacking spice and overloaded with leftover bread.

A few times during the first six months, Mr. Continental tried to speak to Mr. National about the noise and debris in what he considered to be a low-key, reasonable way. But the Nationals had not appreciated his "attitude" at all. They had been living in that community far too long to take advice from a "damned foreigner," which is what people working for National called those working for Continental. Just because that damned foreigner had to get up early every day and trek into the city to pawn off phony policies on the unsuspecting public had nothing to do with them, stated the man from National. If they insist on living out here with the human race, *they* will have to change, not us. *They* will have to learn to smile, and sleep later. All of his cronies on Peaceful Lane would take another gulp of the Nationals' beer in his backyard before shaking their heads in agreement.

Increasingly distressed by the "attitude" of the Nationals—and agitated over a particularly rambunctious party one night, the man from Continental actually dialed the police. But realizing that even cops can't stop people from behaving like primates, he hung up before they answered. Besides, that would have been a major escalation. Somewhat more rational by the next afternoon, he eased into the subject with the neighbors on the other side of his house. His idea was to gain sympathy—and unified action, through a common bond of annoyance. But the couple in white shorts and white sneakers merely listened with blood-shot stares, and he realized, too late, that they had attended the party the night before.

It took only a few minutes for the couple in sneakers to inform their friends at the end of the block that the "city people" had been complaining about them. This might well explain why—in the course of the Continentals' second half year in the not-per-fect-but-airy-house—the noise grew louder, the garbage deeper, the kids brattier, and the dog more adventuresome in its pursuit of bones and places to hide them. During this stretch Continental discovered the extreme limits of his patience. Something, he de-clared to his wife, had to be done about those "reckless fools" who pawned off soap-bubble policies on innocent consumers, "reckless fools" being the name employees of Continental gave to those of National. His wife agreed there were far too many paper cups and roller skates lying around, and that lately the CD player had been going too loud for too long. People ought to be more considerate of other people, she observed. At the same time she did not see the wisdom in trying to change their neigh-bors' habits. It'll just create more sour feelings, said his wife, only make them noisier. Might just as well live with it, she said.

"Live with it?" her husband cried. "I've been living with it almost a year, and I don't intend to live with it any longer!" Something, he repeated, had to be done. And soon. He just didn't know what.

The question of what to do about the man from National followed the man from Continental everywhere—to his desk at the agency, to their Friday evening grocery shopping, lying beside his wife in bed. Staring at the ceiling, which was smeared with nightmarish shadows, he would flip over and over like a pancake for hours—not only because of the squealing and stomping next door, but because he was scraping his mind for ways to stop the reckless fool from wrecking their hard-earned, much-deserved peace and privacy.

"That's it!" he shouted one night, startling his wife out of a hard-earned, much-deserved sleep.

"Go to sleep," his wife muttered.

The man was too excited to go to sleep, and spent at least an hour considering the logistics of cutting off the house with a ten-foot, solid wood fence. But the more he thought about it, the more impractical the idea loomed. First there was the expense. Inflation had continued to kick prices upstairs, especially for products made of natural materials. And the gap between his commissions and his bills was getting wider, ever wider. And living out in the suburbs, they'd been forced to invest in a used car, which turned out to be temperamental, lazy and a spendthrift (nine miles to the gallon—if driven 38 MPH): Every extra dime dripped out of their pockets like burnt oil out of the crankcase. And then there was the work required to put up such a fence, plus the cost and labor of maintaining it, to consider. In the dimness of 2:12 AM his bright idea no longer shined so brightly.

A ten-foot wooden fence was out of the question, he admitted around 2:30, and a five-foot plastic divider just wasn't going to give him the separation he needed, nor the durability he demanded. Galvanized steel was even more expensive than wood. But he was on to something, he felt, and continued to explore the general idea of cutting off the two houses. Not long after 3:00 AM he came up with a brilliant compromise: the man from Continental would let nature do his work for him. He would plant a row of thick shrubs between the houses, and these shrubs would not only build a wall by themselves, but would pretty much maintain themselves, too, with the help of a little water. Best of all, there would be only a one-time, not very great expense, so his wife couldn't nag him about spending money foolishly. Once again he shouted, "That's it!"

His wife didn't bother waking up this time.

A few hours later he sprang out of bed whistling, something he didn't do very often. From his smirk it was obvious to his wife he was feeling very smart. She said nothing, having learned to wait out her husband's outbursts of enthusiasm—like those of any salesman. Of course Continental would've discussed the idea with his wife had he not been certain she would only try to discourage him. These days, she never seemed to back him up on anything. Since it was Saturday, soon as he finished his yellow tea and dry toast, he muttered something about having "a little shopping to do," hopped into the car and sputtered black smoke all the way to the nursery. Stalking through the aisles, he took a long look around: he'd had no idea there were so many different kinds of bushes. At last he approached an attendant: She had skin as splotchy as the bark of a sycamore.

"Something that grows thick," explained Continental, "and needs very little care."

Juniper hedges are hearty, and in five, six years you'll have a thick growth, explained the attendant. Four, maybe five feet tall.

"Four feet in six years?" Continental was disappointed down to the nails on his toes. "I need something that grows big and fast."

You couldn't go wrong with anything in the willow family, said the saleswoman, who pointed a tendrilled finger toward a group of single sticks protruding from burlap sacks.

"Those little things?"

"Fastest growing trees in the nursery," she claimed.

Trees? With trees Continental was afraid he'd end up with no protection where he needed it most—near the ground. Then it occurred to him that willows grew very leafy, and tended to hang down low. What did not occur to him was that an even more compelling vote for trees, rather than bushes, had been cast in the subbasement of his mind: CIC's official emblem and slogan (which appeared in all of its television and newspaper ads) was "The Tree of Life."

"I'll take half a dozen!" he exclaimed, feeling fulfilled in some deep-seated, primeval way.

Down the streets he chug-chug-chugged, whistling again, the tips of the willows sticking out of the trunk. Though he'd slept only a blink, he did not feel tired. Not wasting a step or a stroke, he grabbed the shovel in his garden shed and started digging the first of six holes, two feet deep, five feet apart. His wife stuck her head out the side door and asked what in Lucifer's name he thought he was doing. Without looking up from his work the man replied sagely, "I'm removing a thorn from my side." Biting her lip, she disappeared into the greenish house.

By lunchtime the man from Continental was sweating and puffing and patting the soft brown earth around the last of the skinny whips—before the Nationals had even unwound from their sheets. But their brats had squatted five feet away on their own crabby, uncut grass, watching the entire operation with stretched eyes, scratching their bushy heads. The dog had stared at him, too, convinced the man was burying bones. Continental wanted to ask them what they thought they were looking at, but he had vowed not to speak to them—any of them—ever again. His wife stuck her head out the screen door once more, this time to tell him the vegetable soup was hot. The sight of him on his hands and knees, muddy to the elbows, caused her to bite her lip once more, only harder.

Face-to-face at the formica table they had brought to this kitchen from the city, the wife asked her husband to explain, and he did. After hearing him out, she wagged her head slowly as if to rearrange his words in her head. Then she pointed out the plants weren't big enough to stop a flying ant, much less a flying beer can.

"What do you think I am," he smirked, "a foreigner? I bought six of the fastest growing trees in the nursery."

His wife asked him point blank how much they had cost, and he claimed they were on sale. But she wasn't satisfied, and said that even if they were on sale, and even if they did grow fast, they still wouldn't cut off any noise. Not a single shout, she emphasized.

"Out of sight," the husband smirked, "out of mind."

The wife looked at her husband as if he were slightly out of *his* mind, and swallowed a spoonful of watery, luke-warm soup.

"Maybe now," said the husband, slurping a spoonful of watery, luke-warm soup, "we'll start getting a little sleep around here."

By that time the kids next door had awakened their parents with the news. Soon the man from National staggered out the front door in his striped underwear, pretending to search for the daily newspaper under his dried-out rhododendron. When he saw the saplings, he immediately called for his wife, and when Mrs.

National finally staggered outside, in her see-through negligee, a cigarette hanging from her mouth, he pointed at the sticks. "What do you suppose *that* means?"

His wife wondered out loud why it had to mean anything, especially at that ungodly hour.

"Trust me," he counseled her, "it means something, and I mean to find out what."

His wife shrugged her shoulders doubtfully, and suggested they have some coffee before their heads toppled into the weeds on their lawn. So they went back inside and had some coffee—a whole pot, and then they had some lunch, and later they had some dinner, but National couldn't get those six sticks, all in a row like the bars of a cage, out of his mind. And after the sun had plopped behind the pentagonal silhouettes across the street, and the Continentals had rattled off in a blast of black smoke, National went right up to the saplings. He wanted to see for himself if they were poison oak or something equally catching, but especially to make absolutely certain they were planted on the foreigner's side of the property line. The saplings were so bare he couldn't tell what they were, but they looked harmless enough, and he needn't have worried about where they were planted: Continental had been very careful about legal boundaries, knowing only too well that National would jump at the chance to sue him.

Still the plantings annoyed National. Back in his yellowish house he sounded off on the saplings as an underhanded comment on the company he served, not to mention their way of life. Though ready to argue these points to the grave, he couldn't quite explain why he was certain of their truth. His wife didn't interpret the plantings this way at all, but she had lived with him long enough not to try to talk him out of any idea that got into his head. Instead she pointed out the saplings were ridiculously skinny, and probably wouldn't live out the week. Having been tossed a twig of hope to hang onto, her husband felt a mite less uneasy...at least for one week.

Skinny though they were, the saplings grew, and as they did, both salesmen began to target—from their respective plots in the world—on the progress of the plantings. Continental forgot about having babies, and National dropped the dancing lessons. Their faces took on the blankness of an unfilled out insurance policy. As they moved to and from their offices and their homes and the shopping mall and the church/synagogue, between their clients and their wives and the sales clerks and their priest/rabbi, the mood was one of intense contemplation, as if each were planning the perfect murder. In a few months, however, the saplings had grown several feet tall, and branches had appeared. It was only then that National realized what the plantings really meant and, turning greenish in his neck, he shouted: "The Tree of Life!" His wife, who didn't watch much television, nodded as if she thought he was making sense.

While Continental was fertilizing and watering, National was brooding and plotting. He would teach those damn foreigners a lesson, he swore to his wife—even if that mission had to become his life's work. His wife agreed the Continentals had no right to spoil their fun, that the people next door should loosen up a bit. Even so, she didn't think they should do anything foolish. Certainly it wouldn't change next door's thinking, would only make them think up new ways to be drab. Might just as well live and let live, she said. But her husband replied she was crazy if she thought he was going to let Continental get a free commercial "practically on my front lawn." Mrs. National became vaguely alarmed at the flames in his eyes.

Noticing her concern he assured his wife, "Don't worry. I'm not going to rush in like a fool." He, the man from National, was smart enough to be patient, to think this out very carefully. And he did. Night after night—after their guests had wandered home, or the late talk show on TV was over, lying in bed beside his wife, he would search the grounds of his mind for a clever, satisfying, fail-proof response to The Tree of Life. But in the end, he simply responded to the throbbing in his chest. One moonless midnight, when the young willows were quite a bit taller than himself, and many branches were reaching out from their thickening trunks, he climbed gently (without disturbing his wife's sleep) out of bed, and slippered weightlessly out the back door. In his garden shed he found what he was looking for and, cloaked in a dark robe, crept on hands and knees between the houses. Quietly he snipped every one of the willows three inches from the ground.

Next morning Continental could be heard screaming madly. Neighbors two blocks away (they reported at a barbecue later) thought someone had lost a toe in a lawn mower again. It wasn't long before he was storming in his maroon robe up the flagstone path of the last house on the block, whereupon he began pounding on the door. Expecting a visitation of some sort, and having slept peacefully for a change, National had gotten up earlier than usual, and had already had his coffee; therefore he was in a relatively tolerant, and tolerable, condition. Nevertheless Continental's intrusion didn't please him, and he thumped out onto the stoop in his purple silk lounging pajamas. Being a much larger man than the foreigner, National felt no compunction about shaking his fist at him—warning him that he'd better take out plenty of NIC insurance because if he pounded on his door one more time he was going to pound some sense into his skull. "And drive you back to hell, where you came from."

Continental, being a much smaller man, demonstrated a certain wisdom by backing off, turning on his heel, and bounding away in a huff. But when he was safely on his own turf he swore over his shoulder: "I'm going to call my attorney and sue you for everything you've got, you reckless fool." National placed his hand over his heart in mock horror and demanded to know on what grounds. Continental waved a shaking fist at the violated trees lying on their sides and shouted: "You know damn well what grounds!"

National replied, "You better have plenty of proof for that kind of accusation, you damned foreigner, otherwise you'll be hearing from *my* attorney."

Though Continental *knew* National was responsible, it was true—he had no proof whatsoever. For the first month or so after the plantings he had kept watch over the young trees, as if they were a set of new-born sextuplets. But growing accumulatively more tired, and beginning to think the threat had petered out, and responding to his wife's nightly pleas for him to come to bed, he finally stopped waiting up at the window. Now the worst had come to be, and he had no proof. It was all his wife's fault! Up the stoop of his house he kicked in a rage, slammed the door shut, and could be heard all day, a block away, stomping and ranting about the house. His wife spent the afternoon straightening up the basement.

In the city next day, on his lunch hour, the man from Continental called the attorney who had closed the sale on the house, and he was given the number of a civil lawyer. His hand was shaking so badly he punched a wrong digit and had to redial. But the conversation merely confirmed what he already knew: He didn't have much of a case—no case at all, and would only be throwing his money into the attorney's vacation fund. The way his sales had been going, Continental didn't have a nickel to waste. Exasperated, he stared all day at the list of customers, never thinking to notify them of premium increases, or sending out past-due policy cancellation warnings. In the evening he brooded all the way home on the train. Dragging himself up his driveway, he saw it—a large American flag nailed to the front of the house next door. True. The Fourth of July weekend was almost upon them. But a striped flag appeared in all of NIC's advertising, so Continental knew precisely what National had in mind: "The Banner of Security!" he cried. The dog helped to intensify the tension in his stomach by barking at his heels right up to his own kitchen door. Continental turned yellow with outrage, and would've kicked the dog in the teeth had he not been certain he was being watched—more or less constantly.

The moment he entered the house, he called a war council with his wife, and she detected a fearsome foreboding in his outcry. After she had quieted him down a bit by agreeing with everything he said and by pouring him two glasses of red wine (she kept one cheap bottle on hand for such emergencies) and taking into account that her husband's sales would never break any records—would never permit them to move anywhere else, Mrs. Continental suggested as gently as she knew how that it might be sensible for them to try and make the best of an admittedly bad situation. One of these days, she concluded, I'd like to stop thinking about the next-door neighbors and start raising a family. Her husband couldn't believe his ears—how could she think of bringing kids into a world which let the enemy advertise right next to their own home? "It's immoral!" he roared. "It's anti-Christian!"

Since his wife was being "no help at all," Continental resolved to plan his next move by himself. Whatever his course, he was determined not to jeopardize his situation—such as through a counter-legal action, or a row of knuckles in his jaw. At the same time he intended to make it clear what he thought of National insurance and the fools who peddled it. No matter how long and passionately he considered the problem, however, he couldn't get past the suspicion (which finally evolved into a fact in his mind) that National would be standing behind the curtains of his bow window all night, waiting for him to try and do something about the flag. It was bait, and he knew it.

After several consecutive nights of lying awake, the man from Continental reacted to the lead in his guts not by taking action against the banner but by taking advantage of the distraction it provided. When National had finally shut out his lights, and went to keep watch at the front window, Continental eased off the king-sized mattress, then slippered out the back door and through the shadows into his garden shed. On his belly he crawled into the backyard of the Nationals, as if behind enemy lines; there he snipped the plastic seats out of half a dozen lawn chairs scattered about—one for each tree he had lost. The retribution wasn't of equal value, he realized, but it was a start.

That night he slept without dreaming about cranking a vise tighter and tighter on National's head, as he had dreamed so many nights. But he didn't sleep as long as he would've liked, having stayed up later than usual, and having heard, late next morning, the shouts of National, his "Ks crashing like pins at the bowling alley: "I'll *kill* him! I'll *kill* him!" Not bothering to don his lounging pajamas National stumped in bare legs up the slate path of Continental's house and started pounding on the door, loosening its woodwork. "Come on out of there you god damn foreigner!"

Impressed by National's snarl, and noting again the size differential between them, Continental came to the open window rather than the door, but said nastily: "You are trespassing; if you don't get off my property immediately, I will have the police throw you behind bars, with the rest of the criminals." National felt like hurling the plaster birdbath frisbee-style through the bay window, but that would have given them a legal branch to climb on. And the man from National, though riled up, was too smart for that. While he knew Continental was responsible, he had no proof whatsoever, so the best he could do was clear his throat and spit on Continental's front stairs as he stumped back to his own property in a fury. When she heard the door slam, National's wife ran out the back door to quiet her nerves.

For a week or two the daily sales calls made by National and Continental were more abrupt than usual, and in the evenings a wisp of steam seemed to rise off the roof of each of the last two houses on Peaceful Lane. On Saturday and Sunday respectively, they prayed the other would be struck by lightning. But there was no open conflict. Continental was tempted to think the loss of the willows had achieved, in the end, what the planting of them had not. Still he was highly suspicious. It was *too* quiet. As it turned out, he had every reason to sleep with one eye open. Not only did the dancing lessons start up again, but National's stereo system, wired throughout the house, was turned so high it shook Continental's windows; soiled napkins landed in their yard with the regularity of jets at International Airport; cocktail glasses were smashed in the driveway for "good luck"; and their kids made a baseball diamond out back, using the lids of garbage cans for bases.

Now Continental was sleeping with both eyes open, getting even less sleep than before, and this affected his work even more. He grossly under-quoted a blanket policy for a medium-sized business, in writing, and since it was the agency's mistake and the bill had already been paid, the client threatened to pull its business if forced to pay an additional amount. Another time he got into a loud argument with a corporate VP over the interpretation of a rider he had prepared. His boss began to watch him with increasing concern, calculating how much money he might lose as a result of his employee's errors and indiscretions. By this time Continental's sales curve was sagging so badly he began to fear he might not be able to keep up with the mortgage, that his job itself might be in jeopardy—despite years of loyal service.

To prove he was still a dedicated member of the CIC team, Continental humbly but earnestly appealed for permission to do some door-to-door selling in the area where he lived. On his own time, of course. "It's all upper middle-class, two-car, professional families," he said with the bright eyes of a recent graduate of the CIC Sales Training Course. His boss gazed at him as if to ask how *he* had gotten into the community, if that were the case. Nevertheless he assented to look into it. A few days later his boss happened to be speaking to the Regional Department on another matter, so he inquired and found out the territory was not serviced directly by a local agent; the Home Office gave him the go-ahead to send a man out there. With quite a bit of pomp—as though he were doing him a great favor, the boss delivered the news to the employee. Continental rose five inches off the floor. It was the best thing that had happened to him since the going-away party in the apartment building where they used to live.

Cautiously but distinctly encouraged, that weekend Continental packed his briefcase with fresh literature and applications, started up his car on the first try, and drove around the corner and parked—so as not to arouse the suspicion of the nosy fool, never thinking his suit and tie might tip off his neighbor anyway. Then he started knocking on doors. No thanks, they said, we're already covered by National. Continental's blood gushed into his head. But the rejections only made him more determined. And after several weekends of roaming along the curved lanes, smiling till it hurt—hitting them with every statistic, every chart, every angle within the compass of his experience and trained imagination, he managed to interest three or four families in comparing "certain rate discrepancies" and certain "loose coverage" from National with certain "price breaks" and certain "extended benefits" offered by Continental. In a few important areas these prospects were shown, to their horror, that their protection had "swampy spots," leaving them "wide open." What they did not notice, and which was not pointed out to them, was that their current policy covered them more completely than the Continental policy in certain other areas.

When the word got back to the National agent, he nearly went through the awning over his deck. "That damned foreigner is working *my* territory, calling on *my* customers," he squealed, a bluish foam at the corners of his mouth. "It's burglary in broad daylight! It's anti-Semitic!" Then he grabbed the long knife off the carving board. His wife immediately jumped in front of him and insisted he take her shopping before the stores closed. He knew his wife didn't like to drive at night, and she knew full well the stores were open late that night. Otherwise they'd have no beer and potato chips for the party the next day. The idea of a party, of any day without beer was abhorrent to his being, so he grunted something nasty in the direction of Continental's house, threw the knife on the picnic table, and reluctantly got out the car. Mrs. National kept Mr. National walking through the supermarket, and then the shopping mall, until past closing, wearing him, herself, and their children out, but managing to side-track her husband from doing something, as she put it to her friends later, that could destroy their whole life.

By next morning he had simmered down, and instead of going next door and "tearing Continental apart limb by limb," as he'd threatened several times in the mall the previous night, he packed his briefcase with literature and drove around the corner to park. "I'll show that foreigner who can sell and who can't sell," he said grimly, yanking his tie straight in the rear-view mirror. That day, and several days thereafter, he spent many hours and much energy making promises to the "traitors" (as he thought of them) and demonstrating that the Continental policy would not protect them the way they ought to be protected in "certain crucial areas," leaving them "wide open." Now the insureds were profoundly confused, and during the week they phoned the Continental agent and said they wanted to hold off on their decision. Continental felt too discouraged to try to sway them back, especially over the telephone. After having boasted to his boss that he had pulled three new accounts out of NIC's paws, and was depositing them into CIC's pockets, it now looked as though he would not be able to deliver them. His sleep went from poor to pathetic.

Complicating matters was that National and his wife, and Continental and his wife, had gotten into the habit of bickering over every item on the grocery list, every gas/electric/oil/phone bill.

Plus Continental's car broke down again—it had to be towed twenty miles, and National's roof developed a leak in the center of the living room. However, National had the consolation during this difficult period of winning back the clients he'd seemed to be losing. Continental had one consolation, too: to his great surprise, sprouts had begun to appear on the stumps of the willows. In a few days they were four inches long, and each day, it seemed, they grew a few more inches. While the nursery attendant had promised they would grow fast, she had not mentioned the willows could survive such severe cutting back. This new development gave him an ironic pleasure, not to mention new hope.

Every time Continental accidentally glanced at the yellowish house next to his, a sourness spread through his stomach. Every time National saw the greenish house in the corners of his eyes, he got heartburn. This bitterness did not infect the soil, however; the willows continued to grow rapidly, and it wasn't long before they had stretched three feet tall—the height at which they had been purchased. Of course National had also been keeping track of the willows' progress. He too had been astonished at their amazing aptitude for survival, at how quickly they were coming back. But he had more disturbing problems to keep him awake. With all the running around to reclaim clients, and getting to bed so late every night—watching over his flag, he found himself worrying more and more about his business, not to mention his health. Some days he got up so late he didn't even bother to open his office, falling farther behind on sales calls, policy renewals, bill collections. Not only that, a sharp pain had developed in his chest, and it hung there day and night. Nothing was quite right: Hamburgers were beginning to taste foul, the beer flat.

Late one evening Mr. and Mrs. National got to yelling at each other over the shrubs, and the bills, and the household economy again; that's when the husband blurted that he hadn't been feeling well, that he was falling behind at the office, and that she couldn't care less about what he was going through. Mr. National rubbed his chest tenderly. It was no surprise to her, snapped Mrs. National, since he was worrying himself into knots over the people next door. You'd better learn to be more tolerant, advised his wife, or you're going to end up with a heart attack. That comment added considerably to his concern, having thought of that possibility a long time ago.

Though he tried to appear confident over his position toward things in general, as well as things in particular, in the succeeding days National forced himself to take a somewhat different perspective on the war with Continental. Maybe he and his wife would be better off, he thought—as if it was his own idea, if they stopped fretting about the plantings. With a row of willows, he told Mrs. National, "I won't have to look at that green dump infested with foreigners." Besides, no one would know who had planted them; it might look like the greenery belonged to him, and would make his home appear more estate-like. Then he could raise the coverage on his house. Feeling clever, he got a little sleep that night.

The willows were allowed to live, indeed received tacit cultivation from both properties, and they thrived. In the meantime, both salesmen tried to act as if the other did not exist. Which was not easy since the loyalties to their respective companies and, therefore, the hatred for their competitors, remained steadfast. Somehow they managed. Perhaps it was because Continental felt the rapid growth confirmed the righteousness of his cause, and because National felt the rapid growth would increase the value of his property much sooner than expected. Whatever the reasons, National went so far as to think that one day he might sell his property for a big profit, and open a swanky full-service agency in the city—far away from those damned foreigners. But he cut this idea short—"Why should *I* sell out when I've been here all my life?" he thought out loud. "If anybody moves it'll have to be *them*." Lighting her fifth cigarette in a row without a break, Mrs. National peered at him through the smoke as if he were slightly foggy in the head.

In a month the shrubbery had shaped up as small, sturdy trees. Other residents along the block had noticed how swiftly they had grown, too. At long last a chill filtered into the air, however, and the freshness faded from the grass, and the young willows let go of their slender leaves. All of Peaceful Lane had turned brown, then gray. In another month or so the lawns went smooth and white, in accordance with the temperate succession. Even so, Continental and National, both of whom spent part of every day lurking behind their curtains to see what the other was up to, would've testified in the highest court that the trees were continuing to grow right through the cold season, leaves or no leaves. This surprised, and yet pleased, the salesmen.

With prices of oil, gas, and electric jumping during the winter, National and Continental had to put in more hours, more energy to produce more sales. As soon as Continental dropped into his seat behind his desk, he would get out his electronic Rolodex and start making calls—badgering someone to pay up, or to expand his coverage, or to dump National in favor of The Tree of Life company. As soon as National dropped into his seat behind his desk, he would call up his customer list on the computer and start making calls, badgering someone to pay up, or to expand his coverage, or to dump Continental in favor of The Banner of Security company. These efforts helped a little, not enough, for the economy was continuing to droop at a rate faster than they could recoup their loses.

By spring, two of the willows had grown as high as the electric wires that ran from the street to the greenish house. So high that Continental, feeling prudent one morning, set up his ladder and snipped off the errant tips. After another day or two, however, these particular willows had reached even higher, and the other trees had spread their reach even wider. Since they were now threatening to snap the wires, he decided to cut the intruding limbs entirely. No great loss, he assured his wife. "Not the way they're growing," he said with a certain pride.

In the meantime a thunderstorm had torn away the flag next door (along with a few leaves and twigs from the trees), and National had seen it happen so he couldn't accuse Continental—though he was tempted. In what seemed a related development, the kids stopped holding Cub Scout meetings in the garage. But Continental didn't get much satisfaction out of these gains: He had trees, rather than fools, on his mind.

Other branches of other trees were soon pressing against the side of his house, twisting in under the slats of greenish siding. These branches too he trimmed off. Several days later, however, he noticed that lower branches were reaching toward the wires, toward the siding, toward the windows again. Continental, deeply perplexed, summoned his wife and had a long, serious talk. While the trees seemed to be helping to get "the reckless fool off my back," he declared, they were also becoming a threat to his house and property. Quietly and carefully his wife suggested it might be in their best interest to consider removing every other willow. Her husband protested loudly. Suddenly, without carrying on too long, he gave in—having been harboring similar ideas for quite awhile, even if unwilling to admit it. The trees would then be ten feet apart, instead of five. But at least the nuisance of wayward branches would be eliminated, and they would keep most of the privacy provided by the trees. Just then, quite unexpectedly, he had a faintly conciliatory thought: maybe he should save some of the shoots and give them to next door for planting in their yard, a gesture to prove that he for one could be reasonable and neighborly. Way down in his heart, however, he was certain the NICs would only interpret this as an act of weakness on the part of the CICs, and that galled him into an even greater rigidity than existed before his generous thought.

When National got up not-too-late the next morning, and saw the gaps left by the missing trees, he did not gloat as Continental might have expected. Instead he felt quite distressed, even sorrowful. Though not in a position to say anything about the matter to Continental—indeed, they never spoke to each other—he couldn't help thinking Continental had cut down the willows to spite him. National called a summit meeting with his wife, and a serious discussion ensued; the husband said he was going to plant three trees on his own property, to replace those that had been "callously struck down in the prime of life." But his wife pointed out the existing willows would grow many more branches, and would still provide lots of shade on their side of the property.

National grew silent, and looked at the stained rug, looked at the leaky spot in the ceiling, looked everywhere but at his wife, and finally let his idea drop; he didn't feel like digging holes and poking sticks into the ground anyway. Nevertheless he continued stewing over the lost trees, which he had come to think of as his own. To compensate—despite the fact that funds were low, as his wife mentioned several times—the next weekend he threw his first big party in a long time. And later that week the Cub Scouts *and* Brownies were seen setting up their tents near the willows. Continental's stomach began to feel as though it were stuffed with raw, skinned, flaming-hot red peppers.

After a few weeks sprouts began to appear where the trees had been cut down, and the remaining three had stretched out their sinewy arms to the garden shed, and seemed anxious to extend their domain toward the house, and the electric wires, again. By late summer Continental had become greatly alarmed; even his wife didn't know what to make of it all. He cursed the nursery out loud on several occasions, but it didn't help. At the office his sales continued to decline, and his boss actually alluded to his "situation in the company." At home the three living trees were raising the roof of the aluminum garden shed;

and tearing up the siding on the house; and dislodging shingles; and choking the drain pipe; and crawling under the screens in the windows. Meanwhile the three dead willows had grown to three feet tall.

The eaves of his house had been loosened, forced out of alignment by the powerful branches. Continental climbed onto the roof, hung off the edge, and tried to nail it straight—a gust of wind nearly blowing him away. Shaking as he climbed down the ladder, he blamed it all on the Nationals. If they hadn't been such reckless, thoughtless, heartless, mean and nasty fools, he would never have planted the trees in the first place and wouldn't have these troubles now. If it's the only thing I do with my life, Continental swore to himself, I'll make him pay for starting that tumor in my stomach, which was an idea that had possessed him of late. Mrs. Continental saw a ghoulish gleam in his eye, and it made her afraid, as though she had glimpsed the monster inside the man she'd been living with all these years.

In the yellowish house, National was amazed—and tickled—by the progress of the willows: He looked upon their regrowth as proof that he was in the right and that his company was efficient and fair to its customers, while Continental mistreated and mishandled its customers. True. He had recently lost a few clients by neglecting to take steps to get them to renew their policies. But that was entirely the fault of that damn foreigner, who was also responsible for his palpitations, not to mention the arguments with his wife. As for Mrs. National, she didn't know what to make of any of it, so she responded less and less to her husband's outbursts, finally taking up jogging to get out of the house.

In the greenish house, after a long and sometimes loud exchange with his wife, Continental decided, with tears in his sockets, that the willows would have to be destroyed. All of them. "We'll just have to learn to ignore those fools," he said, unaware he was echoing what his wife had suggested a long time ago.

It was better than having to worry about branches tearing up everything he had worked so hard for, he said, proud of his mature attitude toward the horrors of living lawn-to-lawn with the Nationals. His wife, judging from her silence, agreed. That Saturday the Continentals, working side-by-side, sawed every one of the willows to the ground—not even leaving a stump, poured motor oil over the six spots, and placed a ten-pound cinder block over each place where they had been growing. That, he said to his wife, is that.

That side of the house now seemed naked to them, and Continental cringed at the full view of the yellowish house, unfiltered by the thousands of slender leaves. But he felt relieved, too. Especially by the time darkness dropped like a truckload of dirt, and they had chopped and sawed and, finally, began burning the branches in their barbecue pit. Since the trees were still fresh, however, the sap made the fire smoky: A thick, pungent cloud unwound over the house on the dead-end street, activating a harsh cough in National, aggravating the pains in his chest. But what really got the man from NIC to wail insanely was that all the trees—*his* adopted trees were "going up in smoke," and that now he would have to look at the joyless house next door every day of his life. His heart felt as if it had been filled with hot coals.

Mr. and Mrs. Continental went about their business, repairing the siding, boiling bland soup, taking out the garbage, taping up the hoses on the car, making sales calls. Mr. and Mrs. National went about their business, emptying beer bottles, popping popcorn, blasting the stereo, shouting at the kids, making sales calls. One Saturday, while Continental happened to be mowing his lawn, and National happened to be searching for his putter in the wilderness of his front yard, they both noticed shoots coming up out of the ground, around the cinder blocks, at every one of the six planting sites. Both men were stunned into stillness. Then the man from CIC began jumping up and down on the shoots, and the man from NIC clapped and laughed loudly, and gave up looking for his putter—he'd found something even better to amuse him.

Later that afternoon the dog noticed Continental running out of his house, and watched the man stumble into his car, finally getting it started, and rattle down the lane. The dog did not see the car pull up at the hardware store, smoking heavily, shaking nervously as it idled. Afraid to shut off the engine, the man left it running as he ran inside, and demanded advice. The shop owner didn't like the man's tone at all, but a customer was a customer, so he sent his clerk in the back to look for a particular, not-often-called-for item. At last the clerk returned with a black cylinder, and the owner assured the customer that it was the most powerful stuff of its kind on the market. "It better be," said Continental behind a weird smirk, tucking the package under his arm, running out, leaping into the driver's seat and rumbling home—almost running down a kid on a bike before bringing the car to a lurching halt in his driveway. Next door's dog pulled its snout out of the bone hole it had dug in Continental's lawn, and watched the man race along the side of the house. Continental's wife was as curious as the dog. "Now what you are doing?" she inquired through the screen door, though it was plain to see: He was driving holes into the ground with a stake—like a stake into National's heart—in four evenly spaced places around each upstart sprout. Then he filled the holes with white powder—a triple dose for good measure, and watered the holes mercilessly. The dog, apparently trying to be helpful, raised its leg and emptied its bladder at the last sprout.

The rest of the day Continental sat out on a folding chair, hands clenched together, watching, watching out of hollow dark sockets. From the upstairs window next door National was watching, watching—praying too, his brow heavily gashed with concern. Remarkably, within hours, the sprouts had shriveled and wilted to the ground. Continental called his wife to hurry out and see, and when she came, very slowly, and saw, her eyes

104

rolled in her head toward heaven. It had long been her nightly prayer that the entire mess would be ended, and that they could begin to think about having babies. If they didn't get started soon, she feared, it would be too late. Next door National waved his wife to the window, and when she saw the dried-up stems, she gushed a grateful sigh. Even her husband, though he tried not to show it, felt considerable relief.

Each evening, as soon as he got home from the office, Continental would trap the air in his lungs as he walked cautiously up to the planting site, and then he started breathing again, aloud: not a sign of life. This went on for about three weeks, and still no greenery pushed its way through the reddish crust. Silently he thanked God, as well as the hardware store owner—who obviously knew what he was talking about. Over the following weeks Continental began to get a little sleep; his car didn't break down; his sales stopped declining. Though the dark circles under his eyes did not disappear, he felt better than he had in months. Next door, National began to sleep and eat better, too; he managed to patch the leak in his roof; a few new accounts were added to his Rolodex. But the gashes in his forehead would never go away.

It was about one month later that Continental spotted the crack in his foundation. He knew that foundations cracked from time to time, what with the ground settling, and water getting into the spaces between the cinder blocks and then freezing. But his house had been around quite awhile and should have finished settling and cracking a long time ago. Even so, the crack didn't occupy his mind to any great degree until it began getting larger. At last he decided he'd better investigate.

One evening, after consuming half a plate of mushy macaroni, he got the shovel out of the shed and started digging alongside the foundation—a job that was a lot harder than the planting he had done. When he finally got down nearly four feet, he saw the very thing he had secretly feared—the deepest roots of the willow had not died after all and had worked their way over to the foundation, probably to avoid the poison. The hairlike tips had curled into a tiny crack in the foundation and then began, it seemed, to draw the vital minerals they needed not from the poisoned ground but from the lime and sand of the cement. And as the roots expanded, they had begun to separate the blocks, almost as if it were an act of revenge.

Now that a section of the earth had been removed from against the foundation, chunks of dry cement facing crumbled and fell into the hole; Continental was afraid the entire structure might be weakened—that after a time the house itself might shake loose and, in the end, tumble to the ground, and that he and his wife would be ruined, if not killed. Standing up to his neck in the hole, he wailed mournfully, "Why me? Why me?" National, who happened to be having a beer on a repaired lawn chair out back, wondering what the digging was all about, heard the cries, and thinking—hoping—someone was being murdered, came at a jog. For the first time in a year, they spoke.

"What's the matter?"

"None of your business," said Continental, slipping repeatedly as he climbed out of the hole, his muddy limbs and bent-over back making him look like an ape.

Grinning, National's eyes beamed at the deep hole, then at the crack. "Well, well," he said, "I hope you've learned your lesson."

Continental turned totally blue: "It's all your fault!"

National mashed the beer can with one hand, dropped it at his feet, and kicked the crushed aluminum can into the hole at the foundation. "Hole in one!" he exclaimed, then started toward his lawn chair, looking back at the crack and laughing loudly. Continental felt like rushing after the fool, leaping on his back, and strangling him until his face turned blue. But he barely had the energy to think such strenuous thoughts.

Meanwhile, in National's mind, a mildly generous thought had emerged without warning: The foreigner had a serious problem, and National for one could see it would never be resolved by one pair of hands. Maybe he ought to offer to help. But he was convinced the foreigner would only refuse his kind, neighborly gesture, making him feel like a fool. So National told himself Continental was only getting what he deserved. And he popped open another beer, then settled back in his chair to listen to the pleasant sounds of a shovel breaking the earth.

Next evening, after work, Continental decided to get to the bottom of the problem—to dig up all the roots of all the trees. Unfortunately he couldn't afford to hire someone to help him, and this was a major undertaking, especially for someone used to selling insurance all day. Nevertheless he began digging, and he dug until after dark; then he got up at first light and started digging again; all day Sunday he dug, dug, dug. On Monday, though aged with fatigue, and though it made him very insecure, he called in sick just so he could dig. And dig he did, though much more slowly, much more wearily. The light rain didn't make it any easier. Next door, National took the day off from the office to make sure Continental didn't throw any dirt on his property. Throughout it all the two wives didn't utter a meaningful word to their spouses, but it occurred to both of them, in their separate worlds, that the women ought to meet each other, and speak, and try to make some sense out of it all.

The deeper the Continental salesman dug, the farther the roots seemed to spread. His grounds, he thought with a sadness that went deeper than the roots, were being ruined: The grass had been torn up, there were mounds of dry reddish dirt and wet brownish clay all along the side of his house, the area smelled foul, and too many stones had been tossed into his wife's flower beds by mistake—far away from National's property. Yet he continued to dig, rather the way he had felt driven to reach a certain sales tally by the end of the fiscal quarter. And while

107

he was working on an especially tenuous, especially far-reaching root, trying to tear it out of the earth with his raw, gritty hands, inch by inch, he collapsed partly from weakness and partly because of a remarkable discovery: This very thick root extended a long way under the ground toward National's property, right in the direction of a crack in the fool's foundation.

Though numb with exhaustion, Continental was unable to sleep all that night; he couldn't get that root, that crack in National's foundation out of his mind. Sometime during those sluggish, miserable hours it occurred to him that if he told next door about their mutual problem, together they might be able to dig out all of the roots, and save both of their houses, their marriages, their livelihoods, their health—their lives. But he knew this root, extending from his house across the property line, would finally give National something concrete against him; he knew the reckless fool was just waiting for him to take one step over the line so he could sue him into extinction. Continental wasn't about to let that happen. If his world was crumbling around his ears and eyes and nose, at least he had the satisfaction of knowing the roots were slowly tearing down the world of the man from National, too.

BY MUTUAL AGREEMENT

The blinking red light forced Jane Nilson to realize how much speed she'd gathered, and as she peddled to a full stop at the railroad crossing, the rude smell of brake linings tainted the air inside the Toyota. Six leads—postcards people had gone to the trouble of self-addressing and mailing—**Yes, I am interested in learning more about Mutual Funds**—had led nowhere. Now there was only one left. The freight train thundered past, and the saleswoman shifted into Drive.

At two locations the respondents hadn't answered the door, though at one of the houses she'd noticed a shadow of someone through the folds of drapery. In the next town, a middle-aged woman in a baggy sweat suit had held on to the door knob: "I never sent *any* card to *any* company." And yet there was the handwritten address on the card. Later a man with an open boil on his forehead, like a third eye, kept the chain hooked while Nilson introduced herself. *How can long-term security be sold through the links of a chain?*

A slow-handed, silver-haired woman had let her in at the last stop, and had listened to her patiently. But the more the saleswoman explained, the less the elderly woman seemed to understand. Nilson went through her pitch anyway, growing more annoyed to hear the sound of her own voice going over the details once again, knowing all the while that this woman wasn't about to invest her savings in mutual funds. When Jane Nilson had first gotten into mutual funds, a retired army sergeant who didn't seem very well off had sat at attention for half an hour and then signed up with a surprisingly hefty investment. Others came along for the ride, too. That early success had made her feel she had chosen her career and her methods wisely—she wasn't the kind to sit at a desk all day long, working a telephone and hoping for the best. She would get out into the bushes and stir them up. Get them to sign up by the *scruff of their necks,* as she had boasted at the office. But she had come to learn that those kinds of quick hits were as rare as finding true love on a barstool.

As the compact thumped alongside the painted white line on the country route, Jane Nilson clicked off the noise gushing from the radio, adding silence to the time and space which surrounded her. Only two or three hours of each day actually went into selling, dealing directly with people. The rest was burned up getting from one town to another, and locating a residence or office, and drinking coffee in roadside diners, and adjusting her lipstick in grimy gas station restrooms and, lately, spending time with a gin and tonic or two in long, small-town nights.

Under a slow gray burn in the clouds, at eighteen minutes past three, she swung off the road and rolled into a combination gas station and convenience store. As the attendant—elongated and rigid as an open-ended wrench—began releasing gasoline into her tank, Nilson pulled her tall, fleshy body out of the car.

"How far off is Potter Hill?"

"'Bout fifteen miles—straight on," said the split lips set in a porous face.

An extra thirty miles round-trip from nowhere, she thought. Nilson thought about the cell phone in her purse, wondering if she should call ahead to see if the Kalp household actually had any interest. Since it was much easier for a prospect to say "no" over the phone, however, she decided to push on. But with an enlarging suspicion that Potter Hill wasn't going to pay off either, the saleswoman said to the gasoline pumper: "This place yours?"

"Uh huh."

"Running a garage these days must be tough, with gasoline prices going right through the roof."

"People are always complaining 'bout the price of gas," he admitted, notching the nozzle into the pump's shoulder. "But they dunno what it costs me, and all the other expenses I got."

"I'm surprised more smaller businesses don't try to stretch fewer dollars into bigger returns."

The garage owner, up to his neck in green, grease-stained overalls, squinted at the saleswoman, who was up to her neck in a loose white blouse. "How's that?"

"Mutual funds: They give the local business operator a fighting chance in today's tight retail marketplace."

"That'll be $19.50."

Slowly down the main street she drove, looking for movement in the barber shop, the hardware store. Potter Hill, one of too many towns like it, she felt, wasn't large enough to have its own Burger King. Having driven through lunch as if it were a back-road stop sign, yet less out of hunger than a sense of duty, she pulled up at a wooden-faced diner the town had neglected to tear down. The brakes shrieked in the dry, still air. Over the door hung an oval Coke sign which had melted from red to pink in the sun and dust. Silencing the engine, Jane Nilson tried to remember the name of the man she'd met in the motel bar in Worcester the previous weekend. After talking awhile with her, he'd slid off the stool and walked out the door, and she'd felt deeply alone, as if abandoned by a life-long partner rather than a total stranger.

Overpowering the smell of fresh licorice and boiled tomato soup in the diner was the languishing ammonia of a recent mopping. An elbow on the stained formica counter, Nilson consumed only one of the grilled cheese triangles, the thin slices of sour pickles, plus two mugs of surprisingly flavorful coffee. *A good omen,* she thought. Two seats to her right sat a balding man in business slacks and dress shirt, no tie. *The local insurance agent,* she thought, *or the mayor! Or maybe both!* It came into her head to slip an earnings graph onto the counter and study it, just to see if she could strike up a little curiosity in him. But another head-on rejection might've tempted her hop into the car and wheel north—just keep driving all the way to Hollow Run, New Hampshire. Unfortunately the sad, splintery house in which she'd been brought up could never again shelter her.

Without ever having gained an understanding of what her mother had wanted out of life, Jane Nilson had watched her being removed from that house by strangers in white and, weeks later, lowered into the decayed earth by strangers in black. In the succeeding months, she had watched her father from the kitchen window, caning along the pond-shaped slabs of slate as if trying to catch up to his wife. To Jane it was a mystery how they had managed to establish such a close, lasting connection, one that continued even beyond death. To her, these days, relationships seemed so much more complicated, so short-lived that they could hardly be characterized as human connections. Rather more like business associations. By the end of the year, she had moved out of that house of crumbling curtains, that town of immutable oaks. While she felt guilty about leaving her father by himself, she had sensed the old man wanted to be alone with the memories of his wife. And by that time, she had become desperate to get away from some of those same reminders.

Her confidence was dragging like a rusted muffler as the compact rolled between the muscular trees, the car's beige enamel scarred by the scratchlike shadows of the branches. At that moment she would rather have crashed into a telephone pole than stand before the intense green eyes of Bierce, District Manager, and tell him that not one of the leads he'd handed her "looked promising"—*promising,* that lowest step in the climb toward signing up a client—of extracting money from someone who didn't necessarily want (or could afford) to part with it. With Nilson being less experienced than the rest of the staff, Bierce had closed the last sales meeting by asking her to stay, and had finally sent her out on the road with these words: "I know the company can count on you." A chill had pirouetted down her spine.

During her first six months of selling mutual funds, Jane Nilson had kept a careful watch over that self-drawn line between statements to potential customers that were true and not-so-true. One day, however, while speaking to a newly-wed business couple who struck her as good prospects, she noticed that the line had partially washed away like chalk on an old slate sidewalk in New Hampshire after a rainstorm. Soon the line was gone altogether, and by this particular day she was prepared to say almost anything to return to Providence with a signed application in her briefcase.

At the end of a narrow, disintegrating tar road stood the Kalp house: a frame structure that was, oddly (considering the abundance of undeveloped space around it), built upward instead of outward. Its cracked, stuccoed foundation was inadequately hidden by a row of unruly, aimless shrubs. Where the pebbles ran off into the weedy lawn she slowed to a smooth halt. The overgrown grass was not a good sign. Nilson lifted her tweed jacket off the back of the seat beside her, and worked her arms into its satin-lined sleeves. Forcing the rear-view mirror to face her, she patted her hair, which was the color of a river bottom, and looked pensively into her pale green eyes. Now she smoothed her skirt with both hands. Then she gripped the hard handle of the briefcase and climbed out from behind the hot plastic steering wheel.

As she stepped along the islands of broken stone, she anticipated the Kalps' first excuses: *Friends coming over shortly? What time? Perfect! I'll be out of your way long before then.... Your son mailed in this card as a joke? Smart boy! This could be your ticket to a vacation in Europe, or a new camping trailer, or even an early retirement.... Changed your mind? That's quite alright. One is required to have a certain line of credit, a certain level of assets to be qualified for mutual funds. As you know, it takes money to make money. Oh, really? You own this fine house? Two cars? With saving certificates in the bank? Maybe we'd better review your qualifications after all....*

Jane Nilson depressed a black button the size of an aspirin, and in half a minute the door opened jerkily as if operated mechanically. A man in a pale green short-sleeved shirt, whose vague face looked as if it had been sandpapered, seemed surprised to find a young woman at his doorstep.

"I'm Jane Nilson," she said as cheerfully as she could manage, "from Mutual Management."

Extending her arm straight out, he said, "Thought you might be a little earlier." His hand felt mushy, as if beginning to dissolve.

The saleswoman stepped up into the cramped, musty vestibule, ducking away from the hanging, wide-brimmed brass lamp. "Sorry. My other contracts took a little longer to finalize than I expected," she said, adding, "but we can go over this quickly without interfering with your plans."

"We have no plans," said Mrs. Kalp, equally truncated, equally gray, appearing at the opening of a dining room that was larger than the living room. The woman in the faded, sand-colored dress attempted a smile, and said, instead: "I'll put on the coffee."

Coffee! Jane Nilson had to be careful not to be disarmed by their receptiveness. Mr. Kalp urged her toward an armchair that looked as if it were made of shredded wheat, but she found it to be firm, uncompromising. Then the man and his wife sank into the hollows of the sofa, which was jammed between two end tables at a right angle to the armchair.

In the moments it took the couple to get settled in the crispy-looking cushions, the saleswoman evaluated their circumstances. Though the house was compact by the standards of when it was built, and its paint had evaporated into shadows, the china cabinet in the dining room, as broad-chested as a father-image, had plenty of thick lead crystal on display. A pair of candlesticks on the mantlepiece, centered over the cemented mouth of the fireplace, had the tarnish of silver. The leaden rug was beaten down by years of treading, but there was a well-crafted heaviness in its oriental design.

"Beautiful country around here," Nilson offered.

"Do you live in Providence?" Mrs. Kalp inquired.

"Yes, but I was born in a small town in New Hampshire, a town a lot like Potter Hill."

"You're quite a ways from home."

"You never really leave that kind of upbringing behind."

"Guess your folks are still up that way."

When she told them her mother had passed away, and that her father was occupying the big, gray, clapboard house alone, Mrs. Kalp rose heavily, though she didn't look very heavy, and said, "Coffee must be ready."

As cups and saucers clinked against each other in the kitchen, Mr. Kalp said: "What brought you to Rhode Island?"

Silently the saleswoman thanked him for the convenient lead-in: "Mutual Management Corporation—a really solid company that works hard to make lives for folks like you more secure."

When Mrs. Kalp returned and set the round tray on the low rectangular table, the saleswoman used the distraction to slip printed materials out of her briefcase onto the table. As soon as the woman had poured the darkly winking fluid from the porcelain nozzle, Nilson began unfolding the story of mutual funds: the diversification not normally within the reach of the modest investor, the buying power of the group, the bonanza yields of certain select years—without mentioning that the past is not a reliable indictor of the future.

Though she had been there too long, though she didn't care for instant coffee, Jane Nilson accepted a second cup with a grateful show of teeth. By this time she had enumerated the principal points with sales-manual economy, and had even managed to repeat the financial terms without making her prospects edgy. They had listened politely, apparently with interest. Suddenly, however, while the Kalps were staring indecisively at the fund literature, the saleswoman was overtaken by a feeling that nothing she'd said added up to good common sense to them.

With a scooped-out sensation in her middle, she commented, "If you have any questions, please feel free to fire away."

"Why aren't you married?" Mrs. Kalp was pointing at the ringless finger on her left hand.

With a faint laugh that was partly embarrassment, partly annoyance, she replied, "I guess I'm not ready to settle down just yet."

"There must be a special young man back in Providence," Mrs. Kalp persisted, causing her husband to shift his slight frame uneasily on the sofa.

Before Jane Nilson could consider a response that might satisfy them and also change the subject, her lips and tongue had released these words: "A couple of years ago I was engaged, but that's over." Her own impulse of candor distressed her—it was none of their damn business; and yet that fissure of honesty sputtered with a desire to tell them more: to describe the remoteness that had built up, inexplicably, around her life; a sense that she was on one side of an endless counter and everyone else was on the other; a suspicion that she owed all of them something far beyond her emotional means to pay back, ever.

"Shouldn't wait *too* long to walk down the aisle," advised Mrs. Kalp, who tried and failed again to smile.

"If you want kids," added Mr. Kalp, "better to have 'em while you're young."

An angry desire to wake them up to changing times, to tell them she had things to accomplish that had nothing to do with marriage—dried up in her throat. And looking for an indirect means of returning to the business that had drawn her to this speck of coffee grind on the map, the saleswoman relaxed her face with a practiced warmth: "I'll bet you folks have some fine grandchildren."

"Our daughter never married."

Most of the silvery sheen had gone out of the thinly penciled clouds, depositing a fragmented gloom in its wake, and Nilson felt disoriented, no longer in control. Somehow she managed to refrain from looking at her watch. But she longed for the taste of a gin and tonic.

"How did you happen to get into this line of work?" said Mr. Kalp.

"It's a long and dull story. I'd rather not bore you."

"We wouldn't be bored," Mrs. Kalp assured her.

Jane Nilson stretched out a smile. "I'd much rather help make you folks well off."

Mr. Kalp made a low rumble that sounded like an atmospheric disturbance. Remarkably still beside him, Mrs. Kalp made no sound at all, her eyes pinched and unblinking.

Gambling, the saleswoman started digging into her briefcase for the dividend graph—the jagged mark of lipstick climbing sharply over the vein-blue crisscross pattern of years and dollars, a weapon she was taught to save for those times when a deal could go either way. But the graph didn't seem to be where she usually kept it. And the Kalps watched her with such frank curiosity, such obvious sincerity, the saleswoman stopped searching.

"Originally I was going to teach mathematics. By the time I was a Junior at the University of New Hampshire, the outlook for teachers was dismal, so I switched majors to economics. After my engagement ended, I wrote to several companies in the financial field, and finally moved to Providence and accepted this opportunity with Mutual—best move I ever made," she said half-heartedly, wondering why she had launched into her own past. "It's a growth company, and I'm pleased to say I've been able to help many good people like yourselves solidify their financial future."

"Our Jennifer studied bio-chemistry," said Mrs. Kalp.

Though his expression remained unaltered—the flat resignation one finds in a person who has lived too long for no particular reason, Mr. Kalp turned his eyes on his wife.

"Must be excellent opportunities for advancement in that field," Nilson said, her tone bright.

"If you work at it," Mr. Kalp qualified emptily, "and don't give up."

Again the saleswoman tried to angle the conversation toward the "smart people" enjoying beachfront property in Florida—the ones who had foreseen these "cloudy economic times" and had "mapped out their future." But the Kalps replied with details of their daughter's past accomplishments—"graduated with honors," and platitudes on life—"you look away for a moment and years pass by."

"Seems like only yesterday I joined Mutual Management," Nilson agreed.

"After college Jennifer accepted a position with a research laboratory outside Boston."

It occurred to Nilson that the Kalps, though dull as a book of computer definitions, had spawned a bright daughter, an only child like herself; and now, getting older, they were anxious, perhaps even desperate to have grandchildren, to somehow carry their uneventful lives into a promising future.

"Be nice to meet Jennifer sometime, especially if she's as friendly as you folks."

118

Something in the next voice she heard went metallic: "Our daughter's dead."

Jane Nilson's confusion prevented her from saying anything, and an urge to get out of that house swept over her. But the face of Bierce sprang up in her head like a life raft that had been held under water and released. Though Nilson knew she should've been saying something else, the saleswoman heard herself say: "Is there anything else you'd like to know about mutual funds? Anything I haven't made clear?"

"It was days before they found her," Mr. Kalp said.

"Her body carried into the harbor," Mrs. Kalp added.

Realizing their daughter had been involved in a tragic accident, Jane Nilson sensed the Kalps were lost to her—at least for now, too tangled in the past to consider the future seriously. The saleswoman decided to lie to the District Manager. With the muscles of her face all in place, she would tell Bierce that a contract with the Kalps was ninety-nine percent wrapped. Just a matter of how much they wanted to invest. Later, she would try to pull the deal together, try to bend her lie into a reasonable facsimile of truth.

Quietly the saleswoman said to the couple: "Maybe I'd better come back another day, when you're feeling more…." Even as she spoke, Nilson knew that Bierce would never buy that story: Bierce would probe; Bierce would find out. "I'll leave this literature with you, and you could look it over at your leisure. In a few days I'll call you, and see if you have any further questions. And then…."

Throughout Nilson's closing speech Mrs. Kalp gazed out the window, her mind lost in the unkempt backyard that was closing in on the house. Having run out of things to say, the saleswoman sat rubbing the blue leaflet between her thumb and forefinger, a "Fact Sheet" handled so often she didn't realize it was in her hand.

It was Mr. Kalp who broke the barrier of dead air: "Jennifer didn't even leave a note to tell us why she did it."

Quickly Jane Nilson began collecting the literature off the table and stuffing it into the wrong file folders in her briefcase, the interior leather raw against her knuckles. Now she spotted the graph she'd been looking for earlier, but it was too late. Much too late. About to snap the brass latch closed, she looked up: The eyes of Jennifer's mother and father were upon her, silently begging her not to leave. Suddenly the saleswoman saw it wasn't too late after all. They would do whatever she asked of them: commit to a long-term plan, spend more than they could afford, write out a check immediately. All they needed to be spared their immense guilt at that moment was to scrawl their names on one of MMC's printed forms.

TO EACH HIS OWN

Stunned into a state of innocence known only to commission salesmen after three or more days on the road, I hauled my suitcase out of the cab supremely oblivious to what lay in store for me. It was as if the most powerful environment in a person's life—one's home (in my case a ten-year-old ranch house fifty miles out of Chicago), does not transmit through its TV antenna, window panes, or chimney stack, signals of impending drama within. Not even when I found the front and back doors locked on a Thursday afternoon, and searched impatiently for keys, was I sufficiently alerted, humanely prepared to find 22 Sunnyside Drive cleaned out to the last light bulb.

I thought I had the wrong house...until I recognized the gash on the vestibule wall: inflicted by my umbrella one morning as I raced for the 7:38. Having settled that point, I decided a very thorough gang had pulled off a wholesale burglary. That theory collapsed the moment I established—"Is *any*body home?"—that Marge, Morty Jr., and Spot were missing too. Along with the understuffed sofa, the home entertainment center, a pair of back-deforming bean bag seats, one wobbly lucite coffee table, a 19-inch Sanyo. And, why not, the fibreglas rug and drapes. Even the framed Picasso reproductions were AWOL; only their rectangular imprints remained on the walls like ghosts of the artist's clowns and lover. Standing out in those wide-open spaces, I found it impossible to resist the conclusion that my wife, son, and pointer had run away from home—lock, stock and crockery.

To say I was astonished would be like writing a check for five grand with only five hundred in the bank, for as far as I'm concerned, no words could have covered the feelings which crashed around inside me. With my jaw locked open as if dislocated, and my neck as stiff as a two-by-four, I squatted on the edge of my suitcase and, under the sway of some mad rationale, proceeded to hum a tune that had been popular decades earlier. Around the time I had started working at Midland Wholesale Meat Products and began dating Marge (she was MWMP's book-keeper). "Something in the way she moves...." It didn't hit me until later that the song was in bad taste at that particular moment. Not that it would have stopped me. The humming was an attempt at self-protection, a slipping into the past so as not to have face the present...at least not too quickly.

Once my neck had loosened, I stood up to face that alien living room. For without the goods that had defined our lives together, the place truly felt remote: not the Wickman's room at all but four walls that could be fitted with the reproductions and chairs and lamps and end tables of someone else's life. As I plunged into that space, my crepe soles crunched unseen sediment, the crumbs of our way of life, sending aloft a thin, eerie echo. My eyes scrutinized the floors, the corners, the window sills, ferreting out minute details with an unhealthy fascination. I noticed, for example, that along with the hanging spotlight even the curtain rods had been pillaged.

Back and forth across the floor I marched like the chief of *La Policia* in one of those tragic operas, trying to encompass (with limited emotional capacity at the time) the meat-car load of implications in all that emptiness. It was like trying to service the Midwestern, Eastern and Western Sales Districts all at once. The more belongings I realized were missing—my *personal* re-clining chair, the carbonated water-maker, my collection of Beatles' albums (they're going to be worth plenty one day)—the more difficult it became to remain calm. Soon I was charging through the house in desperate want of a single relic of my life, as if I might lose my claim to existence without it. In every room it was the same—desk gone, tools gone, towels gone, toys gone, beds...gone. Through the side window of our former bedroom, I gazed—the Ford was gone. Out back, the dog house had disappeared. The cyclone fence, thank God, remained—too deeply imbedded, I suppose, to have been removed. As did the apple tree. But it had never borne fruit, a fact that brought to the surface the question I'd been avoiding: *Why did Marge leave, and with everything but the bathroom tiles? Perhaps because we too had not borne fruit. There was* Junior, but even the lad was noticeably empty, bordering on incidental: a product of our lack of attention to preventive maintenance rather than an expression of our optimism. That inauspicious start is probably what had deprived him of his fair share of personality. Morty Jr. seemed so unlike me that an old friend had once kiddingly asked—but with underlying seriousness, I believe—if Morty had been adopted. Observing Jr.'s sluggishness of speech and spirit, I too occasionally wondered where he had come from.

What mystified me most about Marge's decampment was that, from all outward appearances, she had been a willing participant in our life together. Just like me. While it's true our marriage had largely boiled down to an exchange of services, a series of acquiescences, we accomplished these transactions with very little inconvenience to each other, and nearly always without friction. It's also true we didn't pay much attention to each other, like a footrest you continue to live with as long as you don't trip over it. But that never struck me as remarkable either, living in a neighborhood where haircurlers and newspapers were standard equipment with morning coffee, where every one of my neighbors was consumed with the process of selling one product or service to someone, anyone, every waking moment of the day.

To some degree Marge's involvement in the relationship had been sustained, I guess, by fantasies of a material windfall: that I would sell my way up to V.P. of Pork/Lamb Sales, or at least win the lottery, catapulting us into a house with fourteen rooms, three baths, paneled basement (with bar), three-car garage (including cars), and matching dog house. I couldn't cut her down on that count. I wanted the same things. Maybe my career hadn't moved along fast enough to sustain those dreams in her. Or maybe my fair good looks, at forty-three, were fading to a freckled blandness more quickly than I cared to admit. If the medicine cabinet had been left behind, I'm sure I would have inspected the creases around my eyes just then.

Possibly I should have taken affirmative action when I'd noticed, a year or two before, that we were connecting less and less in bed. I passed it off as mutual fatigue, preoccupation with our daily routines—my selling dead, slaughtered pigs, and her keeping the books balanced at the company. By now, though, sex had become a novelty. If we both happened to get enough sleep the night before, and both happened to have a few minutes on our hands—that is, nothing decent to watch on TV—and both happened to be relatively naked at the same time and in the same bed, then it might sort of come about...like rain. Otherwise we didn't make an issue of it, as if we silently took pride in overcoming the human frailty of desire.

Once I stopped kicking the question of "why" around the house, another immediately took the floor: "What am I going to do?" Before I could begin dragging the bottom for answers to that one, the door bell went off—the first five notes of "I Love You Truly." Couldn't have been Marge—she wouldn't use the chimes. With nothing to hide behind, I hauled my weary body and soul down the hollow hall to the door. When I went to hook the chain latch I found it was gone, so I set my foot a few inches behind the door, and stuck one eye out: It was Teresa Blumbetter, of all people, from next door. I was in no mood for company, particularly not a lackluster snob whose husband, Bert, I had never particularly cared for with his "I've got the greenest lawn on the block" perspective. (Seems he fed his roots a special formula, and his grass *was* greener.) With a curtness calculated to get rid of her quickly, I said: "Yes, Teresa, what can I *do* for you?"

Teresa Blumbetter looked remarkably peculiar, as usual, zipped up on a weekday in what I took to be her shopping mall finery—a baggy, rust-brown lounging suit with a rope sash that, coupled with her short blonde bangs, gave her the countenance of a monk. What was even more peculiar was that she stood staring at me without answering my question. "What is it?" I snapped, anxious to climb back into my mind, to look around for any options that might be within my reach.

"Welcome home, Mort."

What the hell is that supposed to mean? "Thanks," I said abruptly, avoiding conversation so she couldn't pick up any clues. Then I remembered, with horror, that the windows were bare—anyone could see there had been some changes around here.

"The truck loaded up last night," she informed me.

That's just terrific, I thought—*the whole damn neighborhood knows!* But her voice was so pathetically empathetic I opened up and let her fill a bit of the emptiness, swiftly slamming the door behind her. Uneasily we shifted our feet in the drafts several moments until I said: "Well now you know our little secret. We didn't want the neighborhood to find out. Everyone just would've tried to talk us out of moving and our minds were—"

Teresa Blumbetter had the decency not to let me go on too long, interrupting me in a tone that revealed she knew the truth: "Is there anything I can do?"

The only thing she could do was leave me alone. I had political reasons for not telling her that, however. Already judgments were being handed down in the neighborhood, I knew—having rendered a few myself in the past, as to who was the guilty party in the break-up: me, Marge, Morty Jr., or the mutt. Advocates would be hard to come by. "If you don't mind," I heard myself say, "it would be nice if you could hang around a few minutes, until I...get used to the idea."

"Oh, I have all the time in the world," she said.

I faked a smile. "Well, there's plenty for you to take care of at home," I reminded, not wanting her to hang around too long. "Just until I get used to the idea."

"You mean you don't know?" she asked with an earnestness that rattled me. "Your Marge left with my Bert."

I had an urge to faint. Unfortunately I'd never developed the skill. "Where did my Marge...run off...with your Bert?"

"No one knows."

"That figures!"

"I came to ask if you'd like to visit with Bert Jr. and me ... for a day or two. Until you get straightened out. At least we still have furniture next door."

"How considerate of them."

Teresa Blumbetter nodded glumly.

I thanked her for her kind gesture, but she quickly admitted her reasons were mostly selfish: "I need someone to talk to, until I get my nerves untangled."

There it was—an option, a point at which to begin, born of mutual need: I needed to get used to the idea, and she needed to get her nerves untangled. Undoubtedly we both wondered what the neighbors would think. But we must've felt entitled to a little human company under the circumstances, for when she started moving toward the door I collected my suitcase, scanned the forlorn emptiness of 22 Sunnyside one last time, and followed her out like a runaway child who had been brought back to justice.

Although the drive between the even, facing rows of houses exhibited the same gentle curve as before, and the maples planted by the developer brandished the usual pointed leaves, the setting felt only vaguely familiar...like a locale I'd visited once, a long time ago. Lagging behind Teresa Blumbetter, I wondered just how long Marge and Bert had been "buddies," and how I could've been so dumb. Even though the two of them had always acted as if they had a powerful dislike of each other, I should have noticed a sly wink, a wistful gaze—*some*thing. They were probably in the sack that very moment, having a big fat laugh at me and Teresa. I would've become angry, but I didn't have the energy. Anyway a weekend was approaching. Why not torture myself at leisure?

Creeping along the crushed marble path to the Blumbetter place—freshly painted sheet white, and substantially larger than my ex-house (Bert, the show-off, had added a wing), I stared at the stubby pines he personally had set into the ground last spring: young, needled symbols of his commitment to that quarter acre, that life. Why had he bolted? And with my wife? Partly convenience, I supposed. And partly because Margery Wickman did have one or two admirable qualities left—a sense of drama for minor events, and a certain flair of wickedness in her dark eyes. Or so I've overheard at backyard barbecues.

Why Marge had picked on Bert was an even bigger mystery, considering his paunch and thinning hair and hot air. The reasons became clear the moment I entered 24 Sunnyside. Yes, the braggart had done pretty well for himself and family: a grandiose Italianate archway had been constructed between the living and dining rooms; plus a walk-in white brick fireplace (with solid brass fire dogs); three thousand bucks worth of CD and DVD multi-plex gear; a room-long blue velvet sofa in a very long room; a jungle-thick shaggy red rug; a teak cocktail bar with six cushioned stools; and what must've been a 56-inch insta-focus, flat, projection TV screen hooked up to 500 satellite channels. Obviously Bert's line of work, advertising, was a growth industry.

"Looks...comfortable," was all I chose to say.

"In some ways," she admitted, "Bert took good care of us."

While I was wondering why they had taken *my* stuff, and left Bert's behind—maybe Marge's dramatic streak had gotten the best of her—into that showplace of high-tech suburbia strode Blumbetter's pedigree Great Dane, Rover, not quite as large but every bit as personable as King Kong. Upon spotting me, he commenced to rumble with a menacing, guttural, continuous growl through his long teeth. I did not dare move even my eyes.

"He won't bother you," Teresa assured me without conviction. "Have a seat. Can I get you anything?"

Holding my ground, I tried to throw my voice across the room so the dog wouldn't know it was me who was speaking. "Right now a martini would save my life—do you mind?" The growl grew louder, nastier.

At the bar Teresa Blumbetter stirred up a pitcher of sales-clinchers, and then escorted me in safety to the sofa. Silently she poured, and silently I drank—with one eye on Rover, who paced under the archway licking his purple gums, as if waiting for the lady of the house to throw him my bones. In a few moments, I poured, and she drank. Then we repeated the cycle, the two of us trying desperately to climb out from under the stupendous pressure in our chests. She cried a little; I sighed a lot. Later, I cried a little; she sighed a lot.

In half an hour our minds had been pillowed sufficiently by the alcohol for me to say, "What are you going to do?"

"Do? Why should I do anything?"

"You're absolutely one hundred perthent right," the martini agreed. "Why should we do anything!"

This compact led to another drink, and that in turn led to an ever-expanding sense of comradeship in misfortune, which in turn led to another drink. I forgot Rover, and Mrs. Blumbetter forgot herself. By the time Bert Jr. had jumped out of the yellow school bus, and had kicked his way through the back screen door, Teresa and I were wrapped around each other like a couple of sentimental octopi in Blumbetter's king-sized oval bed—more or less naked, immeasurably drunk, but at least not alone in this coarse, clammy world.... All we were trying to do was fill that awful vacuum in our lives temporarily, supporting the walls of our spirit before they caved in. Besides, it served Marge and Bert right!

"Take milk and cookies," Teresa called out to the kitchen from the east wing. "Mommy's not...feeling too well so I'm taking a...rest."

Two hours later, I was awakened from a tempestuous sleep as Teresa, somewhat recovered, somewhat embarrassed, untangled her limbs from mine, bound herself in a robe, and staggered out into the main annex. I staggered out of bed, got dressed, and opened the door a crack. While Teresa was grilling a burger for Bert Jr.'s dinner, she broke the news to him: "Daddy's gone away on a long, long trip, and I'm not sure when he's coming back, so Morty's daddy is staying with us awhile."

What worried me about this report was Bert Jr.'s lack of response. Until I moved into a motel, I didn't want to go around being stared at the way a butcher stares at a side of beef; or be the victim of a hot foot if I happened to doze off in the family den; or be ground to chop meat by a Great Dane trained to obey Jr.'s every command. Beyond my own fears, I was concerned about the impact of the flight of his father, as well as my own presence, on the youngster. Poor kid hadn't asked for any of this. As for Morty Jr., I didn't feel especially concerned, or lonely, for him. Possibly because there had never seemed to be much to say to each other, so little spiritual linkage between us. He had always clung to his mother like I was an intruder. And maybe it was true. For all I knew, he was Bert's son!

Friday morning at the Blumbetter breakfast table, when I had my first audience before Bert Jr. himself, with Teresa out in the kitchen, I got a hint as to what to expect. Looking me over from my sand-colored hair to my bone-colored ankles, he said: "Good morning, Dad."

Awfully good-natured of him was my initial reaction ... then I ran it through my head again: The rascal had either blocked out that I was someone else, or was so sophisticated that one slob was just as good/bad as another when it came to fatherhood. Either way I didn't like it, so I made a point of stating my name, rank, serial number: "You remember me, don't you? I'm Mr. Wickman from next door. Morty's dad."

"I'm late for school," he shouted toward the kitchen, darting out of the breakfast nook before I'd had an opportunity to wring a reaction out of him.

After my second cup of good-tasting coffee, and wound up in Bert's velveteen robe, I said: "Teresa, your son called me 'Dad.'"

Nipping her lower lip first, she said, "He seems to like you."

Her eyes were so close to overflowing, I dropped the matter. That threat of human rain also prevented me from getting around to apologizing for my behavior the day before, under the influence of too many sales-clinchers. Not that she expected it. I just felt I owed her some guilt. I also felt as if all my energy had escaped through a slow leak during the night. Though I honestly tried, I couldn't manage to get dressed, so I finally called in sick. "Just a slight temperature," I said hopelessly into the receiver. My boss accepted it reasonably well, reminding me, however, that he needed a full rundown on my sales trip. "I'll tally my orders today and bring them to your office first thing tomorrow."

All morning I hung around like a leaden cloud that was harboring a storm, but by noon my outlook brightened. For lunch Teresa broiled a slab of flounder especially for me, with paper-thin slices of fresh lemon (not that bottled so-called Real Lemon Marge uses); plus a home-made tartar sauce; asparagus lightly sprinkled with paprika; fluffy wild rice under the spell of exotic spices. All served on genuine Delft. Once that Four Star luncheon had been digested, however, I took up worrying again. Bert Jr. had not reappeared at three-thirty and I easily convinced myself that he too had run away.

"Your son is late from school," I ventured gently, so as not to set her motherly instincts a-flying.

"Don't worry, Mort," she half smiled, "he's at baseball practice."

"He's a ballplayer?—that's just great. Wish Morty Jr. had some interest in the great American pastime."

By the time Bert Jr. came busting through the screen door early that evening, I was feeling entirely agreeable: Teresa had washed, dried *and* folded all my business trip laundry—nearly everything I had left in the world; the central air-conditioner was set on HI; and I was planted in Bert's plush leather recliner (mine was naugehyde), smoking one of his smuggled Cuban stogies, reading the *Herald Dispatch-Examiner.* (The Cubs had won their third straight!) Sighting me in the living room, the boy stopped short under the sweep of the arch, his fielders mitt notched under his arm. I looked him straight in the eye and said, "Did you have a good practice, Son?"

Bert Jr.'s face melted into a charming, Cheerios sort of smile. He didn't look at all like Bert Sr., I realized, his sandy hair crackling with vitality, his eyes green and swift—somewhat like mine, at certain angles. "I got two hits!" he exclaimed.

Teresa entered the room just as I was patting Bert Jr. on the shoulder and saying, "That's terrific, Son." And smiling boyishly at Teresa, I added: "I was always a good hitter, too."

Glowing, the boy dashed toward the bathroom as if it were second base, and I thought about the fact that Morty Jr. didn't even understand the mechanics, the beauty of a double play. I took a puff on that snappy cigar, and ogled Teresa proudly. She looked positively huggable in her cherry-dotted apron, her hair shining like strands of much-combed silk, a chrome mixing whip in her hand. And before returning to the kitchen, to finish creating a dozen French-style strawberry custard tarts—edible works of art, really, she set the soft tips of her fingers on my neck and rubbed gently a few moments. I felt like a man who'd returned home after two weeks on the road in a rented Cavalier ought to feel—welcomed back into the comfortable fold of a kind routine, the perfect antidote to selling ribs and chops and the ham hocks of hogs across mid-America.

Saturday brought sunshine the color of peaches and a continuation of the previous day's felicity, a rich mixture of home and family I had never dreamed was within my grasp, a mode of living I believed had passed out of currency a century earlier. During those wonderful hours, Terry and I spoke with refreshing openness about our childhood, our hopes, our needs, our failures, our successes—even about baseball and politics. (We were both Democrats at heart, there in that hotbed of Republicanism.) Everything seemed to interest her! Throughout it all, we never mentioned the names of our spouses. It was as if they no longer existed.... Both of us seemed to sense our lives had become meaningful again.

In the afternoon Bert Jr. and I played catch in the double-wide driveway. (He can really burn 'em in for a ten-year-old.) I learned he was not shy in school, and a good student (which, no doubt, he got from his mother's side). Toward evening Rover, the last holdout, stepped up to me and, as I stood as still as a monument, licked my hand without gnoshing on the fingers. Gingerly I patted his head, and he sniffed his way up both pant legs, then strolled off benignly. Unlike Spot, Rover rarely barked, so I managed to slip in a peaceful nap before dinner, out in the hammock strung between two pear trees clustered with fruit. Rover was stretched out on the grass beneath me, apparently to make sure no harm came to me.

Most impressive of all about Saturday, I think, were the three extraordinarily satisfying meals we shared, remarkable not merely because of Terry's mastery of stove and oven (she baked whole wheat bread with honey!), but because of the absence of what mealtime generally drummed up at 22 Sunnyside: canned this and dried-up that, often burnt, dished out late, served with the grimmest details from the *Herald-Dispatch-Examiner* as a side-order, and culminating in the inevitable gloomy silences over some nondescript, lumpy dessert.

Primarily because Terry happened to mention that Bert Sr. had always refused to go with them, I entered an Episcopalian church for the first time that Sunday. To my surprise I enjoyed the entire service, especially the sing-along. Very different from the synagogues of my youth, where only the cantor was allowed to reach out to God through song. I sang out lustily, attracting the approving eyes of the congregation. The service made me feel hearty, full of the spirit of life on God's earth. And late that night, I heard someone creep into my room, and within the halo of Terry's arms and legs, I found religion all over again. Her talents seemed limitless, and this time she wasn't drunk.

Monday morning I devoured no less than three cups of Terry's fresh-ground, steaming-hot coffee, three poached eggs—not too soft, not too hard—and three bakery rolls with real butter, not the orange-colored margarine I was usually served next door. Though I can honestly say I'm considerably better looking than he, Bert and I were of similar build, so I selected a suit from the dozen he hadn't bothered taking with him—a lightweight, pale blue sharkskin that, according to Terry, "Looks like it was custom-tailored for you." I patted Bert Jr.'s back supportively, kissed Terry goodbye rather lustily, considering it was 7:10 AM, and drove Bert Sr.'s Chrysler Imperial down Sunnyside without caring a pinch what the neighbors might be thinking. I was whis-tling—actually whistling—on my way to the train! (In a dozen years of heading to Midland Meats, in the intestines of the city,

I had never whistled before.) For some reason the pollution downtown did not trigger my customary coughing fit. And my boss didn't give me the business for calling in sick; he congratulated me heartily on the carload of sausages I'd peddled in Wichita. Even more amazing, in eight hours I never once lost my temper with O'Connor, a moderately successful salesman (also on commission) whose tactics I despise.

That evening the train pulled into Fairbury at exactly 6:36 PM, right on schedule. Up Sunnyside I drove singing: "Some ... where...o...ver...the rain...bow...." The succeeding days flowed as gently as the previous ones, the only noteworthy differences arising in the degree and kinds of joys. One afternoon Bert Jr. had finished first in a spelling bee; on another I saw him make an over-the-shoulder catch in left field. One evening I was served cordon bleu; the next we discussed the red-meat cancer theories. One night Terry wore a black satin gown with a "V" neck to the belly button; on another a pink see-through scrap of lace! A steady fount of peace and contentment seemed to have bubbled up out of the union naturally, like an irrepressible, bottomless spring of sweet water, and all three of us drank of it deeply.

Bert Jr. never seemed to have that downcast, orphaned look I'd feared, suggesting to me that he had had the kind of relationship with Bert Sr. that I'd had with Morty Jr. And Terry seemed to sparkle with a gladness that buoyed her above the pretty class into the higher sphere of gorgeous. A kind of quiet bombshell. An angel with just enough devil in her to keep life interesting day and night. Never again would my eyes be able to see peculiarities in her appearance or behavior. She was, in two words, just right—at least for me.

Under the protection of these blessings, during the next few days, I became fascinated with the contemplation of the queer situations we are led into in life. Right next door to each other, for ten years, had lived four people who were ideally suited to each other, but which circumstance had not seen fit to put together in the proper combination, at the appropriate time. Had it not been for the perceptiveness and, really, the courage of Marge and Bert, I would have lived out all my days without ever having known the love of Terry Blumbetter, nee Teresa Meadows, a woman who was obviously made-to-order for Morton Wickman. I began to feel indebted to our ex-s. But with these philosophical excursions came a new rush of worry: Now that this extraordinary happiness had been dealt to me like a royal flush, I was terrified some great, envious power would swoop down from the sky and pluck the cards out of my fingers. One night I dreamed that I returned home from a sales trip to Muncie only to find Terry, Bert Jr., Rover—and all the furniture—gone. Awakening in a greasy sweat, I found Terry close beside me, smiling in her sleep. Watching her easy breathing awhile, I kissed her nose gently, and finally fell back to sleep.

One week later, Bert Sr. telephoned. Terry's polite, guileless face grew long with experience as she listened to him explain things. I had made the mistake of imagining that because Terry and I had fit so well into each other's life, the same was true of Bert and Marge. Apparently not. They had been unable to agree on anything—not even where they should run off to; they were marooned, locked up in a motel room less than a hundred miles south—one leaning toward Florida, the other toward California, and both on the verge of strangling the other. The Wickman heirlooms, meanwhile, were collecting dust and debt at a warehouse considerably closer to Sunnyside Drive. Inevitably, when they had stopped speaking altogether, they had gotten around to thinking about what they had done—about Terry and me and, after what they considered a respectable passage of time, commenced to miss us—or so they claimed. I suspect Bert missed his surround-sound entertainment center, and Marge missed my acquiescence. In any case they wanted to come back home. They wanted to forget and be forgiven. They even wanted to forgive us! At these revelations Terry's eyes stretched wide with confusion. Quickly I surrounded her with my arms to stabilize her—to remind her of how well she and I had been getting on. I was trembling in my—in Bert's—tennis sneakers.

After a long spell of uninterrupted listening, Terry spoke quietly into the receiver: "You abandoned your lawful wife and son and home. There are laws, Bertram Blumbetter, and I've had them all explained to me by an attorney. If I see you sneaking around this house, or hear about you harassing Bert Jr. at school, I'll call the police and make sure they bring along their attack dogs."

Cold, hard, beautiful she was! I felt like skipping around the marble coffee table. Then, with a thick sigh, but nary a tear in her eye, Terry held the receiver out to me. Margery Wickman was on the other end. As if she were a distant cousin, I said: "Yes, who is this please?"

"You know damn well who this is—this is your *wife.*"

"I'm sorry," I chuckled, "my wife is here by my side, where a wife is supposed to be."

"The neighbors told me what you two have been doing Morton Wickman so don't you try to get righteous with me besides Morty Jr. wants to see you and Spot misses his backyard—all his bones are buried there."

"Morty?—oh you mean Bert's little boy. Did he ever get those contact lenses?"

"You cut it out, Morton. I don't think this is funny; we need you at home; did you pay last month's mortgage?"

"You don't seem to get it, Marge. I have found my true home with Teresa. And if she'll have me, I intend to marry her as soon as possible." I was watching Terry as I said this, and I saw a brightness enter her eyes. Marge slammed the phone down, making my ear ring: a small price, all considered. Momentarily relieved, I pulled Terry's always-warm body against mine, and kissed her soft mouth and cheeks and eyelids again and again, until our fears had melted into a reaffirmation of our steady, rich feelings for each other. That evening, in the cool flood of the moon, we tried to find solace in the shadowy dips and swells of our bodies. But underneath our nakedness there was a tautness of spirit not even such a finely tuned intimacy could overcome.

Next morning they were set out on our doorstep, white and rigid as garden statuary—Marge, Bert Sr., Spot, and Morty Jr., faced off by Teresa, Morton Sr., Bert Jr., and Rover. It would've been the most harrowing interview of my life if it weren't for the fact that Terry and I knew, with the unquestioning passion of those who cling to religious dogma, that we'd found what we had needed all our lives. We just hadn't known where to find it. Armed with that knowledge, we were invincible. Despite tears and anger and pleading by Marge and Bert Sr., and the blank-eyed stare of Morty Jr., and Spot's continuous barking, and the civilized discussion that inevitably emerged in the aftermath of all that expended emotion, it became crushingly clear to them that those old relationships were over for us. Finished. Kaput!

Though we never actually aired out the philosophical implications of it all, I sense—or at least like to think—that everyone (including the dogs) came away with some personal, intuitive drift of the manipulations of fate. For me, it was somehow linked, intimately yet mysteriously, with my selling of animal parts, which would end up butchered and broiled on plates in the restaurants and homes of mid-America. A kind of ritual sacrifice I'd been engaged in for years without quite grasping its significance—not until the gods had recognized my contributions to society and rewarded me with a new life. As for those on the other side of the counter, all I know is that they were staggered by the reversal of events, stunned to leave their former lives behind forever, and the four of them walked away with a lonely gait, as if wondering where, out in the far, wide marketplace of love, they were going to find those special, one-of-a-kind individuals who could be husband and wife, mother and father, friend and master, to each and every one of them.

Without opening my mouth, I wished them luck in their search.

COLD PITCH

The woman in the flimsy blue bathrobe was passing the table where the phone rested when its ringer was activated. Stopping short, she listened to it ring one, two, three, four, five times more before lifting the receiver and placing it tentatively against her ear. "Hello?"

"Is this Mrs. Helen Walker?"

With a low exhalation she replied, "Yes, this is she."

"I'm glad I found you at home," the voice said brightly. "It would be a shame to have you miss out on such an unusual opportunity."

The tone, if not the voice itself, was one she'd heard over the telephone many times before, and it made her retract within. "I hope this is not one of those 'once in a lifetime' opportunities," she heard herself say.

His soft laughter seemed to coil out of the earpiece. "I assure you, Mrs. Walker, this is not some sort of come-on, not a gimmick of any kind."

"Well now, Mr.—I don't believe I got your name."

"John Swain."

"Tell me, Mr. Swain, just what is this opportunity you're interrupting my life to tell me about?"

Pleasantly the voice replied: "If I told you straight out, without talking things over, I'm afraid you might not believe me—that's how good a situation this is, and then the opportunity might slip away before you could give it your serious consideration."

Mrs. Walker's eyes were streaked with red veins, and she raised them toward the ceiling as if exasperated. "Please, Mr. Swain, I'm terribly busy. What is it you're trying to sell me?"

"Now there you've gone and used that four-letter word when I never once asked you to buy anything."

"No, I suppose you didn't, but if you're not trying to sell me something, then what is it you're trying to do, and why are you tying up my phone line?"

"I want to be your friend."

"Friend? I find your tone quite presumptuous, Mr. Swain," she said with a flash of annoyance.

"Forgive me, Mrs. Walker. Here I'm trying to be of service to you, and I go and say the wrong thing. Please let me explain myself better."

Helen Walker sank down on the sofa, keeping the phone to her ear. "If you insist," she muttered. It was only after she'd taken the weight off her legs that her knees began to throb with pain.

"I only meant that everyone at some time or other needs a friend."

"Did you call to tell me that, Mr. Swain?"

"No, of course not," he replied, his voice trailing off into silence.

Staring at the widening shadows spreading across the pale living room rug, Mrs. Walker rubbed her knees beneath the robe and said wearily into the mouthpiece: "It's past dinner time. I really wish you'd get to the point."

"Ah, yes, the bottom line."

"If you care to put it that way."

"Frankly, Mrs. Walker, I called to offer you my assistance because of the loss you suffered recently."

Mrs. Walker's head jerked away from the receiver, and she looked at the white object in her hand as if trying to figure out how it was able to emit sound. Then she put her sharp dry lips to the punctured plastic disc: "How did you know that, Mr. Swain? I demand to know how you knew that."

"Does it really matter? Isn't it more important that you fill the emptiness that's opened in your life as quickly as possible?"

"I don't think that's any of your business, Mr. Swain, or whatever your real name is."

"All you need to do is give me an affirmative answer," the voice said smoothly, "and we can get started right away. Over the telephone. Isn't that convenient?"

"I have no idea *what* you are talking about, and wish you'd get off this line. I'm…I'm waiting for an important call."

Mrs. Helen Walker sat severely still on the sofa, pressing the receiver against her ear so hard it began to hurt.

"Furthermore I guarantee you satisfaction," promised the voice in the receiver.

"What do you *mean* by satisfaction?"

"I'm afraid I can't tell you that. Not yet."

"Whom do you represent?"

"I can't tell you that, either."

"This is ridiculous!" Mrs. Walker slammed the receiver down on the cradle and stood up, abruptly sliding a hand over her tangled, gray-streaked hair. But the moment she'd let go of the instrument, she felt a wave of loneliness flood over her, and it became difficult for her to breathe. Pulled by a weighty sadness that seemed to surround each of her limbs, she dropped onto the sofa again.

The telephone rang, and it sounded louder than before. With a shaking hand she lifted the receiver to her ear: "Hello?"

"Please don't misunderstand me, Mrs. Walker. It's not that I won't tell you anything. It's just that the circumstances are unique in each individual case. No one really knows what form the service will take until we know more about your specific needs. By that time, I won't have to explain a thing to you. You'll know exactly what to expect."

Reluctant to hang up and experience that sickening loneliness again, she started talking: "What you're asking of me is to accept this so-called opportunity of yours entirely on faith, to believe everything without knowing anything about this proposition. Is that it, Mr. Swain?"

"Yes, that's it precisely; you must take it on faith. But could you please call me John, and may I call you Helen?"

"You ask a great deal of one, Mr. Swain, a great deal."

"Perhaps, but the benefits of our service will make up for that, and they will last a long, long time."

"How can I possibly know whether that's true or not?"

When there was no reply, Mrs. Walker said: "Yes, yes, I know. I must take that on faith, too. But why in the world should I trust you—a stranger who has barged into my life over this electronic contraption? I don't know you, I've never even seen you. What do you look like, Mr. Swain? What do you want out of life? Are you afraid of losing your job? Do you have ill children at home? A dissatisfied wife? Are you sometimes frightened by your own dreams? Have you ever felt completely separated from everything and everyone? Have you ever lost all hope?"

After a few seconds of silence, the voice in the receiver said: "I'm not important. I'm merely the conveyor. You're the important one. You're the user."

The window in the living room rattled, and Mrs. Walker turned her head toward it. Though she remembered opening it earlier, the window was now closed. But she didn't have the energy to get up and open it again, even though she felt she needed more air. "I don't know what to say, Mr. Swain. You're confusing me. It's all so mysterious."

"I don't mean to be evasive. It's merely in the nature of a cold pitch."

"Cold pitch?"

"You know, a spiel over the telephone without the advantage of seeing the potential consumer in person. If you don't hold out information—to establish a sense of mystery, the chance of concluding a deal is greatly diminished."

"There you are—didn't I say you're trying to sell me something?"

"To have a bona fide sale, there must be money involved. In this case, there's no need for money to change hands."

"Are you saying this service of yours is without charge?"

"All you need to do, Helen, is say you trust me."

"Is that all there really is to it?"

"That's right. All I need is your trust."

"And if I agree, can we end this conversation so I can get on with my evening? Or what's left of it?"

"Of course, Helen."

"In that case I'll do it. To get you off this line I'll do whatever you say."

Following a few moments of static on the line she heard the voice again: "You still haven't told me what I need to hear."

"You mean you actually want me to say the words?"

"It's important that you say them so there's no misunderstanding between us."

"Okay, okay, I trust you. Does that satisfy you?"

"You certainly did utter the words, Helen. But if you wouldn't mind, could you say them again only this time with a little more feeling? You know, so that it sounds as if you really mean it."

"This is outrageous," Mrs. Walker said quietly, tempted to hang up again, yet afraid to lose this connection, however slight, with another human being.

"Please, Helen. I wouldn't ask it of you if it weren't important."

"To be honest, Mr. Swain, I can't think of one good reason why I should."

"But there is one very good reason, Helen: If you have faith in me, I promise to bring you peace of mind."

The idea of tranquility in her heart and mind seemed very appealing to Mrs. Walker at that moment, and she said, "All right, all right. Just give me a moment to think this over." After taking several deep breaths, she said quietly into the receiver, with feeling, "I trust you, John. I *really* do trust you."

"Do you mean you have faith, utter faith in me?"

"Yes, I suppose that is what I mean."

"Thank you, Helen. I'm very happy to hear you say that."

Except for the faint rush of air through the little holes in the white plastic mouthpiece, making it sound like the sea, the receiver at her ear was silent. At last she said, "Well, now what?"

"Now I want you to go into the kitchen, put out the pilot lights in your stove, and turn on all the gas jets. Do you follow me, Helen?"

"That's very dangerous, Mr. Swain. I don't understand why you want me to do that."

"Helen," the voice said sadly, "you said you have complete faith in me."

"Well, yes, I did say something like that, but this is different."

"Faith doesn't distinguish between circumstances, Helen. If you trust me, then you trust me. If you don't, you don't."

"I suppose you're right," she said heavily, trying to see out the window: a tall gray hedge blocked the view of the gray lawn and the gray street and the gray houses beyond.

"Do you have faith in me or not?"

"I…I do, yes, I do have faith in you, John."

"Good. Then I want you to go into kitchen, make sure all the windows are closed, put out the pilot lights in the stove, and turn on all the gas jets."

"And then what?"

"And then I want you to open the oven, get down on your knees in a position of prayer, and stick your head inside."

"Prayer?"

"That's right, Helen. I want you to think of the oven as a kind of altar, a great provider, the open mouth of ultimate mysteries."

"You want me to pray to the oven?"

"I want you to breathe in deeply, again and again, and pray for deliverance until you have entirely filled the void in your lungs, in your heart. Breathe deeply in prayer until you feel transported out of your body. Until you are free of all human encumbrances. Do you understand?"

"Yes, John, I understand."

"Good. Now Helen, will you please go into your kitchen and do as I've asked?"

After a pause, Mrs. Walker said, "Yes, I will."

"Thank you, Helen. Thank you very much. It has been a pleasure doing business with you."

Mrs. Helen Walker hung up the telephone gently, and sat staring at the rectangular space on the wall where a picture frame had prevented the dust from settling. This time she did not feel the undertow of loneliness. Nor did her knees ache. Having a purpose—something before her that needed to be done, seemed to make those terrible feelings go away. *John Swain has been telling the truth after all,* she thought. Slowly she rose off the sofa, walked into the kitchen and looked at the windows: They were closed. Now she drifted toward the stove, snuffed out the pilot lights, and opened the black abyss of its oven.

THE STEALING PROGRESSION

Barney Dreer was shocked by what he had done.

One autumn evening, on the way home from his office, he stopped at the neighborhood mini-market to buy a loaf of bread. As he drifted up and down the aisles, he had a powerful sense there was a second item he needed, but he couldn't remember what it was. In the rear of the store he stopped to eye the tubs of butter, quarts of milk, containers of sour cream, trying to remember. The only other customer in the market was up front, checking out her groceries. Always very careful with all of his expenditures, rather than lay out money for something he might not need, he picked up a packet of cheddar cheese, extra sharp, and slipped it into the inside pocket of his jacket.

Knees wobbling on his way up front, he snatched a loaf of white bread off the bakery shelves and halted awkwardly at the check-out counter. When the cashier rang up his amount on the register, he fumbled in his wallet, pulled out two one-dollar bills, and held them out with a shaky hand. As the matronly woman handed him his change, he felt his face fill with blood. Without looking at him the cashier stuffed the bread into a brown paper bag. He thanked her twice and hurried out of the market, sucking in air as if he were suffocating.

Down the track of concrete he fled toward his apartment building, the package in his pocket thumping against his ribs, feeling more like five pounds of potatoes than eight ounces of cheese. All the way home he kept looking back over his shoulder, and resolved never, ever to do such a crazy thing again.

By the time he entered the lobby of his building—a stack of bricks slapped together after World War II—he was genuinely surprised not to have been accosted by the grocer, arrested by a policeman. Upstairs in his kitchen, Barney sat down at the chrome-legged table and, without removing his jacket or loosening his tie, ripped open the cellophane-sealed cheese with a steak knife. He sliced off a corner of the cheddar, dropped the chunk into his mouth, and began chewing uneasily. The soft cheddar had a rich, tangy, heady flavor that dizzied him. Continuing to cut and drop chunks into his mouth, he chewed steadily, unable to remember when cheese—when any food—had tasted so delicious.

Later that evening, as he watched "The Munsters" on TV, he felt calm enough to reflect upon his misadventure, and could not help noticing how easy it had been to get out of the store with the cheese in his pocket, even though he'd made many mistakes—thanking the cashier twice, racing out of the store with a bright red face. Being a person who prided himself on his efficiency in whatever he undertook, he began to consider, purely hypothetically, how the job could've been done more efficiently. It gave him something out of the ordinary to think about.

Barney Dreer considered himself a good businessman, and his mind was quick—especially when it came to numbers. He operated his own one-desk tax preparation office. Each day during tax time he would brush what was left of his dusty hair, and put on a jacket and tie before heading out to do his duty. Unfortunately, his professionalism didn't help him make friends: Clients, neighbors, and strangers mostly steered clear of his slightly out of balance facial features, his five feet two-inch high frame, his three feet four-inch wide mid-section. Even his regulars preferred to do their business by mail, fax, computer, or telephone. Thus Barney learned to talk and laugh to himself, spending nearly all of his time adding up deductions, cooking omelets, watching reruns on television, and maintaining order in his apartment and his office.

The older he grew, however, the less satisfactory these simple diversions became. Though not a religious man, he joined a church social group—where it seemed that everyone ignored him piously. For a time he took up reading paperback romances, but all this did was remind him he was neither heroic nor romantic, not even tragic enough to arouse compassion in those who passed along the fringes of his life. He even ventured into the People Connection on the Internet but received only a couple of incomprehensible responses. It was after he failed to connect on-line that fate intervened to provide a distraction by encouraging him to commit his first theft.

Despite his best intentions, the sweetness of that first chunk of stolen cheese virtually assured that Barney would try again. Next time he shoplifted—a pint jar of strawberry jam—he managed to avoid many of the mistakes he'd made the first time, though not all of them. He was obliged to commit a string of small thefts—chocolate chip cookies, a can of peas, a pork chop, packets of instant oatmeal, a box of tea bags—before he really started to get the hang of it. In the process he learned not to steal heavy, bulky items that would show under his clothing; or something that might break if it slipped out of his pocket; and to avoid certain types of cellophane which tended to make telltale noises when crinkled under the arm. Although he got away with the goods in these new capers, and eliminated his earlier mistakes, he also made several new ones, such as glancing over his shoulder furtively. If he could only eradicate these errors, he believed, he could retire with his accounts in order. And he certainly intended to bring an end to this business; he was not a terribly moral person, but as a tax man with a few small retailers among his clients, he didn't like the idea of reducing the potential profits of the stores he victimized.

The trouble was, stealing had added an element of adventure to his life, and had brought him a certain relief. Each time he consumed some unpaid-for item of food—anything from an apple lifted from the produce stand to a fillet from the fish stall, he noticed he no longer felt quite as downhearted as before. As a

149

result, his compact three rooms in the Bronx—outfitted with a formica table, a chrome-tube kitchen chair, a worn-cushioned love seat, a 19-inch TV, a pressboard desk in the front rooms, and a mattress on a black iron frame, a square night table, and a scratched maple chest of drawers in the bedroom—no longer seemed quite so confining or dismal.

Over the next few weeks, however, something as difficult to pinpoint as a change in the barometric pressure set in, and he realized that consuming stolen food was having less and less beneficial effect on his moods. One afternoon, overcome by a panic at the thought that this balm might no longer be available to him, Barney did something out of the ordinary: He called up a new client who had come to him over the telephone via his boldfaced directory listing. The gentleman had spoken kindly to him, and his tax return had interested Barney more than most.

"I need...to go over your return...in person," the tax man stuttered into the mouthpiece.

Next morning a stocky, icy-haired man in mismatched trousers and jacket stepped breathlessly into Barney's office, which was not much wider than a grade school wardrobe closet.

With a quivering finger, Barney pointed to the metal chair alongside his desk. "You got a potential problem with these medical deductions," he rasped, staring gravely at the open file folder on his desk.

Having a head-on look at the tax consultant for the first time, the client squirmed in his seat—or so it seemed to Barney. "What makes you say that?"

"I seriously doubt the IRS'll make allowances for depression drugs in such large amounts."

"It's a legitimate expense," the client insisted, inspecting the business school diploma hanging on the wall.

"In my twenty-five years in this game, I've seen the IRS call taxpayers downtown for much less questionable deductions,"

Barney stated with authority, "and the first thing they'll want to know is whether all these drugs were prescribed by a practicing MD."

"I got receipts."

"Between you and me," Barney said in a confidential tone, "I saw a report on TV that showed these depression drugs do nothing except kick up stock prices for the pharmaceuticals."

"That's not the point!"

"Maybe so," Barney muttered, "but as someone who's working on your behalf, I think you ought to know there're other ways to deal with this trouble."

"What trouble?"

"You know, being down in the dumps once in a while."

"What're you driving at?"

"I'm no doctor, but talking from personal experience I just want to say that maybe what you need is less drugs and a little more...excitement in your life."

Gripping the armrests, the man started to tremble. "I came here for *tax* advice, not *personal* counseling."

"You're absolutely right," Barney said agreeably. "I only brought it up because I had a similar problem, and I've managed—"

The man stood up abruptly. "Give me back my tax papers."

"Why don't you sit down a minute and we'll discuss this calmly—no need to get upset," Barney suggested, surprised by his client's reaction.

Reaching across the desk the older man scooped up the folder, tucked it under his meaty arm, and said, "You're nuts!" Now he swung open the door and slammed it behind him.

In the silence that followed, Barney hoisted himself onto his feet, stepped to the open window, and extended his upper torso beyond the sill. At last he saw the white-haired man emerge from the building and disappear around the next corner. For a long while he watched the people shuttle back and forth across the concrete. From ten stories up, they seemed insignificant, not worth the trouble of getting to know any of them.

Noticing the Super Mart on the corner, from which he'd stolen and enjoyed food for several meals, he was struck by the realization that the sales clerks in the stores he successfully stole from were the only people towards whom he felt any real friendship. *Maybe stealing a variety of products from a variety of stores,* he thought, *would be something like having a circle of friends...*

That evening, on the way home from his office, Barney visited a neighborhood hardware store and walked out with a box of nails in his pocket, but no sales slip. The next afternoon it was a bookstore and a pocket book of horror stories, and the following evening he emerged from a paint store with two brushes—and with nothing he wanted to paint. At first this strategy seemed to help lessen his anxiety, but an hour or two after each theft he could feel something begin to squeeze his heart again, making it difficult to breathe.

On weekends Barney began taking the subway down to department stores along Thirty-Fourth Street in Manhattan and riding the bus up to the shopping malls of White Plains, visiting women's cosmetic and clothing departments. Initially this strategy seemed to have little positive effect on the constriction in his chest. After it had occurred to him to sit on the edge of his bed and sniff the pilfered powder puff or fondle the snitched scarf, however, he found that the internal grip would loosen, and the floating panic settled down deeper (if uneasily) within him, as if lying in wait for an unguarded moment to resurface.

Since he tended to feel congenial toward establishments from which he'd stolen with relative ease, Barney looked upon these stores as his best friends. If a store's counters were situated in such a way as to make stealing inordinately difficult, however, or if guards were posted at all exits, he became indignant and would refuse to spend time in that store in the future. If a particular kind of loot—a silky piece of lingerie, for example, seemed to make the bad feelings stay away longer, he would go after lingerie again, using a toilet booth in the men's room to stash a see-through negligee in his briefcase.

The more skillful he became—learning to use his own or someone else's body as a shield, or to tuck stolen goods deftly into items he intended to purchase—the safer he felt. At the same time, because he needed to steal more often and in new situations to satisfy his craving, he was placing himself directly in the gunsite of the law of averages, which to him was as immutable as the law of gravity. To combat what had been characterized in the media as a national epidemic, amounting to billions of dollars in lost goods annually, stores were becoming highly sophisticated in discouraging or entrapping shoplifters. Increasingly he was confronted by electronic detector gates, computer-coded clothing tags, video cameras. All this worked on his mind, especially at night, when he should have been asleep.

His collection of barrettes and tubes of skin cream and silver bracelets and fancy perfume bottles and ladies underwear continued to grow in his chest of drawers, kitchen cupboards, medicine cabinet, shoe boxes under his bed, and in two large cardboard boxes stacked in his hall closet. This accumulation made him nostalgic for the times when he'd been able to consume most of what he'd stolen. Worse yet, the more he gathered from stores, coddling these objects or applying them to his shoulders or rubbing the satin over his face, the less his tension seemed to melt away. Again he could sense the panic rising up out of that murky zone beneath his consciousness. All day at the office, all evening at his apartment, he thought about how he might stave off what now seemed inevitable. His work began to suffer, and his usually tidy apartment began to resemble a Salvation Army thrift store.

Suspecting the relief he found in stealing was somehow associated with the people he imagined buying such products, he thought: *What better way to get closer to someone than by acquiring something that already belongs to a human being?* Even as he came to this idea he recognized that stealing directly from a person is quite a different occupation than stealing from a store. To pick a pocket or swipe a purse one had to assess each opportunity with extreme caution; one needed a light, steady, quick hand; one had to place oneself increasingly in situations where human beings gathered, coming in close contact with them. To steal from a person required a readiness to be confronted, too, a prospect that frightened him. But he had no choice. Though he usually walked to his office—at least in dry weather, he started taking the crowded subway every day, and scanned newspapers for reports of forthcoming parades, festivals, demonstrations. And he began to carry a thin-bladed folding knife on his person at all times.

Barney Dreer undertook a series of dry runs in which he did everything but actually swipe something from the individuals he had targeted. These dry runs occurred in the subway, in the lobby of a hotel, at a parade along Fifth Avenue, and it didn't take him long to acquire a grasp—at least theoretical—of the fundamentals of picking pockets and purses. In the process he learned how to turn the attention of a victim in another direction without raising suspicions—and, though it both intimidated and excited him—how to bump into a person and make it seem accidental.

Riding the Fordham Road bus on a Friday evening—dozens of passengers jammed together with their packages—Barney dipped his hand into the shopping bag of an elderly gentleman and got off at the next stop with a small brown bag containing a pound of ground beef. Though he'd fried up a fat, juicy hamburger an hour later, the pressure in his chest had not diminished, and he wondered if it was because he hadn't stolen something that was personal to the old man. Next morning he moved up behind a teenage girl in a local variety store and, brushing against her, used his thumb to slide a cigarette lighter up out of her back pocket and into his hand. She never even glanced his way, causing Barney to beam with a sense of accomplishment as he walked out of the store. Nor did he feel quite so down as before.

In the ensuing weeks, he stole mostly from women because, in the past, he'd been able to loosen his miserable tension more effectively with female goods, and because, in general, women did not seem to be as attentive to the dangers of being victimized. The range of things that could be stolen from them, furthermore, was considerably greater, and more intimate. Fancy handkerchiefs, perfumes, necklaces, lipsticks, scarves, earrings, an extra pair of shoes. What he coveted most, however, was a woman's wallet—though not for the cash: Money belonged to everyone rather than to individuals and therefore never seemed to chase his moodiness away. Yet he'd managed to appropriate only two wallets—one that was without interest from a school boy, and one from an elderly woman wearing a thin black coat, looking as if she were in mourning. In her wallet he had come across pictures of her husband, children, and grandchildren. As he looked them over, Barney imagined himself into these photos—out on the stoop, in the backyard, surrounded by smiling family members. It was a life that he, the son of an alcoholic father and unstable mother, had never known.

As Barney soon discovered, moving targets were not always cooperative, and once he nearly got caught by a college student, narrowly escaping by bouncing out of the subway car just as the doors closed. Afterwards he started taking the subway at a different station and time. Yet Barney refused to revert back to stealing from stores, understanding in some primitive way that going backward would only make him more depressed. He merely kept alert—a predatory beast, waiting for the right victim, the right moment. Meanwhile, the unwholesome weight continued to collect in his chest, as though, each night, someone were placing another heavy stone inside his rib cage as he slept, making it increasingly difficult for him to haul his body out of bed each morning.

One evening, with his stomach coiled like a rattlesnake as he rode the subway home, he spotted a young woman—hair the color of peaches, lips as bright as strawberries—holding onto a passenger hand grip directly across from him. Her beauty startled him, causing him to forget that he should never stare at a potential victim. On her way home from her job, like everyone else in the train, she seemed dazed by the long workday. Aside from her beauty, what excited Barney was that her eyes were closed and her left shoulder supported the strap of a floppy handbag without a clasp.

When the train stopped with a jolt at the next station, and the passengers fumbled like bees to get in and out of the hot, airless subway car, Barney edged toward her, pretending he was being forced in that direction by the incoming crowd. The closer he got to her, though, the lonelier he felt. Her smooth-as-ivory hands, her mass of curly hair, her pointy nipples in the sweater she wore shot a pang of longing through his body—sensations that staggered him with their sudden force. For the first time in years he pictured himself caressing a woman's breasts, and this shocked him, for his feelings of separation had never struck him as carnal; rather he'd always associated them with the absence of innocent companionship. Sex was a totally different matter, as far as he was concerned.

Edging into position adjacent to the young woman, Barney checked out the passengers—to make sure no one happened to be looking toward him. Next he folded his arms across his chest. Then, his left hand dangling free under (and concealed by) his right elbow, he waited for the train to rock back and forth (as it always did), and when it did he tilted sideways toward her and eased two fingers into the open corner of her handbag. Gripping a corner of her makeup case, he straightened up and, in doing so, his little finger tugged the strap of her bag slightly. The case slipped out of his fingers and back into the black leather womb.

The young woman glanced at him, her eyes open as wide and as blue as morning glories. A shiver traveled the length and breadth of his body as the train stopped and the doors grunted open. Blindly he backed out and pushed through the crowd that was poised to gush into the car. When he reached the exit turnstile and heard the train doors close, he peered toward the car and spotted the red-headed woman: She had turned to look out the window and follow his progress across the platform.

Up the stairs out of the black hole of the subway he climbed, biting off a corner of his thumbnail as he emerged into the cool moist evening. Weary, impatient figures pushed past him, in a hurry to get home and sit down with loved ones at the dinner table. Having gotten off three stops too soon, Barney began the long journey to his apartment, passing through a parallel row of dreary storefront buildings that were losing the battle against the corporate tide of competition from giant retailers. The night seemed murky. As he wobbled along the commercial street, his eyes focused on an ancient couple in front of him; they were holding hands like teenagers strolling through a park.

His failure on the train undermined Barney's confidence to such a degree that, by the time he'd entered his building, he resolved to stop stealing altogether. "No percentage in going up against the law of averages over and over," he muttered. It wasn't merely because he might be arrested, possibly locked behind bars. Even more he feared that his picture might appear in the *New York Post* —TAX MAN NABBED AS PICK-POCKET. All five boroughs of the city would have a long, hearty laugh at his expense. His nose swelled at the thought of such public humiliation.

At his kitchen table, while making a bologna sandwich for dinner, Barney experienced a sharp clasping in his chest and, though he felt certain it wasn't so, he half wished it was the onset of a heart attack. Dropping the slices of bread, he hurried to his hall closet and pulled out an orange crate that contained his favorite purloined items. Into the bedroom he went, sitting down on the edge of his mattress. One by one he began fondling these objects, whispering endearments to them, placing them around his neck and on his shoulders. But the gold heart on a chain, the rhinestone broach, the pure-silk scarf, the transparent negligee, the lace brassiere—none of his treasured items helped to lessen the pain. That night on his lumpy mattress he was able to sneak away from consciousness only intermittently.

More mistakes started showing up in his calculations at the office, and he had reason to believe other clients might not return to him the following tax season. His sleep went from poor to miserable, and he began getting forgetful, one time leaving his keys stuck in the deadbolt lock of his apartment, forcing him to go all the way back home to be able to unlock his office and get a day's work done. A scowl carved itself into his face, and although he'd never been communicative with his neighbors—he used to nod at them upon occasion—now he clenched his fist whenever someone passed him in the corridor. The slightest annoyance—an abrupt waitress, a shoelace that came undone—would launch him into a rage.

The grim weight started spreading from his chest into his stomach and groin. But it was this new level of despair, this desperation that enabled him to see what he needed to do next. The only way he'd be able to regain his confidence would be to steal from the woman who'd nearly caught him. Calling up the image of her face in his mind, he indulged himself in the fantasy of sliding his stubby fingers very near her flood of red hair, her creamy skin, as he reached into her handbag, into her soul. These thoughts made him feel more relaxed than he had felt for days.

Next evening Barney Dreer, wrapped in his best jacket—a dull blue serge—and choked by a thick gray tie, with dark-rimmed prescription sunglasses notched on his nose, stationed himself on the subway platform where the first car of the train normally stopped, the car in which he'd failed to secure the makeup case from the young woman. Chewing on his cuticles, he waited for five forty-five because office workers tended to board the same car at the same time every evening. The train screeched to a halt, humming and trembling electrically in the station. Once the riders had poured out of the doors, Barney entered and scanned the car to establish her location before weaseling toward her—but he couldn't find her anywhere.

Barney's shoulders slumped as the train jerked forward, rolled into the long tunnel that lay between stations and began rattling through sheets of flowing, harrowing blackness. He felt like baggage being carted to some distant, indefinite point in time and space. Occasionally the lights in the train blinked off, on. He unfolded his newspaper and raised it in front of his face, pretending to read. Glancing around for a possible replacement, he thought: *Maybe I should just be patient and try to find her tomorrow.* But he shook his head vigorously at this idea. *Who knows what'll become of me if I don't do something tonight?*

At the next station people pushed out of and into the car, jostling him toward the middle. He moved without resistance, keeping his eyes sharp for any opportunity that might present itself. From this new position, through the windows of the sliding doors between cars, he spotted the red-headed woman seated in the second car. Her delicate facial bones and swanlike neck were poised over an open magazine. Barney's heart started thudding so fiercely he was afraid others might be able to hear it pounding, pounding.

With a burning sensation in his stomach, he made his way through the crowd, elbowing passengers aside as he passed out of the door of the first car and into the door of her car. Subway riders glanced at him with annoyance, and he realized he'd made a mistake in attracting their attention. Afraid she might recognize him, he kept his face turned away as he snaked between passengers toward the place where the woman was seated beside the doors. The train clattered furiously through the dark tunnel, faint lights flashing by the windows like a horror house ride at Playland. His legs shaking, the newspaper folded under his arm, he nudged a schoolboy out of his way and sidled into position next to her. Not having noticed anyone watching him, he opened the tabloid in front of his face and observed the woman from behind his sunglasses. Her hair was brushed out to its full length, and she wore a pleated black skirt and a short brown jacket that was unbuttoned. At the open neck of her cream-colored blouse, he saw a pendant on a chain, which looked like a thin gold scar across her throat. Her black leather handbag, sticking out of the shopping bag on the floor, caught his eye, but just then he was more interested in the fact that she wasn't wearing a wedding band.

Barney didn't like reading newspapers very much any more—too many murders, too much sex—yet he often carried the *Daily News* because it was a versatile tool. In addition to hiding behind its pages, he could use it to stash pilfered items. And if someone was on to him, he could toss the tabloid into a trash can while it still contained the goods—to be retrieved afterwards. The *Times* was too large and unwieldy for such operations. Folding his newspaper like a pair of jaws, he bent down at the waist as if to scratch his knee. What he really did was reach toward the woman's handbag, concealing his hand with the paper. For a second he thought he would be overcome by the rose scent of her hair, and when he touched the soft skin of her handbag, his heart fluttered wildly like a trapped bird. But he had set his feet firmly and, with a fluid motion, slid his hand under the flap and lifted out the first thing his fingers touched—instantly clamping the newspaper over it. Then he straightened up. Though it had all taken just three seconds, it had felt like three hours.

Her wallet was in his pocket! But he forced himself to temper his excitement, knowing the moments immediately following an episode were just as critical as those preceding it. *Take a look around. Slowly. Is anyone watching? Does the woman seem to be aware of me?* The red-head continued to read an article in the magazine—"Great New Hair Styles for Spring!" The rest of the passengers seemed lost in the tunnels of their minds, too. Turning away from her gradually, he gazed out the window at the steel girders of the approaching station as they whipped by until the train began to slow, and came to a halt. He had timed it perfectly.

Perspiration oozing out of his forehead in droplets, he stepped out of the train the moment the doors slid open, and he was carried forward by the crowd emptying from the car. In half a minute, he heard the doors snap shut. After he'd drawn a deep breath, Barney whispered to her from afar, "You really ought to keep your handbag on your person at all times," glancing at her through the window of the car that had begun to pull out of the station. Six minutes later, he got on the next train and rode it two more stops to his neighborhood.

Triumphantly he strode through the damp evening air toward his apartment building, thrilled by each bump of the stolen wallet against his thigh. Not only had he managed to steal from someone who had noticed him previously, but he'd gotten away with her wallet. "I'm going to flush all that stress out of my system tonight. Who knows?—maybe I'll get rid of it forever." By the time he had inserted his key into his front door, another delicious thought had come over him: *Her whole life is in the wallet, and now it belongs to me.*

Wrestling his body out of the jacket, he withdrew the wallet from his trouser pocket and dropped down on the edge of his mattress. Made of smooth red leather, the wallet seemed like a human heart lying in the palm of his hand. He removed its contents and arranged the pieces in rows—like numbers to be added on a sheet of accounting paper—along the parallel ribs extending down the stained white bedspread. Three photographs were in the collection—one of the young woman upon graduation from Fordham University, according to the banner behind her; one of a middle-aged couple; one of a good-looking blond fellow in his twenties. Barney wondered if he was her boyfriend.

A couple of quarters were in the coin pouch. One ten, three fives and four one-dollar bills were in the billfold section, but he was vaguely disappointed to notice they were not placed in numerical order. He found, too, a torn ticket to a play. An ATM card. A lottery ticket. A phone calling card. A discount coupon for Tampax. And assorted paycheck stubs from a small brokerage house off Wall Street; since the amounts were different and not very much on each stub, he thought she might just be getting started selling stocks and bonds on commission. And a folded newspaper clipping—FORDHAM GRAD, 23, DIES IN AUTO CRASH. Was it the young man in the photo? Well, no matter. He had her history in his hands, and looking over his bounty, out of raw delight he burst into laughter.

The most useful thing he found was her driver's license. Not only did it provide a more recent, though blurred picture of her, but it revealed her name was Laura Fahnestock and that she lived on the other side of the park, less than half an hour's walk from his apartment. Removing his glasses, Barney brought the license close to his face and flattened his lips against the image of the young woman. Now he lay down on the bed, closed his eyes, and waited. Within minutes he could feel a wet warmth begin to seep from his mid-section into the rest of his body. After another couple of minutes, however, he realized something was wrong, and he sat up. The tension had not gone away.

Barney Dreer could not continue losing sleep, making mistakes at his office, living in a disorderly apartment, losing keys and clients. "I'll bring the wallet to the red-head," he said, squeezing a pimple on his chin, "and tell her I found it in the subway." With tremulous hands he slipped each item back into the wallet, making sure the pieces were placed in the order in which he'd found them. Then he put on his jacket and forced the wallet into his breast pocket. In the bathroom he scraped a comb through his wispy hair, straightened his tie needlessly, and shined his teeth with a piece of toilet tissue. Minutes later he was stepping resolutely down the stairs of his building.

A mist was in the air as he walked along Fordham Road. He did not notice the people he passed, nor the stray dog that had followed him a short distance before giving up, as if realizing the short round man was not likely to befriend him. Soon he turned off the commercial thoroughfare and headed down a tree-lined street. After walking a few blocks, he found himself moving along the black iron fence of a spacious park, faced off by a row of squat, two-family houses. The street was hazy with a glow that sifted out of aluminum buds suspended from curved poles. Though each day was remaining lighter a little longer, the evenings still retained the dull chill of winter, and it would be another month before the warmth of the day carried fully into the night. Except for a distant drone of automobile traffic, all was quiet—so few people were out on the street this time of evening, most being at home watching the evening news together and the workaholics not due to arrive until hours later.

By the time he located her residence—a wood-frame two-story dwelling with tan, fake-stone siding—much of the mist had melted away and the sky had darkened as if rubbed with charcoal. The lonely man stood under a broad, twisted tree, looking up at the lighted window on the second floor. He wondered if the house belonged to her parents; the thought made him edgy: *Suppose they see me out here, staring up at her window. They might*

163

call the police. And the police'll question me and find out I stole her wallet. Pressured by the powerful immediacy of his need, however, he tried to reassure himself: "With no lights on downstairs," he whispered, "there's probably no one else home." And not having seen a wedding ring on her finger, he decided she probably wasn't married and lived alone in the upstairs apartment. Aware of his heart throbbing against the wallet—against her heart—under the desultory flutter of leaves, Barney found himself moving through the swaying shadows toward her house.

At the door he took hold of the knob and twisted it, and the door opened into a compact vestibule. He went in. Through the curtain of the glass inner door, he could see the stairs that led up to her apartment and, holding his breath, he gripped the inside door knob and twisted it gently—locked. Checking out the pair of doorbell buttons, he saw the bottom one read ADAMSON, but the upper had no name tag. *Maybe her parents don't live downstairs after all,* he thought, and whispered her name: "Laura Fahnestock." The sound of her name on his lips reminded him he would have to look her in the eye and speak to her. If she recognized him, she would surely cry out for help or jump back inside and call the police. And what if she had a boyfriend upstairs, or someone really was home downstairs?

Backing out of the vestibule, profoundly discouraged by the fact that he lacked the courage to place himself face to face with risk, he stepped down the stairs and moved heavily to the sidewalk. For several moments Barney felt entirely devoid of hope …until a vague white light came into his inner vision. The more he focused on that light, the more he could see it had a shape—a small round white thing, and he was comforted to remember he had hundreds of these tablets in his medicine cabinet, waiting for him to return.

Passing under the branches of the broad tree, Barney heard someone emerge from the house, and he saw her red hair glistening in the porch light. The handbag from which he'd stolen her wallet was dangling from her shoulder. When she turned to lock the door behind her, Barney ducked behind the wide tree, his breath coming in short uneven gusts. Pulling the woman's wallet out of his inner pocket, he compressed it in his hand and had a distinct sensation that it was throbbing in his fingers. Out of sight in the thick shadows under the tree, amidst the soothing whisper of the leaves, he felt less apprehensive than at any time since first entering this neighborhood.

The young woman moved down the brick steps and turned onto the sidewalk in his direction. After she had passed well beyond his tree, Barney stepped out onto the sidewalk and followed her down the block. Because he did not have to look at her directly, he found himself able to cough out words: "Excuse me, Miss, may I speak with you a moment?" Startled, the woman spun around and let out a shriek as her eyes settled on him.

"You needn't be afraid," he said, attempting to shape his mismatched lips into a smile.

The woman began to run down the empty sidewalk, clutching her handbag, and Barney wobbled after her, calling out, "I've only come to return something that belongs to you!" He held the wallet out toward her. But she continued scurrying parallel to the spiked iron fence, toward the street lamp on the corner.

Glancing over her shoulder the woman cried out, "Leave me alone!" But looking away caused her to lose her step, trip and she fell, scraping her knee against the concrete. Near the gate to the park, a long way from the corner, she lay on the sidewalk, moaning and rubbing her knee.

As Barney closed in on her, he noticed something bumping against his thigh, and reaching into his trouser pocket he found the white-handled folding knife. By the time he stood over her he had put away the wallet and opened the blade of the knife.

Bracing her arms and legs to rise, the woman gasped at the sight of the chrome-plated blade.

Barney said, "You needn't be frightened. I only want to return something of yours. It's back at my apartment, on the other side of the park."

"I don't want to go anywhere with you."

"But you must come with me," he said, "don't you see?"

When the woman had managed to stand up, Barney pressed the blade hard enough into her ribs for her to feel its point through the jacket, causing her to emit a low squeal. Barney felt elated to be standing so close to such a beautiful young woman.

Wild-eyed, the woman looked up and down the block, but no one was on the damp street. "What do you want with me?"

"That's what I've been trying to tell you—you lost your wallet in the subway and I found it. I just want to return it to you."

"You're the man from the subway!"

Instead of being disturbed that he had been recognized, Barney experienced a rush of gratitude.

With the point of the knife pressing into her side, the woman stopped struggling, making low noises like a mouse caught in a trap.

"Why don't we go by way of the park—so much more pleasant, don't you think? The winding paths, the new grass, the trees beginning to bud."

Maintaining the pressure of the knife against her ribs, Barney led her through the iron gates into the park, and they moved down the black ribbon of tar, passing shrubs that had grown out of control last summer only to dry into a tangled mass by winter.

"Keep all the money in the wallet—just let me go."

"I'm not interested in your money," Barney said softly.

"*Please* let me alone," she whimpered.

"Look!" Barney pointed. "The moon is breaking through the clouds. It's turning out to be a pleasant evening."

166

The pale, cold light of the half moon was scattered by the branches, staining their faces with shadows.

"This time of night we'll have the park all to ourselves," he said, his eyes scanning the dark rows of dormant bushes, their spindly branches reaching out as if aching to burst into bloom.

The woman cried quietly in the darkness.

"Ah," Barney sighed, "a very romantic evening for a stroll through the park."

Barney, a short, bulky man, and the woman, tall and lean, moved haltingly along the winding path, through the broken lamp light. Far down the lane, a young man jogged across their path in the direction of a side gate to the park. Barney pressed the point of the knife more forcefully into her side, causing her to purse her lips.

Once the jogger had passed out of the gate, Barney said, "He's hurrying home to people who will listen to him."

The woman glanced at him.

Barney gazed up at the sky through an opening in the overhanging limbs of the tree. "The clouds are breaking up, and the stars are coming out. Can you see them?" When she didn't respond, he said: "Don't you see them?"

"I see them."

"What do you say we sit down and enjoy the stars a little while?"

"No, please—it's too chilly."

The man used the knife to prod the woman to the nearest bench. "Have a seat," he said politely.

The woman sat down on the bench. Barney lowered his weight down beside her.

For a few moments they sat in silence, the woman rubbing her sore knee, the man breathing audibly. "My name is Barney," he said, lessening the pressure of the knife in her side. After a time he added, "And your name is Laura...Laura Fahnestock."

Surprised, the woman had an impulse to ask how he knew her name, but she remembered the wallet and drew her handbag close to her body.

"The stars are so big tonight, Laura, I just might pluck one out of the sky and give it to you—a cosmic diamond."

Laura Fahnestock said, "My roommate is going to wonder what happened to me."

"Roommate?" Barney muttered, wondering if she shared the apartment with her boyfriend.

"Your family...friends...must be waiting for you, too."

"You're the only one I have, Laura, and you're here with me, enjoying this lovely evening. Don't you think it's a lovely evening?"

"Yes, it's a...lovely evening."

"Laura, I'd like you to do something for me."

"I'm wearing a gold necklace," she whimpered, "with a real diamond pendant." With a trembling hand she pulled the thin necklace out of her open blouse to show him. "You can have the necklace and all the money in my wallet. Please let me go."

"Didn't you hear what I said? I have *no* interest in your valuables!" Barney spat, poking the knife into her ribs hard enough to tear the seam of her jacket.

A cry escaped her throat.

Suddenly calm again, he said gently, "All I want is to hear my name on your lips. Will you do that for me?"

Slowly turning her head toward him, tears streaking her face, she looked at him head-on for the first time, and her eyes widened at seeing his tiny eyes, thinning hairline, and the suit jacket and tie he was wearing.

"In case you don't remember, my name is Barney. Will you say it for me?"

Wiping the tears off her face with her sleeve, she shaped her lips and forced out the syllables, "Bar-ney."

"Say it again, please."

"Barney...Barney."

"How nice to see you again, Barney—say that, too, Laura."

Stuttering, the woman got out the words: "Nice...to see...you again."

"You forgot to say my name."

"I'm sorry," she murmured. "Nice to see you again...Barney."

"The pleasure is all mine," he said, grinning at her.

The woman trembled.

"You have a beautiful speaking voice, Laura."

"My roommate is expecting me to bring home dinner."

"How can you buy dinner when you don't have your wallet?"

"Oh, my wallet," she said, squeezing her handbag.

Releasing the pressure of the knife in her side, he reached into his jacket pocket and slid the wallet out of the soft cotton lining. For half a minute he rubbed his thumb over the red leather in his hand. "Here," he said, extending it toward her, "this belongs to you."

Silent at first, she stuttered, "Thank you...for returning it. I didn't even know I had...lost it."

The wallet passed from his hand into hers, his fingers brushing hers lightly.

"You've got to be more watchful of your belongings, Laura. All sorts of things can happen to a young woman in this city."

"I see what you mean."

With the knife in his hand pointing at her, Barney stood up and stared at the seated woman—the red hair and blue eyes had lost their color in the shadows. Raising the knife, he snapped its blade shut and allowed it to slide into his trouser pocket. "I've got work to do back at my apartment so I must be getting along."

The young woman did not move, did not make a sound.

"It was a great pleasure speaking with you, Laura," said Barney. "Good evening."

"Good...night," she said, adding stiffly, "Barney."

Barney trundled along the path toward a gate that lay out of sight on the opposite side of the park.

Shivering deeply, the woman continued to sit on the bench, the wallet in her hand, her eyes following the short, heavy-set figure as he grew fainter until he had become one of the bushes of the night. Now she stood up on shaky legs and headed back to the gate through which they'd entered the park. Out on the sidewalk, moving toward the warm, lighted house in which she lived, Laura Fahnestock felt like crying, but no tears would come to her eyes.

As Barney Dreer approached the gate that would lead him back to his apartment, to the tax returns that lay scattered on his desk, a shooting star flashed across the sky, followed quickly by another and another and another. The black sky was crisscrossed with streams of light that sparkled and shimmered like strings of diamonds in a jewelry shop. He stopped to watch the shower of comets against the velvety screen of the sky, feeling profoundly connected to the vast expanses of the universe.

WWW.DEATHMARKET.COM

When the customer opened the door of the neighborhood supermarket, a tiny bell on a spring rang violently overhead—startling him, and a man slid out from behind a gauze curtain in back. Toward each other they moved, the customer wearing a wrinkled gray suit and plain beige tie, the storekeeper draped in a knee-length, white, rubber-coated apron. The two men met at the checkout counter, and it was clear from the way they looked each other over that they had business to conduct.

The customer was remarkable to behold because he was so unremarkable—utterly non-descript, as if his features had been erased by years of effort to maintain mental and physical steadiness. The storekeeper too was remarkable—the arc to his fine, fair eyebrows was almost comical, and his teeth were wide and bright in a fully stretched smile. Every strand of his hair seemed to have been waxed against his pate, giving the impression of a man entirely under control.

"What can I do for you?" the storekeeper inquired cordially.

"I'm John Meddle," he replied, "the one who called this morning?" his voice rising to a question, as if wondering what he was doing there.

"You're late."

"Your store is *not* easy to find."

"Yes, we've heard that before," the storekeeper said. "Was there anything special you had in mind today?"

"Thought I'd look around first and see what you have to offer—if that's all right."

"We offered self-service long before the giant supermarkets moved into the neighborhood."

John Meddle looked around incredulously, finding it hard to believe this out-dated establishment, with its antiquated proprietor, could have been in the forefront of any marketing development. Patterned squares were punched into the tin ceiling, and the floor's wide wooden planks had been shellacked so many times they'd hardened into a thick amber shell. Three short aisles apparently housed all of its goods. The store's drab, dusty appearance was even more puzzling since he'd learned about this enterprise via the internet, which he had always counted on—at least when his computer was cooperating—for the very latest in services and information. Except for the two men, the small supermarket was devoid of people.

"If you need assistance," the man in the apron offered, "don't hesitate to ask."

Backing away from the counter, the customer started down the nearest aisle. Boxes and cans and jars and bottles were lined up neatly on twelve evenly spaced, shellacked pine shelves on both sides. The extent of the assortment surprised him, and wishing to make a decision as quickly as possible, he became concerned the selection process might be delayed by the large number of choices.

"I'm afraid I need help already," Meddle admitted over his shoulder.

Unfolding his arms with satisfaction, the storekeeper left his station between the black dial telephone and the tarnished brass cash register. "That's what I'm here for," he chimed. "In point of fact, this section is generally frequented by customers considerably older than you."

"I don't understand."

"These cans and cartons contain processed tranquility, a favorite among the elderly."

The customer tried not to allow his face to reveal he was mystified. "Which brand is the most...popular?"

A veined, bloodless hand wrapped itself around a squat tin can. "Many go for this recipe in a big way," he said, continuing to display his teeth like a miniature storefront window. "Easy as closing your eyes and falling asleep."

The muscles around the customer's mouth tightened.

"Of course the less the pain," he hastened to add, "the higher the price."

"I should think so," the customer muttered almost inaudibly.

Carefully replacing the can on the shelf, the man in the apron spoke as he floated—that's how it seemed to Meddle—down the aisle. "Some prefer to be awake, to be thoroughly involved in what's going on down to the last breath." When the customer's faint eyebrows twitched, the storekeeper felt obliged to clarify his statement: "They don't want to miss out on a once-in-a-life-time experience. Yet they still want a certain amount of serenity, especially for that kind of money."

"How much are we talking about?"

"Ten thousand dollars."

The customer released that high-pitched whistle which denotes an outrageous price.

"Worth every penny," the storekeeper defended, losing one corner of his smile. "Besides, when you shop at this supermarket, you never have to pay any sales tax."

Since the customer didn't seem particularly impressed by this news, the storekeeper plucked a short-necked bottle off the closest shelf and aimed it at him. The bottle had the same style label as the cans: white, with a black border around its edge, and black lettering too tiny to read from where he stood. Every item in the store, Meddle now noticed, seemed to be labeled in this manner, with nothing packaged to be more attractive, more saleable than any other merchandise.

"This dressing is a bit less pricey and works faster than the product I just showed you, but the experience is rather more jarring."

"I've never cared for abrupt beginnings or endings," the customer asserted.

"To each his own," he replied, placing the bottle back in its line up with dozens of others. Immediately he began drifting toward the deep end of the store. "This department is preferred by people who can't be bothered with confessions or expressions of regret."

"A waste of time," Meddle agreed.

Pointing an unusually long fingernail at a group of cylindrical cardboard containers, the storekeeper snapped his fingers: "Munch on one of these sugar-coated cookies, and the whole thing is over in an instant. No waiting. No fuss. No bother. Very neat."

"What...is it?"

"Comes in several flavors." The storekeeper slipped the spectacles out of his breast pocket, hooked them over his tiny ears, and stuck his glossy face close to the cylinders. "This one is Cardiac Arrest," concluding enthusiastically, "a chocolate treat that's ready to eat!"

John Meddle scratched his darkish hair, which in recent years had begun to acquire the color of cigarette ashes. "I don't think I like the sound of that," he said, rubbing his chest involuntarily.

"In that case, you might want to examine the next shelf down, where we offer a variety of strokes—you know, different strokes for different folks." The storekeeper grinned, well pleased by his little joke.

Seeing he was not amused, the storekeeper tried to alleviate the customer's uneasiness. "Of course you don't have to decide

174

right away. Take your time. That's how the smart shopper does it. It's your right—your duty to make the best possible choice."

The storekeeper drifted along the shiny floor, turned left, and began moving up the second aisle, the customer shuffling along several feet behind him. Even though the evening had been cool and damp on his way over to this supermarket, which was jammed between two brownstones at the downtrodden edge of the city, John Meddle felt as if the store was growing warmer, stuffier, and he unbuttoned his suit jacket and loosened his tie.

"Here is our rather fashionable Long-Sufferers Department," the storekeeper said with a casual air, as if pointing out a fresh shipment of iceburg lettuce.

"Does that mean…diseases?"

"Among other varieties."

"Would these be more reasonable than the other items you've shown me?"

"Depends upon the particular preparation."

"With four kids, a mortgage, a lease on the van, I was never able to put away all that much."

"We don't give credit here," the storekeeper warned, relinquishing his smile momentarily. "Absolutely no lay aways, no time payments."

The customer looked at him self-righteously. "Don't worry. Your website stipulated cash only, and I've got it right here." He patted his breast pocket. "I just need to make sure it's within my means so I don't leave my family holding an empty bag."

"Very considerate of you," said the storekeeper, "but we must make sure each customer understands this is strictly a cash-and-carry business, and it doesn't take much imagination to see why."

When John Meddle had come across the black, one-inch ad on the obituary page—containing nothing more than **www.death-market.com** —and had logged on to the website, he experienced a tidal wave of relief. For the first time, it had seemed possible to slip out of existence respectably, and on his own terms. No self-respecting family man would commit suicide and leave his wife and children behind to carry that emotional burden—that public humiliation—the rest of their lives. Not when a socially acceptable death was available for purchase through the internet. Now, confronted with numerous methods of achieving this end, however, he no longer felt quite as confident in his plan.

"Was the ad I saw part of a brand new campaign? I don't remember seeing any ads before."

"Our advertising has been appearing in newspapers and magazines for many, many years," he replied, "but an individual has to be ready psychologically before he can actually *see* our advertisements."

"Are you implying that I'm already one hundred percent committed to...making this purchase?"

With a haughty flare, he quipped, "I would say that's rather obvious, wouldn't you?"

Though Meddle felt like challenging him on this point, in good faith he couldn't disagree. After he'd gone on the internet and read the prepared responses to several "Frequently Asked Questions," he had begun putting money aside that very payday, never mentioning it to his wife, children, or anyone else. Madeline would have gotten very upset, and this was a step one had to take in a composed, rational manner. Besides, she might have blamed herself for his outlook, and the truth was that he had nothing against her, or his kids—or anyone else for that matter.

"Your website also mentioned strict confidentiality."

"Absolutely guaranteed. That's another reason for our cash-only policy—no credit card records, no check statements, no receipts."

Meddle wanted to ask how a dead person would be able to know if confidentiality had in fact been honored, but he held his tongue.

"Before I show you additional wares," the storekeeper sighed, "it would be most helpful if you could tell me why you have come to us so early in life. Has some personal tragedy befallen you?—the death of a child, found your wife in bed with your best friend, drug addiction, or perhaps you've been caught embezzling from your employer."

"No, no, no, it's not anything like that."

"I mention these possibilities only because they are among the most common motivations for...early retirement from life."

Somewhat defensively the customer replied, "My wife and children are alive and loyal, and I've been a trusted employee of the same company for twenty years."

"Splendid! But I assure you we have no desire to invade your privacy, Mr. Meddle. We do these informal surveys merely to help us serve our customers better, now and in the future."

"I'm in the business world, too. I understand completely."

"Well, then, if it's not an unhappy home or business failure or trouble with the law, what brings you here?"

Pinching his forehead as if to pluck an answer out of his brain, the customer said at last, "It's a question of stamina."

"Ah, ha! You have a terminal illness and want to beat life to the punch."

"Nothing so dramatic as that," he half whispered, lacking sufficient vigor at that moment to explain.

The man in the apron repeated with quiet persuasiveness: "I can be much more helpful to you, Mr. Meddle, if you can help me understand your needs better."

"That makes perfectly good business sense," the customer admitted, and as soon as they had agreed it was better business to be forthcoming, he found himself able to proceed: "It's the life-long accumulation of trivial, yet necessary duties and errands and paperwork, the ceaseless, overwhelming maintenance of existence."

Once he had begun, John Meddle couldn't stop the words from pouring out of his throat, trying to expunge all that had become abhorrent to him: "Jarred out of sleep by the alarm clock every morning, riding trains back and forth to a job where I'm on my feet from 8:30 AM till 6:30 PM, dealing with customers, personnel, bosses; paying off the mortgage, electric, oil, gas, phone, traffic tickets, credit cards, internet service, repair bills, cable TV; correcting bank and credit card errors; checking the kids' homework and bolstering Madeline's sagging spirits; replacing everything from shoes and shirts on my body to shingles and paint on the house; monitoring blood pressure, cholesterol, sugar-levels, eyes, cavities, and daily vitamins; cleaning drain pipes, raking leaves, servicing the furnace, scraping snow off the roof; grocery shopping, church services, choir practice, benefit dinners, school plays, basketball games; remembering birthdays, anniversaries, holidays, buying cards and gifts for dozens of people; attending to the needs of my aging mother and father; visiting my in-laws; sorting the garbage into categories; carting clothes to and from the dry-cleaners; keeping up tax records, paying off income, school, property, and water taxes; auto inspections and registration, driver's and dog licenses; renewing auto, home, medical, life insurance policies; changing spark plugs, air and oil filters, tires, anti-freeze for the van; avoiding foods I love while cutting down on after-dinner cocktails and cigarettes; and stopping myself from throwing my temperamental computer out the *damn* window...." John Meddle's voice had continued to rise until he was nearly shouting at the end. "That's not the half of it, and they keep making it more complicated every year!"

Throughout this outburst, the storekeeper had listened patiently, allowing Meddle to get to the bottom of his frustration.

178

At last, when the customer seemed to have used up all his breath, the man in the apron said in a quiet, soothing voice: "I understand perfectly, John. It's the little things."

In the ensuing silence of understanding that had evolved between them, John Meddle could feel his heart settling down to a more normal, less painful rhythm, and looking over the shelves before him—stacked with limitless manifestations of death—he realized that, despite the modern conveniences of a selected fatality, he still didn't know how to accommodate the dark space that the impending loss of life occupied in his mind.

In the midst of these ruminations, the customer thought he heard the storekeeper saying something about sclerosis of the liver, so he tried to pay attention. "On the other hand," the storekeeper went on, "Kidney Failure is delicious spread on whole wheat crackers." The man wrapped in the rubbery apron was holding up a squat jar, the kind used for pulverized baby foods.

Trying to make the storekeeper think he'd been listening all along, he said, "How long does it take to work?"

The storekeeper checked the label, but he obviously knew the answer already. "This blend requires a couple of months to activate, but before long," he added cheerfully, "you'll be hooked up to a dialysis machine. Ultimately, however, both kidneys will fail and no organ transplant will be available to you." He glanced at the label again. "In all, you can figure on nearly a year."

"Works rather…slowly."

"Believe me, that's quite an improvement over how long it might take under normal circumstances."

The customer fiddled nervously with the butane lighter in his pocket. He needed a cigarette badly, but there was a NO SMOKING sign over the front door, which struck him as odd, given the nature of this establishment. "I'm afraid I'd be much too impatient for such a drawn-out process."

Replacing the jar with a bit of impatience himself, the storekeeper quickly recovered his composure and said in a confidential tone: "Customers of this inclination are willing to wait it out to get the attention their souls have been thirsting—think of it, nine or ten months of constant personal care, first by one's family, and then by a series of pretty nurses. Pro-rated, it's a very good buy."

"In exchange for their breath," Meddle replied too low to be heard.

"What did you say?"

"Nothing—I just wanted to ask you something."

"That's why I am here."

"I'd like to know if...if you're...*him*."

"Him?"

"Are you...Death himself?"

A rumbling chortle rose out of his wrinkled throat. "I would never presume to represent myself in such a grand manner," he said with what seemed to be genuine humility. "I'm merely an agent, a broker, a rep, a clerk. But I thank you for the compliment."

"It wasn't meant as a compliment. Just wanted to understand your operation better—I mean, are there supermarkets like this in other cities?"

"Throughout the world!" he announced proudly.

"In that case, you must have a headquarters somewhere."

"Naturally."

"Is that where...Death keeps his offices?"

"Let's just say his offices are everywhere, just as he is everywhere."

"You mean, like God?"

"One could make such a statement without being terribly far from the truth."

"Are you telling me God sells life and death the way I sell suits and coats?"

Growing pensive, the storekeeper replied guardedly: "Since you're a salesman yourself, John, I'm sure you understand I cannot divulge all of our trade secrets without eliminating an element of mystery. After all, mystery is our stock in trade."

To give himself time to absorb this comment, John Meddle looked up into the fixture, an age-yellowed bowl hanging from three chains. Light spread out from it like dust after a rug has been beaten. But it did not carry far, the air seemingly thick enough to slow down the spread of light.

In an attempt to revive his stalled sales effort, the storekeeper complimented the customer, "You certainly are a tough sale! But I think I have just the thing for you. A product that has satisfied millions."

"Millions?"

"You don't imagine all the deaths reported in the obituary columns came about in the normal course of life, do you?"

"Never really thought about it one way or another."

The storekeeper strutted down the aisle, stopped abruptly, lifted a rectangular box off a shelf, and declared, "Total Paralysis!"

A low growl rattled out of the customer's larynx.

"Despite one's inability to move any bodily parts, this remarkable powder enables the brain to carry on with business as usual. You can see and hear everything, but you never have to lift a finger to do anything about all that goes on around you. *Never, ever again.*"

Unable to prevent the horror he felt from consuming his face, the customer spat, "Dreadful."

"Come now, Mr. Meddle, you already admitted you came to us to get out from under the accumulated weight bearing down on your life. By rejecting this product purely on an emotional basis, you may be losing out on the ideal solution to your dilemma."

By not moving a muscle, and holding his breath several moments, John Meddle was making an unconscious attempt to synthesize the condition described by the storekeeper.

"An added bonus is that this product gives one a glimpse of what to expect from the next world."

The sanded face looked at the glossy face with an expression of bewilderment, as if the storekeeper had just spoken in a different language.

"Because the user is unable to do anything but see, listen and think," the storekeeper explained, "one is entirely free to indulge in experiences such as love and hate, but all physical manifestations of these emotions are quite impossible."

"A living death."

"Precisely!" he said brightly. "You'd be surprised how many customers appreciate a preview of what they're getting into—especially when they've saved so long for a decent passing."

"That's definitely *not* for me."

"Far be it from me to sell you something you do not want."

"I'm *sure* you wouldn't."

The tone of the customer's voice did not go unnoticed, and the storekeeper said resolutely, "I happen to be a great believer in matching the person with his own particular brand of death—in accordance with the kind of life the person has led."

Not a sound was made by the customer, who was in the midst of a struggle to quell the rising resentment he was feeling toward the salesman and his establishment.

"A woman who's been well-fed all her life is not likely to purchase a jar of malnutrition," he continued, looking over the customer rather closely. "While a man who was an artist, chilled to the bones in his unheated loft, might prefer liquid pneumonia to every other product on the market. All a question of life style."

"Why are you looking at me like that?" Meddle asked.

"I've been in this business a long time," he replied. "After a while you get to know the types."

"Are you saying you know the kind of…demise…best suited to me?"

"Mind you, I am not telling you what to buy, but I've sensed all along that what you are after may well be waiting for you in the last row," and he immediately moved down the aisle and took a sharp right turn.

Though reluctant to allow such an important decision to be influenced unduly by a salesman, John Meddle shared that curiosity with his fellow human beings about how others assessed his life. And death. Soon he was tip-toeing between the last rows of shelves, as if moving down the aisle toward the casket in a funeral parlor. Stopping a few feet from the storekeeper, the customer couldn't stop himself from eyeing the closest shelf.

"In the Violent Death Department, we offer natural disasters *or* unnatural causes."

"What makes you think I'm suited to a…violent passing?"

"Because you're too young to be coming around here. About forty-four, I'd say."

The man in the apron had guessed his age exactly, but when the customer tried to estimate the storekeeper's age, Meddle discerned elements of youth as well as age in his make up.

"Moreover, throughout our interview, you have seemed rather … frenzied, if you don't mind my saying so. That's another reliable indicator of violence in the offing."

"I feel perfectly calm," Meddle insisted.

"It's in your eyes, in the way you carry yourself. I've seen it too many times to be mistaken."

"Not in *me* you haven't."

"The customer is always right."

"You're awfully sure of yourself."

"I know my products. I know my customers."

"If you knew this all along, why didn't you say so the moment I entered the store?"

"The company has a strict policy against leading customers into purchases they may regret later—unless, of course, they can't make up their minds."

"It so happens I've been considering what you said about long-term sufferers; it's beginning to make a lot of sense to me. I just might purchase a can of stomach cancer. My family has listened to me complain about gastric disorders for years."

"I am at your service, of course. But since you only get one chance, you might as well get it right."

The storekeeper's patronizing tone infuriated John Meddle, but he managed to refrain from lashing out at him.

"All the pressure that has been building up in your heart and soul for decades must find a way out, and that is precisely what a violent death represents—a cataclysmic release from life. The most satisfying discharge you will ever experience."

John Meddle stood there wondering how the storekeeper could know it was a satisfying experience since a dead person couldn't possibly convey such information to him.

Afraid he might be losing momentum, the storekeeper stepped up his pitch: "With a violent death one is catapulted out of life in a blaze of glory—rather like being shot out of a cannon!" he said gaily. "Yes, the more I think about it, the more I am convinced that violence is the only way for you to go, Mr. Meddle."

By this time John Meddle was raging within—so angry he couldn't coordinate his thoughts, and he felt like striking the storekeeper. Until it occurred to him that such an act would have been a verification of what had made him angry. "Look, I didn't come here to be psychoanalyzed."

"Certainly, sir, but rest assured that an explosion is only one of countless violent deaths available." Wiping his scaly palms on his apron, as if warming up to the bargaining at hand, the storekeeper slid to a shelf lined with rows of soda pop bottles.

"Of all the violent deaths, I daresay this comes closest to the *real* you."

Under the sway of an increasing, if morbid curiosity, Meddle approached the shelf. Leaning close to the bottles, he saw that each had the word MURDER imprinted in black on the label. The customer began to tremble involuntarily.

Lifting a bottle off the shelf by its neck, the storekeeper declared, "Murder is our best-seller. And it's on sale this week— $5,000, down from $6,000."

A muffled groan emitted from the customer's tight, pale lips: The sale price quoted was the exact amount he had sealed in the business envelope in his pocket.

"Twelve ounces of this refreshing, naturally flavored seltzer will give you courage you never dreamed possible," the storekeeper said. "Within twenty-four hours of its consumption, you will attempt to aid someone being mugged on the streets of our fair city, and you will be stabbed to death. A reasonably quick, remarkably bloody, and most valuable conclusion insofar as achieving a noble death."

Meddle asked himself whether death was ever really a noble event, or if people fastened the idea of nobility to the despair of mortality so that passing into the universe, via a hole dug into clay and dirt, wouldn't seem quite so meaningless. Or did the true nobility of human existence lie in the carrying out, without complaint, of the daily burdens of life? Suddenly all the weight of forty-four years of maintenance and responsibility sailed out of John Meddle's mind, and it seemed to him as if these obligations, when stretched out over a lifetime, became light as air, nothing more than aspects of change, symbols of being alive.

"The newspapers will publish several paragraphs about your heroic act," he declared, "perhaps with a picture of you. Your story may even be picked up by television. Just the thing to make your family and friends proud."

Before the storekeeper realized what was happening, the customer had flicked his lighter and touched the cellophane wrapped boxes with a yellowy flame. Instantly the crinkly paper flared up.

"Stop!" the storekeeper wailed, rushing to the flames, smothering them with the bottom of his apron.

In moments the customer had started fires at several points along the shelves and then dashed into the next aisle where he began setting new fires. Soon the supermarket contained a dozen blazes and they spread crisply in the dry air, clouds of smoke swiftly filling the store. The storekeeper rushed up and down the aisles, desperately trying to snuff them out. Several pine shelves had taken up the fire as well, however, and the shellacked wood crackled viciously, flames licking up to the ceiling.

His smile wiped entirely off his face for the first time, the storekeeper jumped about frantically to smother pockets of fire, scattering the burning cartons onto the floor and stamping on them. But the flames continued to sweep down the aisles, climbing up the walls, and through the swirling smoke he spotted the customer hurrying out the door. The bell rang furiously.

John Meddle ran through the dense, smoky mist down the night-shrouded street—ran for his life. At the intersection, gasping for air, he stopped and looked back. A long, lean, colorless fire lapped through syrupy vapors, engulfing the ancient wooden storefront, and a flaming rafter crashed onto the sidewalk, showering the gutter with sparks. Stunned by what he had done, he turned sharply away to put more distance between himself and the disintegrating supermarket. In a flash, two headlights were upon him and at the moment of impact, though it was hard to say for sure—and impossible to remember—he caught a glimpse of the storekeeper, smiling appreciatively, at the wheel of the silvery, speeding van.

POND WITH NO NAME

On my way back to Philadelphia from a client presentation in Columbus, I decided to bypass the interstate and steered the rented sedan onto a secondary road which meandered quite a bit, though in the same general direction as my destination: a feeble attempt, I suppose, to drive out from under the disenfranchisement I'd been feeling long before the meetings began. Marketing budgets were being slashed, and competition for new accounts was swelling on all fronts, creating a business climate of over-reaction. Clients were packing up their advertising programs and shifting them, in the face of soft sales, to other agencies the moment their contracts expired. In the process, jobs were being lost.

The back road curved and rose and dropped through the vague towns and eroded hills of the Ohio Valley, yet I was unable to leave behind that sense of loss, clinging to me the way a vine of poison ivy winds itself around the bark of a failing tree. With the vibrations of the steering wheel electrifying my hands and the sawing sound of radials over tar working like sandpaper on my nerves, I pumped the brakes, pulled onto the wide graveled shoulder, and turned off the ignition somewhere in southwestern Pennsylvania. Dropping my neck back against the head rest, I sat absolutely still, eyes shut, taking in the ticking sounds of the engine cooling under the hood. It too needed to rest.

After several minutes, however, I still felt edgy, so I climbed out of the bucket seat into warm, still air, and took a stroll to see if my legs would work. They did. From this new vantage point—a fairly steep slope covered mostly by wild grasses and thorny bushes—I saw a small pond tucked away at the bottom. *Home to some neglected smallmouth bass,* I thought. Collected at the base of the wind-softened hill, the bean-shaped body of water was polished as smooth and luminous as an opal. The pond was pretty enough to be kept a secret, and I wondered what it was called. But whether its name was reflected in the serenity of its pearly waters, or one that borrowed the surname of an early settler of the region, to me it was a pond with no name.

What I did next was not the result of thought. I went back to the car, opened the trunk, and slid out the vinyl case which contained a two-piece fishing rod. With my other hand I hooked the handle of the rectangular tackle box. The morning I'd left Philly, an earlier impulse had caused me to drop my spinning gear into the trunk. Without believing it would happen, I'd fantasized that I would find the time and place to fish on my way out to Ohio, a Thoreauean gesture that might help clear my head for my client presentation; that might provide a little mental space to help me comprehend what was happening at the office, and what it might mean to me and my family.

Glancing at my fishing gear in the sketchy light three mornings earlier, my wife Barbara had remarked, "I can see you really work hard on these business trips."

"Fishing's hard work," I'd replied, expressionless as I dropped the striped overnight bag on the back seat.

Barbara's wide mouth stretched into a fishy smile as she hung my dark blue suit (sheathed in a thin, clinging veil of loose plastic) on the hook over the rear side window of the sedan. My wife was unaware that Lundagen had called me into his corner office the day before and said: "Don't mean to sound melodramatic, Luke, but your presentation is vital to this agency's future in the automotive market." The whites of his eyes looked like molten lead, and I knew what he really meant was that the presentation was vital to my own future at the agency.

I'd been with Barlow, Tucker & Fenner fourteen years. While I didn't have the same *corp d'esprit* I'd started with, as an account executive in a shrinking marketplace, I'd still managed to keep most of my clients in the BT&F fold. Earlier in the year I'd lost Crimson Hall—a major account for a medium-sized agency. But that had been entirely out of my control. They'd decided to consolidate their advertising for all media at one larger agency, where they were already producing their radio spots. At least that's how I saw it. Only recently had I begun to understand that my agency may have interpreted that loss differently.

At the edge of the slope, I drew in a full breath and let it out slowly, listening to the sound with an odd detachment, as if it were the breath of Barbara as she slept beside me. Now I began my descent, carefully lodging each maroon oxford against a clump of grassy roots before lifting the other. The slick leather soles nearly slipped out from under me, but soon I was level with the pond and moving along a narrow footpath toward the water. The scratching sound of thorns against my trousers seemed to sharpen my senses, making every stone, every reed, every leaf appear distinct and separate from the rest of the natural world. Half a dozen feet from the pond's ragged edge, I halted.

The water was at peace, disturbed only by an occasional, gentle stroking of air—until I was surprised by the slap of a fish not twenty feet from shore. Hastily I unzipped the sheath, pulled out the pieces of the rod, and forced the ferrules together. It was only after I had screwed down the reel, strung line through the guides, and dug an imitation worm out of the tackle box that I realized how incongruous I must've looked, wielding a fishing rod in shiny business trousers, white shirt, and tie. Without a soul in sight, however, I could be as unconventional as I pleased.

As I was clipping the soft plastic worm to the leader, my mind changed channels back to the conference room at the previous day's meeting. A manufacturer of automobile parts was venturing into national television advertising for the first time, with a start-up budget of two and a half million dollars. BT&F was one of three agencies invited to show off their ideas. Our creative services department had poured a lot of brain power and overtime into this project, and I had done my homework—studied not merely their product line but the history of the company and their current sales strategies. During my presentation, their marketing people had seemed attentive to our concepts and impressed by our storyboards: a first-time advertiser on TV had special opportunities as well as limitations, and we'd taken this into account. Better yet, one of their execs was also an alumnus of the University of Pennsylvania, making me feel I had a slight edge: People want to feel comfortable getting into the same business bed with strangers. Despite all this, when he had accepted my hand in early evening, after my presentation had been completed, there was a looseness in his grip that made me feel uneasy. Even though official notification was not due for another week or two, I knew that I hadn't landed the account. Back at the hotel I went over my presentation point by point, wondering if our concept just hadn't been solid enough, weakening everything built on top of it. Or perhaps I simply hadn't presented it as well as it deserved. All night long I turned over and over in those strange sheets, bedding that belonged to everyone and therefore to no one.

Attempting to cast beyond the splash I'd seen in the pond, I swung the tip of the rod back over my left shoulder and thrust the length of fibreglas forward. The lifeless worm brought rings of motion to the silvery stillness, landing five or six feet to the left of where I'd wanted it to drop. I watched my line coil slowly until it merged with the loose vegetation along the perimeter of the pond. Why couldn't I do the same, allow myself to drift out of this job just as I had drifted into it? From my first job after college to my present position, I'd never been out of work, changing companies only three times in twenty-six years. To me the prospect of being without work was like losing my identity, a pond with no name. Maybe that's where I'd made my mistake—I should've been jumping from agency to agency, building a track record, inflating my market value. What had my years of loyalty gained for me, after all? Like the communications technology in our offices over the past decade, I had become not merely expendable but in urgent need of replacement in order for the corporation to remain competitive.

I began jerking the fake worm at the end of my line, trying to simulate life but succeeding only in stirring up the smooth surface of the pond. Nothing offered itself to my imitation worm—not until the small brass hook snared a stalk that was rooted to the bottom. Impatient, I yanked it several times, willing to lose an artificial to the pond as long as I could be free of the entanglement quickly. At last the hook cut through the reed without breaking my line, though I'd undoubtedly terrified every fish that might've been in the neighborhood.

Reeling in the line, and raising the dangling pink plastic over the water-soaked vegetation, I stepped through the soft, black, soggy earth along the rim of the pond, muddying my oxfords, the hook swinging freely—dangerously near my face. I established a new position beside a convention of cattails. After I flipped the chrome line guard on the reel and pinned the monofilament against the rod with my forefinger, I cranked the rod back over my shoulder and powered it forward. With an abrupt halt in my thrust, I sent the imitation flying into the bluish haze of late morning. The line sailed out cleanly until a knot snagged on one of the guides—the worm's flight died in mid-air like a mallard taking buck shot. It dropped straight down, plinking into the water, tossing leadlike drops a few inches into the air.

Frustrated, I let the line drift out there awhile, a dozen feet short of where I'd wanted it to settle down. As if she were standing beside me, I could see the pensive, childlike eyes of my wife, her cheeks palely suggestive of life, like strawberries picked too soon. Just before I'd backed the car out of the driveway the morning of my departure, Barbara had asked, "Is something bothering you, Luke?"

"Just wondering if I'm forgetting something."

My wife had given up teaching after the birth of our third son, and even though the school had attempted to lure her back into the classroom, she had no desire to return to what she often called a "deterioration of discipline in the educational system." Now it had been many years. Barbara assumed I was doing quite well at BT&F, that I would pay the mortgage, car loan and credit cards on time; just as Butch, Lenny and Sam assumed they would have everything they needed for school in the fall. I hadn't mentioned my concerns about my job because I felt humiliated, the way I'd felt the day I was introducing representatives from a prospective client to a senior vice president and momentarily forgot their names.

I began cranking the worm toward me, finally lifting it out of the water and allowing it to dangle a foot below the tip of my rod. Again I cast out straight ahead. As I waited—*yes*, I thought, *fishing is an act of waiting and therefore an act of faith* —I could hear the clear, high, solitary trill of a bird across the pond. Searching for movement in the trees—they seemed to be mostly maples huddled close together, as if having an impromptu meeting, I couldn't see any sign of the bird. Nor could I identify its call: just another pointless cry that apparently signified nothing.

Yanking and jiggling the artificial, I let it rest again. A few bubbles danced up from the bottom, popping on the surface, and I stood very still, listening keenly, watching severely. The rubbery worm lay undisturbed beneath the surface of the water twenty-five feet from shore. Though I should've kept the worm moving to make it seem alive, at that moment I didn't have the courage to disrupt the tranquility. Not a leaf moved, not a wand of grass stirred. Not a murmur from the reeds. Then a mosquito landed on my neck and I reacted, breaking the perfect calm with a slap. I missed the mosquito and jerked my hook several feet toward shore, setting the world in motion again. Bushes rattled nervously behind me, and a blue jay let out a shriek, and a lumpy frog sprang out of the grass into the water, shattering its smoothness like a mirror struck with a hammer.

Needing to start all over again, I reeled in. This time I cast at a sharp angle, and the line stretched out far, the worm landing neatly, well behind the patch of just-under-the-surface growth. I waited, but after a minute or two it struck me that no sensible fish would bother with such a presentation, such an obvious fake. Deciding to call it quits, I began reeling in—that's when the rod sprang in my hands. My line darted left and right in the water as the fish succeeded in hooking itself. It felt not heavy but urgent, and its evident terror made me feel more in control than I had for some time. Calmly I raised the tip of the rod, slowly cranking up the line, maintaining an easy but steady pressure so the fish wouldn't wriggle free. Swinging the flat dark fish—the biggest black crappie I'd ever seen—onto the slick, muddy bank, I saw that the hook had just managed to pierce the hard corner of its lip. It had been an eighth of an inch from freedom.

The fish's body was bloating and collapsing, bloating and collapsing, and its round eyes looked as desperate as those of a man in a soup kitchen line. When I gripped its tail to keep it from squirming away, the crappie extended its jagged dorsal fins, which resembled the rays of an Aztec ceremonial sun. It seemed dangerously beautiful. Now its tail squirted out of my fingers. Quickly I trapped the fish between a stone and the side of my shoe.

"Take it easy," I said. "I'm going to free you if you'll give me a chance." The crappie flapped again, not succeeding in freeing itself from the hook. "Lie still or you're going to hurt yourself."

Obediently the fish lay quiet, bloating, eyeing me and, curiously, no longer extending its protective fins. In a few moments I dislodged the barb. About to pick up the fish to drop it into the water, I was suddenly struck by something agreeable in its helplessness, and I rose up out of my crouch. The crappie flapped furiously, as if outraged that I had broken a silent understanding between us. Again it convulsed, landing in a patch of muddy grass a foot closer to the water.

Increasingly closed in by my overextended credit, I had watched the growing gap between the money going out and coming in, not with distress but a curious detachment, as though it were occurring in someone else's life. I had always believed it got easier as you went along, yet I'd continued to lose ground: an unrelenting process that I hadn't been able to view whole at one time, and therefore never quite felt threatened by. Not until lately. By this time I was convinced I was going to be let go shortly after the results of the Columbus presentation came in. While uninspired by the idea of spending the rest of my life analyzing demographics for clients, attempting to reassure them that their sales would increase dramatically if only they would buy into our marketing programs, I didn't know any other kind of work. At fifty-two I felt too old to start at something new, some place new. My impulse was to cling to what I had and what I knew, to make it work somehow; to compensate somehow for the transgressions I'd committed against the agency.

The pudgy black crappie in the muddy grass flapped again. As I continued to observe the fish, I felt vaguely sorry for its plight, its humiliation. At the same time I felt incapable just then of giving it the bit of help it needed to get past that obstacle of grass, back into the pond where it could thrive once again. Every few moments it would flutter, but it was becoming sluggish, as if trying to shake off a heavy sleep.

Because I'd been concentrating on the fish I hadn't heard the car pull up alongside my rental on the ridge. Only when he was easing himself down the slope, crunching over dry sticks and weeds, did I turn and see the man in the army-green shirt, gray trousers and tan baseball cap. His teeth looked burnt at the edges, and the skin around his eyes was crimped like the bark of a chokecherry.

"I'm with the state game and fish ward," he twanged, looking over my dress shirt and tie as though I were wearing the uniform of a convict.

"Just returning from a business trip," I explained.

"Let's have a look at yer license."

"Fishing license—sure," I said, setting the butt of the rod against my foot and inserting two fingers into my back pocket to grip my wallet. As I slipped the wad of cards out of the leather flap and began shuffling through them, I thought about the crappie in the grass behind me, and I began to feel a web of tension stretch across my stomach. *Where the hell is my license?* I thought. The game warden stood with his large beige hands on his hips, dropping them only when I located the document he'd asked to see. Suddenly I had an irrational fear that someone else's name would be on the license. Before handing it over, I glanced at the typed-in letters: LUKE DELANEY.

"This is fer Pennsylvania. Yer in West Virginia."

"You mean to say I've crossed over the border?"

He shook his head heavily, the way a horse does to chase flies.

An urge came over me to start making excuses—there hadn't been any signs on the road; the sign had been hidden by overgrown brush...it was the same reaction I'd had when Lundagen had warned me about the sales presentation, about my job. Just then there was a slight splash behind me, and the game warden looked past me. Turning around I saw the ripples stretching away from the edge of the pond, and I stood as helpless as someone with amnesia. The crappie was no longer in the grass.

The game warden's mud-colored eyes flashed with a thought I couldn't decipher as he handed my license back to me. "You better be on yer way."

"Sorry," I said pitifully, gratefully.

"You jus' dunno where you are."

The beige man started climbing up the slope, and I took the opportunity to search for the fish along the edge of the water. But I didn't see any sign of its white belly floating near the surface. Now my eye was caught by the flight of a red-winged blackbird over the placid, silvery surface, and I turned and called out to the game warden: "Can you tell me the name of this pond?"

Having just reached the top, he stopped, twisted his body, and gazed down at me. "They call it Deep Water—the Indians claimed it has no bottom out in its center." In a few moments he was gone.

Unclipping the plastic worm from the leader, I wound up the line, and pulled the ferrules apart. Then I collected my tackle box, rod and reel, and started up the slope. The climb turned out to be a lot more strenuous that I'd imagined. By the time I reached the level, gravel-covered ground my feet felt heavy, as if caked with mud. I marched sluggishly to the car, put my fishing gear in its trunk, and slammed it shut. Opening the door, I dropped into the driver's seat. The rental vehicle was filled with silence, with the smells of other trips taken by other, un-known people to unknown destinations. I inserted the key into the ignition, but instead of starting the engine, I sat there a long while catching my breath, my chest expanding and contracting, expanding and contracting.

FUN & GAMES AT THE CAROUSEL SHOPPING MALL

Around 9:45 AM squadrons of automobiles began rolling into the acres of fresh-tarred parking lots that surrounded the Carousel Shopping Mall, the construction of which had been completed in the fall on a filled-in marsh near a confluence of three highways. By 9:50, the first wave of shoppers stood out in the frosty air, shivering, fogging the green-tinted, impenetrable glass doors with their breath. Just barely they could see vendors lined up along the interior corridors, setting up trays of sugar-coated peanuts, salty pretzels, donuts with 50 kinds of filling (one for each state in the Union), bags of buttered popcorn, gumdrops, licorice, and chocolates sold by the pound. Collectively the vendors served as a kind of buffer zone to slow down the army of shoppers that stormed the Carousel each morning.

By 9:55 many more automobiles were pulling up between the yellow-painted lines, and the swelling crowds at the four entrances were stirring impatiently, quoting out loud prices of sale items they had seen on television and in the newspapers. High above each door was a weatherproof pivoting camera with a cyclopean glass eye that was continually feeding images of them to a windowless compound in the subbasement. Here dozens of video screens were monitored twenty-four hours a day by a rotating shift of security guards in dark blue uniforms and billed caps.

Above ground, the Carousel Mall consisted of a massive rotunda with three floors that surrounded a spacious service area. All shops on each level radiated out from the center, and the front of each was restricted to the same width. This design placed shops on a relatively equal competitive footing, according to the developers, and gave each the appearance of being small enough to be friendly and helpful, like a family-owned hometown store. (A pre-construction marketing survey had indicated that customers desire a "friendly and helpful" shopping environment.) Every one of the stores, in fact, was part of an international retail conglomerate, with headquarters located far away, often in Japan or Germany. Though the original plans had called for windows throughout the building, they were ultimately eliminated from the blueprints in order to achieve a more important goal: the maintenance of climate control and increased security. Every square inch of the Mall, in accordance with the master plan, had been targeted to maximize "comfort and safety." That is, to maximize sales.

At precisely 10:00 AM the four doorways spaced evenly around the Carousel sprang open through the magic of an electronic timer. Shoppers swarmed onto the entrance ramps, draining shoppers down under the building. While a few stopped at the snack vendors, most continued deep into the tubelike tunnels. Along the walls, digitally programmed advertising signs were flashing, and passionate music was blaring from unseen speakers. Many of the children bounded ahead of their mothers, fathers, older siblings, grandparents. Several mothers called out to their fleeing offspring, *Meet me at Burger King at noon! I'll catch up to you at The Disney Store! Don't spend all your allowance on video games!* ... The kids didn't look back, swiftly melting into the milieu of the Mall.

Secretly the parents were glad. With the kids on their own, they would be able to stroll in their favorite shops without constantly being nagged to buy a breast-feeding doll that produced "real" mother's milk or a laser gun that gave off "real" low-voltage shocks. Besides, they knew their children would be safe in the Carousel—if not here, then where could they be safe, the way things were going? Even out here in the suburbs, some school children were wearing bullet-proof vests beneath their sweaters to protect themselves against classmates who hid revolvers under the peanut butter and jelly sandwiches in their cartoon-imprinted lunch boxes. And deadly stabbings were being committed on street corners over outrageously priced designer sneakers.

The mother of one of the kids who had run on ahead entered the subterranean central area of the mall, glad to be inside where it was warm. Here she found herself surrounded by self-service purveyors of breakfast, lunch, and dinner—from scrambled eggs to pasta to tacos to hot dogs to egg rolls to chili. The Carousel Shopping Mall, as its marketing corps pointed out repeatedly in its promotions, was "A Complete Shopping & Dining Experience: Fun & Games for the Entire Family!" The "Fun" referred to the clowns who roamed each floor handing out lollypops to the kids; visits from Santa Claus (armed with candy canes) and the Easter Bunny (packing jelly beans); plus a miniature carousel, which played nursery rhymes while carrying tots round and round. The "Games" referred to hourly drawings for door prizes —one could win anything from a free organ lesson to a free cosmetics analysis; as well as the battery of video games, where electronically devised, virtually real human beings would tear off each other's bodily parts (in color and stereophonic sound) at a cost of mere pocket change.

At the heart of the Mall, the mother stopped to wait for one of the three cylindrical, high-speed elevators to descend. Because these conveyances were enclosed entirely in glass, passengers were able to observe shops glittering stylishly around them as they were propelled upwards. Between the back-to-back elevators were "Customer Conveniences," such as restrooms with diaper-changing stations, information booth, detailed maps of the Mall, baby-stroller rentals, pay telephones, security office…depending upon the floor. On the top floor, a battery of stainless steel water fountains had been installed. Shortly after the Mall had opened, however, the water from the fountains had acquired a marshy odor, so a concession stand selling bottled soda and juices and sparkling water had immediately been installed nearby to make up for the inconvenience.

Soon the mother was swept away by one of the round elevators, and she emerged on the second level, where a tall man at a stall, standing erect in a suit and tie, offered her a free cloth shopping bag if she would sign up for a Carousel credit card. *I already have half a dozen credit cards,* she said, eyeing the carousel imprinted on the free bag. *But you don't have the one card that will take care of all your needs in the Carousel Mall,* he smiled. The mother hesitated, then said, *No, thank you, not today,* and moved past him, vaguely disappointed at herself, and not noticing the momentary flash of anger that had passed over the salesman's face.

Entering the Yarn Barn, she inspected the sale items on tables up front, but none of the scattered craft kits—many were torn open and missing pieces—appealed to her. The deeper she moved into the shop, the wider it became, filling out its slice-of-pie shape, and she found herself surrounded by an ever-widening array of craft supplies and tools to make jewelry out of bottle caps and bird houses out of ice cream sticks. After a few minutes, she handed her credit card over to a pale, dull-eyed clerk, who dropped the block of candle wax and flowery quilted material into a plastic bag, and the mother left the Yarn Barn with a sense of contentment and accomplishment.

Now she walked over to the housewares store, Kitchen Karma. Here she roamed among the gleaming pots and pans, the rolling pins of glass, marble, and wood, the cookie cutters in the shape of stars, daisies, and cows. Within half an hour she had purchased a set of dish towels imprinted with geese and a spatula with an apple-knobbed handle. Already she was looking forward to placing this new merchandise in a special cabinet at home with the other items she had purchased the previous week, the previous month, the previous year, but which—because she had so much to do—still had not been put to use. After drifting along several more aisles, however, it occurred to her she had purchased the exact same items the week before. Her impulse was to go back to the checkout counter and request a refund. But then she realized that possessing these duplicates would give her a good excuse to return to the Carousel in one or two days instead of three or four.

As the morning wore on, and after the mother had slipped her credit card out of her purse several more times, she began to feel tired, and she wondered what time it was getting to be. She'd neglected to wear her wristwatch, an anniversary gift her husband had purchased at the Carousel Mall. Unable to find a clock, she strode over to The Clock Works. None of its mantlepiece or table-top clocks displayed the same time, however, and she wondered why none of the shops was equipped with a wall clock for customers. *It's almost as if they don't want us to know when it's time to go home,* she reflected, a thought that struck her as amusing. At last she stopped a woman and asked for the time. Warily the woman glanced at her watch and muttered, *Eleven fifty-six,* then fled into the nearest shop.

The mother returned to the central service area and, while she waited with dozens of others for the elevators, the circular lights overhead flickered momentarily. Just then the mother noticed she was munching on a large chocolate chip cookie, though she didn't remember having purchased it. Not wanting to spoil her appetite, and having put on a few extra pounds lately, she stuffed the remainder of the cookie into a filled-up waste can, which was surrounded by a spillover of crumpled napkins, soda cans, paper plates with pizza stains, and gnawed chicken bones. At last an elevator settled into position, and she squeezed in. The glass cylinder dropped so swiftly she could feel her stomach jump upwards in her body.

In a few minutes she was standing at the wide-open doorway of Burger King. Unable to find her son, she took a place in the nearest line of customers to save a few minutes while waiting for him. In recent months she had been noticing that it took longer and longer to get served at fast-food outlets, slower really than ordinary coffee shops. But millions upon millions throughout the world were being fed by these franchises, so she knew they were doing the best they could for the public. Just as the mother reached the teenaged African-American order-taker at the counter, her son ran up to her.

What would you like to eat? she asked, straightening his baseball cap. The boy pointed to a picture of a cheeseburger deluxe which came with a large french fries and a super-sized Coke. His mother ordered two of these "combos." When the meals were served, wrapped in foil and cardboard, along with white plastic forks sealed in tissue-thin plastic, mother and son wandered deeper into the interior to find a place to sit. But Burger King was jammed, as usual, and it wasn't until ten minutes later that they leapt into a booth moments before an elderly couple had been able to lay claim to the space. The white-haired, wrinkle-faced shoppers snarled, while the mother and son grinned triumphantly at them.

Unwrapping the foil, the mother took a big bite of her cheeseburger deluxe. All that shopping had made her hungry. That first bite made her realize, however, that they'd had to wait just long enough to make their lunch cold. *Better than walking around famished*, she thought, taking another bite. As she chewed through the bacon, cheese, lettuce, pickles, onions, ketchup, mustard, and mayonnaise that topped the burger, she was reminded that hamburgers, or slices of pizzas, or hot dogs served in any of these national chains tasted exactly alike. *Quality control,* she thought.

Her son was picking listlessly at the fries, and his mother asked: *Why aren't you eating your burger? Just not too hungry,* he replied, staring at kids in the facing booth whose jaws were grinding the ground beef. This had happened during their last trip to the Mall, and it made the mother mildly concerned. *Are you feeling sick?* she asked. *No, I just wanna get back to the video game I was playing—Death and Destruction at the Gates of Hell,* he said with a faint smile. *First eat your lunch,* his mother insisted. The boy looked glumly at the foil and cardboard food wrappers before him, twisted his lips in distaste, then plucked a cold french fry out of the upright container, stuck it into his mouth, and seemed to swallow it whole.

Other parents and their offspring were wandering back and forth along the aisles, balancing burgers and beverages and shopping bags as they searched for seats. Not wanting them to have a cold lunch, too, and wanting to make her son happy, the mother gathered the remains of her hamburger and fries onto the brown plastic tray and told her son he didn't have to finished his lunch. *But you'll have to eat everything on your dinner plate tonight!* she admonished. Her son bounded off the padded seat and into the passing crowds outside Burger King. *Meet me at Carvel's on the second floor at 3 o'clock!* she called out, not quite sure he'd heard her.

Just as the mother was rising off the seat, a woman wearing a ski jacket and hiking boots, accompanied by two young girls wearing ski jackets and hiking boots, hopped into the booth, bumping her aside. She gave them a nasty look, but they only glared back at her insolently. Dumping the leftovers on her tray into the garbage can, the mother pushed her way out of the fast-food emporium. Feeling slightly queasy and vaguely uneasy, she made her way through the expanding crowds, moving in the opposite direction that her son had taken.

As the mother emerged from the elevator on the third level, a gang of "toughs" strode by. The young men had shaved heads and wore black denims, thick black leather belts, and heavy black boots. The young women wore black leotards or ragged cut-off jeans with patches, and had silvery chains with skull amulets slung across their breasts; blue and red make-up was smeared like war paint over their ghostly white faces. Some were cursing loudly, a few smoked marijuana, and one couple kept bumping purposely into shoppers, causing the gang to laugh raucously. Nervous, the mother waited until they had stormed by before crossing over to Fashionable Fineries. Here placards announced several seasonal sales. The prices struck her as high—higher, it seemed to her, than before the items had gone on sale. *No, I'm just losing my memory,* she thought with a smile. Feeling calmer again, she grazed among the cashmere sweaters and cotton body suits. Soon she became lost in fantasies of lingerie, picturing the transparent garments draped over her own plump body. *Wouldn't it be terrific,* she mused, *if I surprised my husband with a silky red negligee and brought some of the old spark back to our bed? Well, there's no time for that sort of thing anymore,* she admitted, *with him working such long hours and my own part-time job just to keep up with the bills.* She let the negligee slip out of her fingers onto the counter.

By now she was feeling weary, as if she'd been harvesting corn in the fields since sunup. But it was not until she noticed the tiny digital clock readout in the register—she was purchasing two pairs of pantyhose for work—that the mother thought about the time. *Three-thirty—a half-hour late to meet my son!* It didn't seem possible that three hours had passed so swiftly. Just then the shop lights went dim, and she noticed it had grown chilly. Voices were rising in the corridors outside the shop.

Finding her way out of Fashionable Fineries, she headed toward the elevators and came upon hundreds of shoppers milling around, murmuring loudly, their hands and legs and heads in motion. Now she realized one of the elevators was stalled between floors and its passengers were pounding hard on the glass as if trying to break through to get air. When the mother asked the clay-faced, skin-and-bones man beside her what had happened, he replied in rapid-fire phrases: *Credit card machines chewing up the plastic! CD's playing backwards! None of the phones working! Heaters shut down and air-conditioners turned on!*

Electronic entrance doors locked automatically! The Carousel's gone haywire! Then the man shrieked, stalking into the crowds with a wild look in his eye.

Alarmed, the mother moved through the crowds toward the door to the stairwell, but it was roped off and a large sign indicated it was closed for repairs. She noticed dozens of shoppers swarming outside the security office. Some were pounding on the door, some were shouting: *My purse was stolen! I've lost my daughter! My nose is bleeding—someone punched me!* But the door of the office didn't open. A network of loudspeakers concealed in vents crackled: *Attention, shoppers! The electronic system of the Carousel Shopping Mall has been infiltrated by a virus on the ground level and the infection is spreading to the higher floors. To protect public safety, no one is permitted to leave any floor until the virus has been isolated and destroyed. Sorry for the inconvenience....*

As soon as the message ended, the music blared back on. Usually the mother didn't hear the background music, but this time she couldn't block it out because the bony man had been right—it was playing backwards, sending eerie, electronic whining sounds sailing above their heads. Now the lights grew dimmer, and this time they remained dim, casting a drab sepia tone over everyone and everything. The voices of the shoppers rose higher, but none of them was intelligible any longer, having become part of the collective roar of confusion and fear.

Suspecting her son was still at the Video Games Arcade, the mother felt a wave of panic swelling in her chest as she entered the closest shop, Jewelry Classics. Winding her way past customers and counter, she felt a sluggishness expanding within her and noticed it was becoming more difficult to breathe. But she forced herself to keep moving. Her idea was to locate the emergency fire exit that was located at the rear of each shop, and use the outside fire escape to make her way down to locate her son at the arcade. Upon reaching the back wall, however, she found a door painted on the concrete surface, but no actual exit leading out of the building. Although certain the Mall's Shop Directory indicated fire exits at the back of every shop, she realized she had never looked for one before. Stunned, she turned and started toward the front of the store, but the air seemed to be thickening like syrup, and her body felt as if it was gaining a pound with every step.

Midway through Jewelry Classics, she saw a man and a woman, both well dressed, reaching into a broken glass display case, scooping jewelry off the gray-velvet-covered trays and stuffing the golden trinkets into their pockets. Shaken, the mother took a different aisle to avoid the thieves. After what seemed a very long time, she passed into the central mall. Amid the crush of people she spotted the young toughs in black leather vests and metal-spiked bracelets, their eyes gleaming, their fists raised. In the blur of movement around her, out of the corner of her eye, she saw a clown with a bulbous red nose strike a child on the head with a wooden paddle. The girl fell to the floor and the crowds, now swaying out of control, trampled over the small, tender body. The child's screams pierced the mother's heart.

Unable to reach the child, the mother pushed frantically through the mob to the stairwell. Here she ducked under the rope, past the warning sign—DO NOT ENTER! CLOSED FOR REPAIRS!—and took hold of the doorknob and yanked. To her surprise, it opened. The mother slipped inside, the heavy metal door slamming with a click behind her. Total blackness enveloped her but, determined to find her son and get him out of the Mall, she placed her hands flat against the wall and began to make her way down, one step at a time. Suddenly she realized she had lost her purse and shopping bags, but this no longer mattered to her. The cold darkness made her shiver as she continued to descend. Her primary fear just then was that she might trip over construction materials left behind by the workmen, and would tumble down the concrete stairs. Yet nothing came in her path, and a strange idea entered her mind: the Carousel Shopping Mall had lied to her, to all of them, about repairs being made in the stairwells, about the existence of fire exits, and a dense apprehension seized her. These weren't ordinary, sales-driven lies, she realized, but lies that had been used to entrap them inside a cinder-block tomb with locked doors and no windows. Frantic, she tried to get her legs to move more quickly down the stairs, but she couldn't seem to gather any momentum.

Some time later her foot stepped onto a landing, and she spotted a thin crack of light. Feeling along the wall, she found the doorknob, pulled weakly, and staggered out of the stairwell. By now she was feeling immensely exhausted, and her body shook from the extreme cold. The lights were dim here, too, and the advertising signs were blinking too slowly, surreally, smearing yellow and purple and red light across the ceilings and walls. Music was groaning at the wrong speed out of the iron grillwork, sounding like a mass of people in great pain, having suffered wounds on a battlefield. Hundreds of shoppers and sales personnel stood all around her in the frigid air, and despite the appearance of movement caused by the blinking lights, each of them was motionless. Their shiny stillness struck the mother as curiously permanent, like things glimpsed in a flash of lightning. By now she felt entirely too weak to move, too spiritless even to be terrified any longer. Her body no longer trembled. It was only when she noticed her son—caught in place at a video game, his skin with an enamel sheen, that she sensed movement, and the last realization that ever passed through her being was that all of them, though frozen in place, were beginning to move in a circle around the central mall, revolving round and round and round and round....

THE SECRET OF SUCCESS

In a dim, stale, paneled motel room in Des Moines, I finger Bowker's bookstore directory, checking off those outlets that seem appropriate for our line—slow-but-sure cookbooks, unauthorized biographies of Hollywood has-beens, household how-to's, novels with enough flesh on the cover to sell almost anywhere. And with the road still buzzing in my body, I try to set up appointments by phone for tomorrow, getting a feel for what I'll be up against: the too-quick-to-laugh male buyer, the assistant eager to wield a little power over publisher reps, the "strictly business" shop manager. In two instances the right person is unavailable; in another the individual refuses to be eased into my schedule just because I'm in town. But I do manage to make connections with half a dozen stores. Spreading a street map on the narrow bed, I pinpoint each, then pencil-in a continuous pattern of movement. The idea is to save the maximum time, to give them the least energy—the least of myself while, hopefully, taking something away from them: like lying stiff and still in bed as someone's organ is emptying into me.

Next morning I order a dark coffee in a solemn, musty luncheonette nearby, finish it off with a few gulps, find my way to the main shopping route, and begin moving in the direction of my first date. For a city built on spacious plains, downtown seems too bunched together, too upright. And the local faces lack desire, as if overcome by their inability to keep the buildings from darkening with age, the edges of the sidewalks from crumbling. I suspect these gray figures—they look straight ahead as they walk—read newspapers rather than books. Yet the directory lists about a dozen outlets in the area. With all that flatness surrounding them, I would think they'd need characters on the page to do some of their living for them.

At my first stop, a general bookstore with "something for everyone," the lumpy leather case (overstuffed with jacket covers,
catalogs and flyers) is hooked to my left hand, leaving my right
free to offer a business card,

Cynthia Mallory

Sales Representative

GINGOLD PUBLISHING CO.

And to shake a hand, if necessary. (Certain buyers want hand-
contact; some, who have been sharpened like a pencil by this
tight business, avoid accepting your hand: They see it as a concession.) Behind the counter a man with a round face peers at
me, recognizing me for what I am immediately.

"Good morning," I say, giving my name and company. "I'm
glad you had the time to see me. Nice looking layout you've
got here." In a minute or two, I lean forward to hand him our
latest catalog, giving him a full view down my loose white, cotton
V-neck.

Flipping through the blue pages, his expression remotely puz-
zled, he says: "We're not ordering very much these days. We
just don't have the space."

"I know what you mean. The shelf situation forced us to cut
back on oversized editions. But you might want to look over
this home improvement line." As I hand him a triple-fold sales
flyer, my fingers brush his knuckles. "Once a customer picks
up one of these, he or she usually comes back for more in the
series."

In the end, as flowingly as a whore swings through a cheap
hotel lobby, I transfer an invoice pad from my case to the buyer's
desk. "These titles will bring you sales, I promise. No matter
where I go, they sell."

"Let's hope so," he says, his speckled eyes taking a gander at my bare knee in the slit.

Once the numbers have been hand-printed on the order blank, and the customary reassurances have been exchanged, out of the back room I move with a sense of conviction as compact as a tube of lipstick, fleshing out my black skirt with each stride. I feel his eyes on me all the way out. But I escape before he notices the muscles in my face have sprung back into their off-duty mold. I am on the sidewalk before he notices he has been seduced...the way I hadn't realized I was being seduced by my father's partner when I was in high school.

At my next stop (two blocks off the Avenue), I move down the aisle gingerly, as if afraid of breaking through a paper floor: This shop is not doing well, judging by the owner's crimped lips, the tidiness of her work area. If the book business is nothing else, it's messy. My appearance draws a cynical glance. Staining her counter with my shadow, I hold my place with an impertinent patience as she runs an index finger down the narrow pages of someone else's catalog. "Be with you in a minute," she says coolly, not looking up. I survey the shop with a pleasant gaze, hoping she'll be able to pay her bills. But the stock on the shelves seems more literary than I was led to believe from the description in the directory, and she is making me wait longer than necessary. Though she had agreed to receive me, I sense she has no intention of buying anything.

Pawing the tight coils of her hair, she squeals, "Won't be much longer."

"I'm in no hurry."

Ten more minutes pass. The owner looks over the rim of her glasses, silently blaming me for undermining another independent bookstore, I suppose, for helping to snuff out serious literature with printed garbage. To her, literature is Shakespeare, Keats. To me, literature is the mailing piece, the sales hand-out. Despite her purposeful delay, I hang in—you just never know when they'll surprise you with an order. Anyway my job is to absorb her criticism, her complaints. Without a crease of expression on her flat face, she goes through them all: the giant supermarket style book stores, competition from remainder houses, rent increases, shoplifting, lack of advertising support, non-return policies of some publishers.... She's been in the business long enough to know I am its professional victim. On the firing line.

"Maybe next time around I'll be able to show you something that will catch your eye."

"You never know," she says.

Bitch! I say to myself, with a wide smile.

In the next shop, too, through every condescending word, every clearing of his loose throat, I smile and listen, listen and smile, altering the shape of my lips (marked bright red for the occasion) according to the arc of his eyebrows, the expressiveness of his voice. It's a passion with this one, his eyes wide and gleaming like he's erect in his trousers. As he moans about the decline of quality in trade book manufacturing—"If you open a book flat, the spine breaks and the pages come out in your hand"—I think that if only his wife had sent him into the day with a decent fuck, I might've walked out of here with a good sale. *Well, maybe I'll get something out of him yet.* While I'm trying to pay attention to him, a pair of faces (shriveled by sun) surface in my mind: my mother and father awaiting death in St. Petersburg, unwillingly locked into each other's lives for more years than they are able to remember.

The streets are gaining momentum in the blunted sunlight. Around the corner, in a hodge-podge store (candy, cards, knickknacks, calendars, books—in that order of prominence), I come up against a blondish, husky guy, twenty-two or three, who doesn't know a thing about the business. *The owner's son?* Softly and deliberately I release each word: "This novel is not going to make you rich. But it's been building sales in all sorts of outlets. Quality shops like yours, and even the hodge-podge stores."

"What's it about?" he says, wrinkling his eyebrows.

"A really strange love-hate triangle set in the Caribbean with snake-worship and stolen jewels. It's got a little of everything—suspense, history, intrigue, and sex—plenty of sex. A real old-fashioned page turner."

He leans back and looks at me warily: "Never heard of the author."

I lean forward and look into his blue eyes sincerely: "Matter of fact he was born and raised in these parts."

After the yellow copy of the invoice is safe in my case, just before I turn to leave, I lick my upper lip, as if I'd just finished going down on him.

"That's one book I'd like to read myself," he confesses with a smirk, ogling the pink breasts on the glossy red cover.

"I think you'd find it very stimulating."

With an assortment of rejections and acceptances in my head and in my case, I start back to the Stardust Motel. On the way I don't see much, or hear much, as if I'm traveling in an empty elevator. Four plastic orange armchairs, a long beige sofa, three brass ashtray stands, two maple end tables, and one walnut desk clutter the lobby, all of it boxed in by more of that thin, grained paneling. The oily-haired clerk behind the counter, eyes gleaning the sports pages of the local daily, doesn't notice me pass by.

Inside my room, in the company of a bolted-down television and drapes thick as sweat pants, I can feel the solitariness fitting into the slopes of my body, the hollows of my mind. Dumping the case on the bed, I sit on the side of the weak mattress and dial those shops I wasn't able to connect with before—especially important since my sales haven't been too hot. The late effort pays off: two appointments for early next day, leaving me late morning to clear out before check-out time. I feel a bit relieved, and food occurs to me.

In a family-style restaurant two blocks away, a square-shaped waitress sets the heavy white plate down quietly before me. The roast beef is as tough as a typewriter roller, and the mashed potatoes taste like the glue on a business envelope. No one else seems to notice. Chubby-faced families are swallowing eagerly, noisily at the round tables. I'm the only one seated alone. Sipping the sharp coffee, I go over the comments that were aimed at me during the day, along with my responses, trying to pin down the precise moment each potential sale passed beyond my reach. But it's elusive, and way down inside a muted sense of distress begins to collect again. If nothing comes of those last two appointments, the trip will barely have paid for my travel expenses.

Leaving fifteen percent of the bill for a tip, I get out into the dull humidity and begin to drift. The people on the sidewalk take short steps, not wanting to get anywhere too fast, it seems. I stride through the high portals of an aged department store—pale green walls and pillars—roam among the cosmetic counters for awhile, then find myself in a boutique down the street with chrome-edged glass cases. Apparently I'm looking to buy something for myself, to take the edge off that dull, unpleasant sensation that comes with lost sales. But what? I try a few other shops, but nothing holds my attention. At last I walk out of a women's specialty store with a white paper bag containing a black lace bra and a pair of see-through panties, red.

It's noticeably gloomier outside, and it occurs to me that Des Moines will always appear overcast in my mind. It occurs to me I have been floating around a strange city without a reference point in time or space, like that day I got lost from my parents at the beach. Though only nine years old, I did not feel afraid, as if being lost had already become a natural condition of my life.

Conceding to evening at last, I turn back, and in fifteen minutes the Stardust Motel—two redwood decks of cubicles flanked by a row of sleeping automobiles, one of them leased to my company—appears as unexpectedly as an unpleasant memory. But it's too early to shut myself up for the night, so I move between the orange striped walls of the corridor to the lounge. I climb up a long-legged stool, and the bartender limps toward me. His face is made of pork-rind.

"What'll it be?"

"Bloody Mary."

"You got it, Doll."

You're damn right I got it, I say to myself, *but you can't have it. And don't call me Doll, you jerk!*

Sipping my drink—the spice stings my tongue, I light up a cigarette and blow a few ghosts into the yellowy dimness. Three people are tucked away into a booth. A middle-aged woman in a peasant blouse is seated alone at a table, staring at an electric beer sign against the plate-glass window. To my left there's a couple hanging over the bar, smashed, arguing loudly. All the while the juke box is flashing and roaring in the corner, as if having a private party.

Ordering another drink, I notice a truck driver (or maybe a local plumber looking for action) in a flannel shirt, sandy-faced, eyeing me from the end of the bar, smiling the way I smile at buyers. I push my red nails up the side of my neck, allowing the hair to flow between my fingers, giving him a feel for its dark softness. I imagine his hard chest forcing itself on me, squashing my breasts. Just about the time he has finished off enough whiskey to stomp over and get friendly, I drop off the stool and walk out the door.

Behind the safety chain of my rented door, I place a call to Jim Carbon, Gingold's sales manager. In another time zone, he is still at his desk. I give him a rundown of sales without getting too specific; let him know about the speeding ticket; bitch about the bleak skies, the blank food—the farm-belt mentality. Suddenly he growls, "Dalton screwed us out of that Washington deal," and adds, "just when The Old Man is putting the squeeze on me to get more sales out of the staff." I express annoyance at The Old Man. But I'm more annoyed at Carbon. I know what he's really saying. Doesn't he think *I* want more sales, too?

Carbon's voice lowers: "Maybe we could have a drink when you get back, Cynthia, and go over your sales tally from this trip."

"Sure thing," I say, thinking: *You'll never get inside my pants, Carbon, never.*

I strip, leaving my clothes on the trampled rug, and move into the narrow bathroom. I step into the shower. Not touching the bar of sticky soap, I turn on the water full blast, as hot as I can stand it. The hot pounding stream sensitizes my skin like a meat tenderizer. The compact room grows misty. Toweling my raw, reddened body, I can't help worrying about those last two shops. Somehow I've got to sell them, and sell them big.

Suddenly I feel inspired. I remove the tiny razor blade from its holder and go naked into the bedroom. Spreading the new underwear on the chest of drawers, I slice off the tips of the lacy cups, and cut out the silky crotch, leaving deep scars in the fake walnut. Now I pull the unlaundered stiffness of the deformed garments onto my body. Moving to the long mirror, the rug gritty against my bare feet, I take a steady look: nipples large and dark as plums, the smooth shaped shoulders, the swell of my belly, the tucked-in-navel, the coiled black wires at the crossroads of my legs. Even with the gathered skin at the sides of my chest and the dark underscoring of my eyes—the price of too much road and not enough sales, I know there are men in a dozen cities who force me to do things to them in their minds. The thought brings a smile to my lips.

Squatting on the sodden mattress—where thousands of bodies have squirmed against each other, leaving their body fluids behind, I pull the purchase orders from my case and, calculator in hand, tap out the totals: the true product of the day's expenditures of time and energy. At last I multiply by twenty percent. When the ultimate figure winks at me greenly from the display panel, the full weight of my dissatisfaction flops over me.

The squareness of the room remains with me even after the muted glow has been withdrawn back into the bulb. In the dark the steaminess which has carried in from the shower settles on my proneness. I shift left and right, unable to get comfortable on the bony coils. Lying still at last, I became aware of my thighs, I become aware of my stretched-out breasts, I become aware of my flattened buttocks. At that moment my body and my self seem to be separate entities, not part of one whole person. I think about the dust-colored hair down the back of my boss' neck, the thick wrists of the truck driver in the bar, the hollow eyes which peered at me from the toll booth, the muscular fingers of the young buyer who ordered ten copies of *Battered Love.* I think about all of them, lusting for me in the porno houses of their minds. But every one of them seems like a shadow tonight, faint and limp, unable to get through to me, to penetrate to my deepest places.

I remember someone from the second shop I visited today—reaching high to slide stock onto the top shelf. A strip of bare back blinked between jeans and jersey. A rib puckered. The hair moved like honey flows. Unexpectedly I feel her small, delicate white hands on my ankles. My nipples are hardening, enlarging, extending out of the open cuts. I touch them lightly with the tips of my fingers. A heightened sensitivity surfaces at the insides of my thighs, and a slow warmth begins oozing within me: tar between the cracks in a summer highway. I watch her head bend down over me, feel her soft lips brushing my calves, sliding up between my knees. I feel her cool breath on my thighs. Her face disappears into my warm center, into my essence, and the dash of her tongue releases a poignant electricity along the ridges of my rawness. My hands become fists as I drink in the sounds of her thirst being quenched.... After not too long, just enough, I push her head away.

My body is flushed and moist, tender with arousal. At last. I think about relieving myself with gently enfolded, wet, smoothly stroking fingers. But I know I mustn't squander this tension, this energy. Closing my eyes, I begin to wait upon sleep, much the way my parents await death. It takes time. Even as I lose my way in the darkness, my strategy remains clear, if not in my consciousness then in my physical sense of things: come morning I will gather up the sensations I have banked in my body and will strut into those last two shops—eyes blazing, lips sticky, legs apart, and they will hear it crackle in my hair, and they will feel it in the damp palm of my hand, and they will smell it under my skirt, and they will tear into my catalog and buy and buy and buy and buy and buy....

SALES CONVENTION

On the morning after registration at the Intercontinental Hotel in Washington D.C., delegates to CCC's 50th Annual Sales Convention awoke as if touched by a live wire. Hurriedly they drew on their trousers and skirts, elevatored into the CCC lounge, gulped their paper cups of coffee and cellophane-sealed pastries, then swarmed into the six-doored mouth of the main ballroom for the official ribbon-snipping of the Convention Exhibit. The crowds of smiling people, the blue and gray banners waving overhead, the bright badges and buttons on their chests, the recorded brassy music lent the ceremony an air of a patriotic parade.

Three rows of booths (draped in blue and gray) housed a photographic gallery of the Corporation's products (and related services) in action, displays of printed and visual marketing aids, glossy copies of national advertising campaigns, a filmed history—*CCC in War and Peace*, models of projected assembly plants, graphs and charts depicting the sales accomplishments of the domestic and foreign territories and, among other features, a presentation called *Safeguarding Mankind's Future,* which demonstrated systems research and development through a continuous clicking of color slides on a 360 degree series of screens overhead.

From morning to evening, delegates in greenish shirts and tannish blouses wandered up and down the aisles, interrupting their pilgrimage only briefly for a sandwich and soda water or, if they had drunk too much in one of the hotel's cocktail lounges the night before, nothing but lots of bitter black coffee. Again their legs would crank up and down the aisles, their eyes coated, their mouths dry. By the time the Exhibit closed for the day, at 6 PM, the delegates were in a trance from all that walking, from so much hot, smoky, dead air, and from being bombarded by so much data and propaganda. Nevertheless, as they were lifted swiftly and silently in steel chambers to the higher realms of the hotel complex, each of them came away with a certain feeling of pride to be connected to all that they had witnessed during the day.

Behind their fire-proof doors, the delegates set fire to another cigarette, or read the Seminar Schedule, or flopped onto the mattress, or dialed their area code back home before smearing rouge on their cheeks, polish on their shoes. Meanwhile the pink flesh of one thousand chicken parts was being toughened in the baked darkness of the massive black ovens below street level; and water goblets (with IH stamped in gold) were being set out on one hundred fifty tables in a huge hall above lobby level. A little before and a little after 7:15 PM the delegates (in steamed suits and dry-cleaned dresses) were lowered in bunches to the mezzanine. Here they became an amorphous mass, buzzing through a funneled entranceway into the dining hall.

The huge hexahedron of space was paneled in walnut-streaked fiberboard, just like their rooms. Of man-made materials too, the rug was tenacious, close-cropped like a GI haircut, and blood red. The cream-colored ceilings were perforated, helping to muffle the noise. Spotlights, each encased in a highly polished bronze cone, lit the expanse too sharply, causing the delegates to blink and waver as they cluttered the aisles—like a swarm of commuters at rush hour who, all in a flash, had gone blind. At last, with chatter in a dozen languages, and with much confusion, they found their way to the tables that held the names of their sales territories on white placards in clear plastic holders.

At 7:47 PM a very white man in a very black blazer (decorated with four brass buttons), standing with his back to the wall, jerked his head toward a pair of triangular windows at the narrowed end of the dining hall. This signal caused the left door to swing open and a column of men—some black, some white—in tight maroon, waist-length jackets stomped up a slope and out into the center aisle. Each balanced over his shoulder a stainless steel tray that seemed as large and round as a radar shield. Once each of the tray's eight covered plates—measured piles of mashed potatoes and carrots-and-peas flanking the bruised, brittle-skinned chicken breasts—had been placed before a delegate, the waiters tucked the rolled edge of the trays under their arms, pivoted smoothly, and scooted back through the right swinging door. Again and again they returned, their trays newly loaded with eight dinner plates containing baked chicken and vegetables.

The teeth of the delegates tore the pulpy flesh off the brittle bones ravenously. It was not an extraordinary hunger (not much earlier they'd snacked on free coffee and donuts at the Exhibit), nor the originality of the fare (hundreds of conventions were serving scrawny, stringy, rushed-to-the-kill birds on the same evening across the land) which incited them. Mostly it was that the meal honored a CCC milestone and, by implication, was a tribute to the delegates, too. As such, the meat and vegetables went down as a deeply satisfying, spiritual food. And in the hours, the days that lay ahead—the meetings and seminars and workshops and speeches and scheduled play—they would require resources beyond the physical to keep them going.

A nod from the man in the blazer (standing in the center aisle now, legs apart, hands at hips), drew the maroon jackets back into the hall, where they began scooping the soiled plates off the tables. When this was finished, they returned bearing a steaming chrome pot and eight dessert dishes, each of which harbored a sad-looking baked apple, a sort of shrunken head up to its double chin in a watery, urine-colored, sugary sauce. Odorless coffee was poured from chrome pots in a long ribbon without losing a drop, sweetened with a promise to provide all the boiled black fluid they desired. But the Convention Committee needn't have worried about keeping anyone awake. To every being under that high, insulated ceiling, the Welcome Banquet was the highlight of the five-day event, for the October issue of *CCC News* had promised (in its lead story) that the Chairman and Chief Executive Officer was slated to be the Keynote Speaker. And even though many delegates didn't quite believe the Chairman would be able to break away from his every-minute-accounted-for schedule to visit with them, they had shown up en masse, on time—just in case.

At 8:55 PM the lead-colored curtains backing the stage stirred, and a very tall woman in a navy-blue linen skirt and crisp white cotton jacket—without a wasted movement of any of her tubular parts—emerged and approached the lectern, where a microphone hung by a wire so faint it seemed to float in mid-air. Though the clashing of voices and spoons diminished, the woman looked at them in silence until the final dozen or so delegates had entirely ceased stirring in their seats, chuckling, rattling their cups, puffing on their cigarettes. Then the cylindrical head at the lectern produced sound, a sleek voice starting way down in her neck and rising steadily to a controlled, surprising shrillness: "Ladies and Gentlemen, welcome to CCC's 50th Annual Sales Convention Banquet.... We hope you enjoyed your dinner, and that you will find the program informative, productive, and profitable.... At this time, I have the great pleasure and privilege of presenting to you the Chairman of CCC, Mr....!"

The name was exclaimed rather than spoken, and in the vastness of the hall, and through the static of the microphone, and in the noisy excitement of the moment, few if any could quite make it out. That name was permanently embossed on their collective consciousness, however, so the proper name and middle initial and surname were whispered to them anyway in the privacy of their minds.

The introduction had come out of the bluish slit below her sharp nose like a slap in the face, smarting the delegates into alertness; instantly they began slapping their hands together. And the more they clapped, the more they wanted to clap, as if their hands had just been unshackled after a long period of bondage. Probably they applauded too loudly and too long, but it was understandable. As far as they knew, few employees from the ranks of any department had ever set eyes on the Chairman; there hadn't even been a photo of him in *CCC News*.

The Chairman's office was located in the penthouse of CCC's international headquarters in New York City, overlooking Wall Street and, indeed, a long stretch of the eastern seaboard. He came and went in a private helicopter which landed at a permanently leased, shielded corner of the heiloport atop the hundred floors. (Or so security guards claimed.) Getting to his office down a private stairwell, through a double set of silvery doors with CCC bolted on them, he was seated at his desk every day of the year—including Christmas and July 4th—at 7:00 AM. The innumerable affairs and ceaseless planning of the Corporation, though under the direct guidance—that is, control—of the Chairman, were delegated through six vice-presidents and thirty-one territorial directors in North and South America, Europe, the Middle East, Indo-China, the Far East, Central America and, most recently, in Africa. But according to talk coming out of the executive secretary pool, not even these administrators got to stand in the presence of the Chairman very often, if at all. This contention seemed to be confirmed by the VIPs themselves who, assigned to the front tables at the Welcome Banquet, sat far forward on their chairs, their eyes narrowed, their necks erect as periscopes.

The woman with the sharp features stalked off, and the weighty, mustard-colored fibreglas curtains parted at the center until a large, square, white, electronic screen was uncovered. Less than a minute later, at 9:00 PM, an image flash upon its surface: A brief, shiny man, with tufts of steel woolly hair above each tiny ear, blinked at them with lizard-like lids from behind platinum-rimmed, perfectly round glasses. The man wore a wide-lapelled, trimly tailored herring bone (with vest) and a cloud-blue collar so heavily starched it looked breakable. He was sitting upright in a tan leather, high-backed recliner, and his long, waxy, squared-off fingers were stretched flat on a simple pine desk.

It was the slightness of the man, and the poor quality of the desk, which made the delegates suspicious. To fulfill their mutual image of him, the Chairman needed to be twice as tall and broad, and the desk had to be made of solid mahogany, perhaps trimmed in silver, and take up half the room. As soon as the man smiled, however—revealed a burst of gold teeth that gleamed with understanding, the delegates began to doubt their own hasty skepticism. A truly great leader, such as Jesus or Mohammed, would after all be a man of the people, a man who was able to relate to each and every one of his followers. Yes, of course. This was indeed the Chairman and CEO of CCC, and the moment they arrived at this conclusion, their hearts bobbed in their chests.

"Good evening," said the golden mouth. "Some of you have traveled a very long way, and others have had to put in many extra hours over the past few weeks just to be here. I wish to thank you all so very much for coming." The voice had the texture of very fine sandpaper accompanied by the vibrations that came from rubbing it over balsawood. His words were offered with such humility, such gentleness, the delegates felt as though they had come not as a business obligation but out of some long-harbored, intimate need.

"It gives me great satisfaction to share this 50th Annual Sales Convention with you, and to help launch CCC into its sixth decade."

While continuing to look out pleasantly toward the audience, the Chairman opened the Corporation's silver and blue annual report on the green blotter before him. "In the course of this year, CCC has stepped up its production capability thirty-four percent...established a marketing beachhead in Nigeria and Zambia...successfully introduced a new line of intermediate hardware ...expanded trade substantially in the Middle East...and, by the third quarter, had increased its global sales sixty-one percent."

A murmur of pride passed as swiftly as a corporate rumor among the delegates, and a crack of gold glinted in the Chairman's mouth. "By any business yardstick, the Corporation is in a solid growth pattern."

Splashes of handclapping washed across the deep spaces of the hall.

"With less than two months remaining in the calendar year," the Chairman went on, "we can project with a high degree of certainty that we are about to conclude the second most successful year in the history of CCC."

This time the applause broke out like a siege of cannon, but it leveled off abruptly, for some of the delegates had sensed a tinge of disappointment in his demeanor, as though the Chairman was asking, indirectly, why it hadn't been the Corporation's *most* successful year.

"That is why I have come before you on this occasion: to congratulate you on your performance, but also to impress upon you that, in the year—in the decade—ahead, the greatest danger before us is"—he grew as pensive as Napoleon seemed in that famous painting of him—"ourselves."

Without speaking for a moment, the Chairman's large yellowed corneas (in the close-up) aimed out of the screen not quite at them, just above their upraised heads, giving them time to digest his statement. Disoriented at first, the delegates soon leaned over to one another and hummed with admiration for their Chairman. For though not everyone had understood the implications of the remark, most were convinced it was profound.

"*Complacency* is the first of the three Cs which comprise the anniversary theme of this convention," said the Chairman, glancing almost imperceptibly toward the expandable gold band on his wrist.

"Once we allow our minds to accept that we have said and done all we can, Ladies and Gentlemen, we have begun to witness the beginning of the end."

The Chairman drew a breath which, amplified, sounded oppressively heavy.

"I would like each of you to take a few moments now to ask yourself, in your heart of hearts, whether *you* might be in danger of resting on your past accomplishments."

A few of the delegates glanced at each other, but then they too sank into the quiet places within them; for ten seconds all of them sat without shifting very much, without looking around, contemplating to the varying degrees of their ability to contemplate.

"In the months ahead I implore you to think not about what you did for CCC yesterday, but what you can do for CCC today, and tomorrow.... If each of you will do that daily, together we can make this year, first of the new decade, a record-shattering experience!"

A tremendous roar rolled through the dining hall like a row of tanks rumbling into a jungle village, and it continued a long while. Finally the Chairman creased his forehead, reminding the more sensitive of the delegates that he had other appointments—perhaps with the head of NATO, or the Secretary of Defense.

When total silence had been achieved, the Chairman proceeded: "Our stockholders have invested not merely their personal resources but their trust in CCC—and in all good faith we cannot, we *must* not let them down."

A splattering of applause arose, fading into the smoke that swirled before the cones of light overhead.

"Our clients too are counting on us, looking to CCC for diversity and dependability, backed by up-to-the-moment technology."

A scattering of applause rose up again, and faded.

"The men and women from quality control and trafficking and inventory and, indeed, from all walks of CCC, depend on us—on you—to set the pace for their own activities world wide."

Several small, isolated pockets of applause sounded.

"But while stockholders, clients and fellow employees look to you for leadership," the Chairman declared decisively, "your efforts would be meaningless without their support."

No applause followed this time, for the Chairman's tone had finally arrived at the solemnity it had been angling toward.

"That is the second C of this 50th Annual Sales Convention—*Cooperation*. In your daily meditations, I want you to consider how you can employ this concept more dynamically in your respective territories."

An oblique movement of the Chairman's head caught the full reflection of the camera lights on his glasses, momentarily turning his lenses into a pair of silver dollars.

"The concerted effort of professionals working side by side on the CCC team, and for the same dream—therein lies the key to wider conquests in the marketplace. *Cooperation*. Think about it."

An uneven, uneasy murmuring worked through the audience: They were unsure whether to contemplate or to applaud first. Ultimately they simply sat motionless and soundless, some blinking at the spotlights, some with eyes lowered, the majority of them thinking about how they could file their sales reports more promptly, how they might detail their orders less carelessly.

"The final and perhaps most critical of the three Cs relates to a condition which confronts each of us every day of our business lives. I am referring to *Competition.*"

The Chairman moved the financial report aside, revealing a black file folder, which he opened but did not look at. "Even though some of our competitors have not enjoyed as enviable a record as CCC, others have registered disquieting gains. And one of them—I need not mention the name—appears to be headed for a higher annual gross than CCC for the first time in history."

A profound sadness seemed to weigh the Chairman's chin slightly toward his chest. (The delegates felt like turning their heads away, but it seemed cowardly.) "In the year ahead the word *Competition* should be on each of our tongues through every day, every night. In the office. On the road. In the home. This will help remind us to keep up our guard, to protect our marketing flanks, to beat the *Competition* to the punch."

The Chairman's purplish irises darted left and right behind the lenses of his glasses like tiny ultraviolet search-lights. None of the delegates had to be told it was time to be undemonstrative, to contemplate the last of the three Cs; lips tight, they stared into their coffee cups (which had just been refilled), some crushing out their cigarettes, and quite a few shutting their eyes.

"Ladies and Gentlemen, I have come here this evening to ask you to take the three Cs—*Complacency, Cooperation, Competition*—into your hearts and souls and to give them your undivided and vigorous attention. Over the next year discuss them with your associates. Elicit their ideas. Be alert to danger, be aware of opportunities. Above all, get the job done!... Promise me that you will. Let me hear you say it—'We promise, Mr. Chairman.'"

In a remarkable unanimity, the delegates responded with a rising chant: "We promise, Mr. Chairman! We promise, Mr. Chairman! We promise, Mr. Chairman!"

After a few moments of satisfied silence, the golden mouth started up again: "Although we have been discussing The Big Picture this evening, the focal point of all our operations is, as it has been for half a century, the people of CCC." Without moving his head the Chairman glanced at his watch again. "Admittedly every person, every job is important to our total thrust. However, in the final accounting, selling—from lobbyists to order-takers—represents the heartbeat of CCC, and that makes you the life blood of the Corporation. That makes you more important than the Chairman himself."

The delegates laughed politely over this absurd, but nevertheless agreeable show of humility.

The Chairman allowed them to draw the fullest satisfaction out of their own delight before assuring them he was not being facetious.

"CCC's Research Divisions may make the technological breakthroughs necessary to keep abreast of a rapidly changing world; and Manufacturing may turn out effective, field-tested equipment; and Public Relations may foster the proper business climate in Washington and other world capitals; and Distribution may deploy our cargoes to the international ports of call with dispatch; yet the Corporation's financial blood will not flow *unless*...unless that sacred transaction occurs: The Sale. And you people out there—*you* are the ones at the point of sale, at the front lines of commerce."

The delegates were inspired by these words, by the fact that the Chairman had pointed his finger at them. And when the Chairman exclaimed softly, "You are the true soldiers of CCC!" the delegates felt as if a grenade had gone off in their chests. Even the man in the brass-buttoned blazer, and the men in maroon jackets, standing around eyeing the camouflaged faces at the tables, looked up at the wide screen that was filled with a close-up of the smooth, waxen face. And as the delegates peered at each other with ignited eyes and shifted excitedly in their seats, the golden mouth declared, "In the challenges of next year, and even into the shadows of the decade before us, I bid you to fulfill the mission of the three Cs—*Complacency, Cooperation, Competition,* and I want you to know your Chairman is placing his total confidence in *you* and *you* and *you!"*

The screen went blank, looming immense in its starkness, for it was much more than a flat, square, electronic, sparkling white surface; it was a deprivation, a void, a blizzard that had swept into their lives, immobilizing them. For a time the delegates felt chilled and hollow and lost and alone; many gripped their chairs and tables as if afraid of being blown into the white-out before them, of being consumed by its oblivion. At last a few veteran lobbyists managed to arise on unsteady legs, and they started slapping the palms of their hands together, slowly at first, then with increasing vigor. Encouraged by this display of fortitude, others stood up and bellowed from deep in their chests. Soon they were all standing and applauding and cheering, a few of the young men whistling, a few of the young women singing. The delegates milled and clapped and called out for a long, long time. Their hands and lungs hurt, their heads throbbed as they gleamed at each other in their shared exultation.

The Chairman did not return, and so, one by one, the delegates sank down onto their seats, and lit cigarettes with shaking hands, and swallowed cold coffee to soothe their throats, and blotted the wetness from their eyes. And when they had recovered sufficiently to express themselves more coherently, they sighed confidentially to one another that the Chairman looked much younger than they had expected; and that the Chairman had addressed them without a written speech—all straight from his head and, obviously, his heart; and that the Chairman was probably already boarding his private jetliner to Moscow or Tokyo or Cairo.... And when they had said it all, and had said it several times in several ways in several languages, the delegates wiped their dry mouths on the soiled napkins, arose, and marched out of the hall, carried not so much by their legs as by the seemingly endless reverberations which rumbled across their hearts and by the glory which flared in their souls.

TRAIN TO NOWHERE

Bruce March had a dilemma. He had a secure job selling ad space for a newsletter and magazine published by a printing trade association in Philadelphia; at the same time, he and his wife Bonnie, and their children Andrew, Barbara, and Charlie, had long outgrown their two-bedroom apartment in the city. Working, playing, eating, and sleeping this close together fostered not a togetherness of spirit but a tightness of mind and body. An apartment with a single extra bedroom would've nearly doubled their rent, however, so it was finally decided—accepted is more like it—that it would be better to acquire a mortgage and commute than to throw a son or daughter or wife or husband out the window.

The house they ended up with was located only eighty-something miles west of the city. It had three bedrooms, a full basement, and came at a lower price tag than expected. At first. Built thirty-five or forty years earlier, it needed roof shingles, windows replaced, doors re-hung, electrical and plumbing repairs, not to mention aluminum siding. These unanticipated expenditures forced the Marches to be more budget-wise than they had been in the city, and if they didn't want to trip over cables and pipe during construction, they had to move about as carefully as they'd had to in their old apartment. Nevertheless the added space seemed to improve their dispositions: Mom and Dad argued less, and the children rarely threw punches at one another. As the workmen cleaned up and cleared out, and as the family slowly began to catch up with their bills, they took to roasting hot dogs in a hibachi in the little yard out back. Life hadn't been this relaxed since they were just starting out together, before the kids had arrived. There was a catch, however, for there is always a catch.

Driving to the station, boarding a train, and being able to read the newspaper en route to work—sometimes abetted by coffee in a paper cup (when he'd gotten to the station early enough to line up at the snack wagon)—was a pleasing change from pushing into a subway car with crowds of strangers, some of whom pressed up against him in a most personal way. But it didn't take him very long, perhaps half a year, to see this adventure for what it really was: a very long haul which, under the continual pressures of the clock, and a continual rattling of one's organs, wearied the mind and body. It took him somewhat longer to learn what it did to the soul.

Each weekday morning Bruce March would fall out of bed at 6 AM, pull on his trousers in the chilled dimness, gulp down a cup of leftover coffee, peck his wife's sour mouth, race the car fifteen miles to the railroad station, and leap into the train just as it was pulling away. In the city he used to get up at 8, sometimes 8:15, and he still got in around 9 AM via the subway—except when they had a derailment or a fire in one of the tunnels. Nowadays he used so many forms of transportation in the course of a single trip that he never knew when he'd arrive, nor in what condition.

First there were the mornings when the four cylinders in the maroon, 1993 Ford refused to kick over. But assuming it did get going, then the train might be held up due to "signal trouble," or the "lights and heat went down," or a "shortage of rolling stock" would force many of them to stand all the way to Philadelphia. These verbal vaguenesses were delivered by men in dark blue uniforms, near as Bruce could tell, to keep passengers off balance, as if the railroad believed the less the passengers knew, the better. Even when the car started, and the train got through without mishaps or a "labor action," Bruce still had to deal with the subway, which had its own tendencies toward instability—and for reasons that were kept equally secret via worthless statements over staticky loudspeakers: "We have encountered a red signal." Bruce March now understood why conductors on trains and subways wore zookeepers' hats.

The distances involved should've meant a two-hour journey in each direction; usually it worked out, door-to-door, to around two and a half hours and, on rarer occasions—a snowstorm, power outage, or a train farther up (or down) the line had flattened a car (and its driver) at a crossing—it could be as long as four hours one way. One morning when the train showed up fifty-four minutes later, a brooding Bruce March tallied the average commuting time and found he was spending five to five and a quarter hours in transit nearly every weekday—about twenty-six hours a week, or more than three eight-hour work days. He was astonished, and immediately shared these findings with the attorney for a collection agency, a regular on the train, seated next to him. Slowly the man shifted his gray eyebrows away from the lined yellow pad he was scribbling on and inquired of Bruce: "How long have you been on this route?"

"About a year."

The attorney laughed with regulated condescension. "There is a woman in the first car who has been riding this line every day for thirty years."

This news stunned Bruce. Pulling the thin calculator out of the inside pocket of his suit jacket, he began poking the yellow buttons with his index finger and figured that the tenacious woman who rode in the first car had been traveling no fewer than 39,000 hours, and had used up the equivalent of four and a half years, twenty-four hours a day, seven days a week, in a train or subway car! And when he thought of how many things could be done with one thousand, six hundred and forty-two days of one's life—the love to be made, the books to be read, the stamps to be put in his album, the movies to be watched on the VCR, the recreation room to be paneled, the camping trips to be taken with the kids...or just that extra hour or two of shut-eye in the morning, Bruce lowered his lids so he could be depressed in private.

A few weeks before Bruce had completed the second year of his tour of duty, the 5:33 PM diesel broke down between stations, halfway home. Everyone was ordered to get off; they had to wait for another engine to arrive and pull the dead locomotive out of the way and then to hook up with the passenger cars. Standing out on the large, unstable chunks of railroad gravel in the bleakness, leaning into the damp, raspy wind with several hundred icy-lipped commuters, he questioned whether it was all worth it. Late that night—when he finally threw his briefcase down on the sofa at home, tired and hungry and frustrated—he complained bitterly to his wife (his children had already gone to bed) about the "constant torture" and "financial drain" of commuting. "One trip takes more out of me than a full day of selling those lousy one-inch ads!"

Bonnie was surprised, and slightly alarmed; her mind had entirely foreclosed on those four rooms back in the city, and she could not have moved back into an apartment any more than she could have gone to work in a coal mine. Patting her brown (beginning to gray) hair nervously, she quickly scraped the stiff pink spaghetti out of the pot onto a plate and said, "But honey, look at all the space we have."

Bruce made the mistake of aiming his bloodshot eyes through the archway into the living room: The armchairs and end tables were cluttered with shampoo bottles and pens and used tissues and earrings and dirty socks and magazines and dog biscuits. It seemed to him that the house was closing in on them, that more space merely created the need for more things they couldn't afford in order to fill that space. Peering down at the sticky jumble of spaghetti before him, he declared, "That's not space, that's chaos!"

"You have to get up early," Bonnie replied. "Why don't you go to bed?"

Next morning, even before unfolding his *Philadelphia Inquirer* on the train, Bruce March said to Jim Bulge, "Our lives are not made of inches or dollars. Our lives are made of minutes and hours."

This comment, out of nowhere, smacked a little too much of philosophy to suit a man who sold hardware wholesale all day, so Jim grew defensive: "The bums on skid row have all the time in the world, but not a nickel to spend or a square foot of their own to stand in."

Although they never had the time to get together "on the outside," Bruce and Jim considered themselves good friends—confidants and advisors who shared the trials of selling goods and services along with the tribulations of the daily commute, and whose perspective, therefore, could be trusted. Just like that, Jim had enabled Bruce to see that he was a lot better off than a lot of other people. From that day on Bruce complained less and less about "the grind," as the regulars affectionately called the round-trip, and thought less and less about returning to the city. Anyway, the rents had tripled since his family had moved out, and he really did enjoy having a yard and basement and all that went with it. On his workbench sat a Stanley plane, plus a circular saw from Sears; he had a dream of one day building his own pool table. Unfortunately, he rarely seemed to have the time to use his tools—at least not for making things. Weekends he spent recovering from the week of travel and repairing whatever had gone wrong with the house and car during the week. By 6 AM Monday he was exhausted.

On a bright spring morning, a young man whom Bruce did not know sat down beside him in the train. Bruce was a little put off because the regulars like to sit with regulars. But the younger man, who seemed as free and easy as a traveling salesman, started talking to him in a friendly way and, to Bruce's surprise, turned out to be fairly agreeable. Employed at a stock brokerage, he was hoping to get his broker's license one day so he could live comfortably without working too hard, he said with a smile. At one point in the conversation about their jobs and homes, however, the younger man said something that made Bruce wary: "How long have you been doing this commute?"

Without flinching, Bruce replied, "Five years."

"Phew!"

Bruce cranked up a superior smile. "You'll get used to it."

"I doubt it."

"There's a woman in the first car who's been riding these rails thirty-five years."

The younger man looked at Bruce with stretched, stricken eyes, and then grew untalkative. Bruce remembered how he'd felt years earlier, before his hair had acquired a salt-and-pepper look, but it didn't seem so terrible any longer. It was just something that had to be done, so he did it. Besides, he had made some lifelong friends on the train—they played cards, analyzed the Eagles football games, discussed the accomplishments (or failures) of their kids, told bitterly amusing anecdotes about their mothers-in-law, read racy passages from paperbacks aloud, described in detail how they'd told off their bosses, rehashed some grisly murder they'd seen reported on television, complained of how increasingly difficult it was getting to sell whatever it was they happened to sell, and in general managed to kill the time very effectively; five or six hours only seemed like two or three at most.

At the end of a long day at the office, Bruce would look forward to pulling himself up on the 5:33 to be reunited with his comrades, to find out how certain situations—the stories put on hold when they'd reached the station in the morning—had turned out for them during the day. Or to resume their card game. Or to tell a hot new joke. Or to hear how someone had landed (or lost) a huge sale. Since the regulars spent the best part of their days and evenings with each other, stimulated by their conversations, as well as by the beer and wine and whiskey some brought on board, by the time they lowered themselves off the train, somewhere between 7 and 9 PM, depending upon their particular destination and how late the train was, their vitality and imagination and equilibrium were shot. After a luke-warm—often cold—dinner, and an hour or so of TV, a quick shower, and another sexless night, the process was begun all over again.

At home on Saturdays, Bruce would keep jumping up out of his armchair, as if late for an appointment. "Why don't you relax?" Bonnie would say with annoyance. This only made him more nervous, and he would stomp around the house barking for no apparent reason, making unreasonable demands on his wife and ordering his children about. Once he even kicked the dog: Andrew, Barbara, and Charlie stared at him as if he were one those escaped lunatics who chatter to themselves on city streets. Since he loved all of them, including Dusty the dog, Bruce knew he was behaving badly. But he didn't know why, having come to believe he'd gotten used to the relentless travel required to enable him to peddle trade advertising all day long in the city.

Each of the regulars expressed this frustration in his or her own special way. Quite a few became functioning alcoholics or got into cocaine (the cocaine crowd, according to his pal Jim, occasionally shared a snort with Nicko, the train's engineer). Some beat their wives and children. One accountant, it was rumored, started embezzling funds from her company, hoping to amass enough to escape the grind permanently. Several tried to write books (in transit) that were loaded with sex and violence. Yet others fell in love on the train, carrying on more or less complete relationships on the plastic-covered coil springs without, as far as anyone knew, meeting in the world beyond the railroad car. And two or three gave their lives in the line of duty. Such was the fate of the woman who had been riding the train for thirty-seven years. As the story was told on the 5:33, the regulars in the first car had simply assumed she was sleeping, as she often did, until her stop came and they couldn't wake her up. A newcomer (only fourteen months on track) in Bruce's car, had joked that she'd died at the office and simply showed up on the 5:33 out of habit.

After years and years of rolling back and forth over the rails, an incident occurred that linked the commuters in Bruce's train in a permanent way. As usual, his crowd began to gather in the last car from about 5:10 PM on, saving seats for their pals who couldn't get out of the office as early, thereby excluding the one-time or part-time riders from their circle. Seats were swung back so that four of them could face each other, and they pulled cardboard ad posters off the wall to use as tables across their knees; this was done in different sections of the car, spreading their domination throughout. Their community had developed to the degree that none of them felt comfortable, safe, until all the regular faces were accounted for, as though they would all be slightly less able to undergo the rigors of the trip unless they all did it together.

On this particular winter's night, just as the train rolled out from under the sloped tin roof of the terminal, Bruce came scrambling up the stairs from the subway and made a last desperate dash to catch up, running so hard he felt a sharp pain in his chest. But the boarding gate was closed, and the train pulled entirely free of the station; with briefcase in hand, he stood there rattling with outrage. It wasn't merely that the last of his energy had been completely wasted, that he would get home late again. What made it much worse was that he would be deprived of the company of his friends, of the beer and potato chips at day's end that made the routine seem less oppressive, of telling the story about a typographical error in an ad which became a profanity in print. Over and over he cursed the subway which had made him late. At last he turned and dragged his feet, like an obstinate child, toward a food stand, where he swallowed two hot dogs (mustard and sauerkraut) without tasting them.

In the last car on the train, his pals felt equally deprived, vaguely hollow; they began, as they did in all such cases, to speculate why Bruce wasn't on the train, starting with the most likely—a late subway train—but including a sales meeting that had run on too long. "Maybe he had to stay downtown to do some shopping," one of them wondered out loud. "Definitely not; he would've mentioned it this morning." After reviewing all the possibilities, they relented, agreeing to get to the bottom of this matter the next morning. The regulars settled into their conversations and card games and drinking and romances. But something was missing inside each of them.

In a wooded stretch of eastern Pennsylvania the 5:33 plunged into a dense, driving snowstorm; the train slowed down, hesitated a few times, then rolled forward more smoothly, though more slowly. When the interior lights went out, the card players moaned with annoyance, and someone called out, "Here we go again!" But the lovers were delighted by the darkness, snuggling deeper into their seats, squeezing each other's knees, touching breasts and brushing lips. The regulars were so attuned to the syncopations of the train that any alteration in its rhythm was a signal to them, so when the train began to pick up speed despite the storm, someone said, "What the hell's Nicko trying to prove? —hope no one gave him a whiff tonight." The commuters laughed nervously in the darkness. Now the train began to hesitate again with a series of short, jarring jerks. Many of the passengers peered out the windows, something they rarely did on the return trip, but it was impossible to see anything in the snow-blown night.

At the station Bruce March entered the waiting room, a cavernous opening between a marble floor and metal-ribbed skylight, and gazed up at the huge round clock: 5:41. He checked it against his watch: 5:41. With forty-two minutes to kill before the next train, he started wandering around between the shellacked wooden benches, finally stopping before the newsstand at one end. Reading the headline of the evening daily—MAD DAD SLAYS SON & EX-WIFE AT BIRTHDAY PARTY—he was tempted to pick up a copy, but he felt too edgy to read. Though he'd been trying to stop smoking, he bought a pack of cigarettes instead and drifted among the white and black and gray faces of the commuters. Occasionally a face seemed familiar, though not enough to speak to. He looked up at the clock again: 5:47. Thirty-six minutes to go.

After another five minutes had passed, Bruce sat down on a bench, not far from a woman with short-clipped hair who was tapping her black shoe impatiently on the shiny floor.

"Missed your train, too?" he inquired.

"Why *else* would I be sitting around this dump!" she spat, getting up and striding toward the coffee machine.

The whole world has gone nuts tonight, Bruce thought. Instead of increasing his annoyance, however, the sight and sound of the woman's agitation enabled Bruce to see his own situation more clearly. He moved to the door of the station, opened the pack of cigarettes, tapped one out, lit it, and took a few puffs. Soon he felt more relaxed. As a result, the hands of the clock seemed to skid along at a more merciful pace, for when he looked at his wrist it was 6:11. By this time he had pretty much accepted the separation from his traveling mates.

Bruce collected his briefcase and went out to where the trains nosed into the station. But the 6:23 had not pulled in at Gate 9. This was unusual. Generally a train would be in the station twenty to thirty minutes ahead of departure to receive passengers; this also allowed time for the engineer to check out the locomotive and for the conductors to clear out the leftover tabloids and coffee cups and snack wrappers. By 6:17 the train still had not arrived, and Bruce's stomach began to tighten like a fist again. By 6:30 the train had not appeared through the fine snow which had begun to fall, and the railroad personnel standing around with hands in pockets could tell the inquiring passengers no more than what was obvious. By 6:37 Bruce was muttering curses at the train, the station, at the unseen figures who ran the railroad.

At 6:44 he decided to call Bonnie and tell her to go ahead and eat dinner without him. The phone was busy. He dialed again and again. "I'm going to beat the hell out of those kids—they've got to stop tying up the phone when I'm trying to call home!" Bruce said this out loud, and as a means of getting back at whatever it was that seemed determined to complicate his life, he slammed down the receiver with a crash. The noise caused him to look around, and standing not fifteen feet away was a policeman in his navy blue uniform and cap, looking directly at him. His left hand rested on his hip, and his right hand was at his hip, too, only the heel of his hand rested on the handle of the revolver, his fingers drumming the black leather holster, as if itching to pull out the gun and aim it at Bruce.

No law against slamming down a receiver, Bruce said to himself, wondering if the cop had heard him threaten to beat his kids. Bruce turned away from the phone and pretended to look for the train, but he could feel the policeman's eyes on him. *You keep spying on me,* he thought with a smirk, *and I'll take that gun out of your holster and shoot you, the dispatcher, the ticket clerk, and maybe a redcap for good measure.* Bruce March was not a violent person, but at that moment he was able to appreciate how that father had gone berserk and gunned down his own son and ex-wife.

By 6:53 there was no sign of his train, nor any indication of when it could be expected, so Bruce left the cop standing there and pushed into the Commuter's Café. He climbed up on a stool and demanded a Stroh's. The bushy-faced bartender growled at the customer's tone. As Bruce took a long, steady swallow from the mug, he wondered who was winning the pinochle game on the train. After a few more swallows of beer, he glanced out the window and saw the cop standing near the door of the café, hands on hips. "What doe *he* want?" Bruce mumbled.

"Did you ask for another beer?" said the bartender, looking away from the television to face his customer.

"I wasn't talking to you."

The bartender slapped a towel across the bar and turned his back on Bruce.

Bruce looked up at the television. It was too early for the 76ers game; instead they had a game show on—the host, flashing long white teeth, was spinning a large wheel with red, green, and black numbers. Four dumpy-looking men and women were standing before the host, giggling. *Typical American consumers,* Bruce thought. To kill more time he fantasized about walking into the television station waving that cop's revolver, and he imagined himself squeezing off four shots until all the contestants lay in a heap. *By the way,* he said silently to the host, *I've saved the last two bullets to blast that grin off your face.*

Bruce wasn't sure what time it happened, but the picture went off the screen and there appeared a man with thinning hair in a pale blue shirt and purple tie, seated at an oval desk, holding a sheet of paper. The words NEWS BULLETIN kept blinking along the bottom edge of the screen as the man spoke in short, tight sentences: "The five thirty-three express out of Philadelphia, destined for Harrisburg, has collided with another train that had broken down earlier in a heavy snowstorm. Initial reports indicate the engineer of the five thirty-three ran a flashing red stop signal. At this hour firemen and rescue workers are attempting to free passengers from the fiery wreckage. While it is too early to assess injuries and damage, authorities fear that many have died. Our news team is on the scene to bring you the following live report...."

A woman in a short fur coat blinked onto the screen and began speaking quickly into the microphone in her hand, the frosty breath shooting out of her bright red mouth, the snow swirling around her blonde head. Now the camera turned away, presenting images of twisted and crumpled steel, of dense smoke pouring out of shattered windows, while men in rubber coats and hard helmets moved like rats over the carcass of the train.

A collective cry arose in the café, followed quickly by silence. Everyone sat so still, staring at the TV, that they seemed to be bolted to the heavy stools, the wooden bar and tables. Wondering if his friend Jim Bulge had gotten out of the wreckage okay, Bruce peered at the scene to see if he could recognize anyone. Now Bruce noticed a narrow white thing lying parallel to a sprung section of track; he realized it was a human arm, and a not unpleasant shiver passed through his body.

Just as suddenly as it had gone off the air, the game show returned, and the host, that same grin stuck on his flat face, was in the act of spinning the painted wheel. The café grew noisy again, a congested sound of humanity rising slowly, steadily. Bruce glanced out the window. The cop had disappeared. Sliding off the stool and pushing through the swinging door, he went out into the station without realizing he'd left his briefcase behind. Others came out of the café, rushing past him, and as the news of the accident spread through the terminal, the movement around Bruce seemed to become as herky-jerky as Keystone Kops dashing about in a silent movie. Peering over his shoulder, he saw no sign of the policeman and, without checking the clock, he entered Gate 9.

The snow was whipping thickly over the platform, but he did not bother to button his coat. For a long while he looked out along the pair of rails, polished by the immense weight they had supported over the years, searching for the great white eye of the train. The distant darkness held together in one piece. Though it was cold in the wind and snow, and though the passengers counting on the 6:23 had dispersed, Bruce March continued to stand out and wait for his train. It was printed on the timetable. Eventually it had to show up. And when it did, he wanted to move close to those shiny rails, so comforting in their parallel harmony, and watch the giant wheels of steel roll toward him.

"Come on over and take a closer look."

"Couldn't hurt, I suppose."

"Little old preacher owned this rig, and he'd still be driving it around if he hadn't been called to his maker."

"Black isn't my favorite color."

"These days most of your finer automobiles are black."

"Too morbid for my tastes."

"This model's worth repainting just to get a really well-built machine—made to last."

"They don't make things very well these days, that's for sure. Look at this shirt: two months old and coming apart already at the seams."

"Then you ought to try this baby on for size and feel some old-fashioned quality for a change. Go ahead, get in. Sit down. Feel a solid chassis under you."

"Well, I don't know if—"

"Sure, get behind the wheel and start 'er up. No obligation whatsoever."

"Maybe for a minute...."

"There! Isn't that a comfortable seat?"

"Kind of...firm."

"Just make sure she's in neutral, flip on the ignition switch, and push the starter button—conveniently located right there on the dashboard."

"No keys? How old is this vehicle, anyway?"

"It's been around the block a few times, but what does that matter when something's constructed with the best materials and workmanship?"

"I guess you're right. Okay, I'll start it up." Err-err-err-err. "Say, why doesn't it start?"

"You have to pull the choke all the way out—any mechanic'll tell you that manual chokes were the best. The automatics are always getting stuck."

"I see." Err-err-err-err-err. "Still won't run."

"Hit the gas pedal a coupla times. That's it. Now try the starter."

Err-err-err-err-err-err. "What's wrong with it?"

"Looks like you've flooded her, that's all. Why don't you listen to the radio while the carb's drying out. You'll love the way it sounds."

"Okay...." Click. "Say, I can't seem to get any stations to come in."

"Oh, then it's probably too late. Most stations have gone off the air by now."

"It's only four in the afternoon."

"Yeah, they've been signing off earlier and earlier. Anyway I guarantee that radio's like new. Little old preacher thought radio was evil so he never turned it on. Ha! Ha! Ha! Ha!"

"I'll try the other end of the dial.... All I can get out of it is some humming noise."

"Maybe we better shut it off—don't want to run the battery down, right?"

"Right."

"Now, don't touch the gas pedal this time; switch on the ignition, and press the starter."

"Okay." Err-err-err—Vroom!

"What did I tell you? Runs like a charm."

"Hasn't been started in quite a while, I suppose—that smoke is thick."

"Listen to that engine purr."

"Not bad."

"Go ahead—rev it up."

Vroom! Vroom! Vroom!

"'Nother hundred thousand miles left in that baby."

"All I want is reliable transportation. Until I can afford something...newer."

"In that case this is the perfect set of wheels for you: couldn't beat this value anywhere, anytime."

"By the time it's spray-painted, and the upholstery gets fixed up, I wonder how much of a bargain it would be."

"Upholstery? Could use a bit of freshening up, maybe. Brush off the dust. Tuck in the edges. Otherwise it's held up real good."

"It's worn thin on the armrests; the cloth has turned yellow. Must be difficult to keep clean."

"Not any more than today's synthetics, and satin's a lot classier. Don't make upholstery like they did in the old days, no sir. And look at all that space in back—a body could lie down and catch a few winks without being crowded."

"Maybe so, but it's kind of...creepy."

"My friend, you are sitting in the lap of luxury."

"Well, I don't know about that, but it does seem to be solid."

"Built like a tank!"

"Say, the smoke has cleared up."

"You kidding? That engine'll outlast all of us. Guess you'd better cut it off; no sense burning up gas standing still."

"Sure. What I don't understand is why this is the only vehicle left on the lot. Last time I passed by here, I saw cars lined up in rows. What happened to the rest of them?"

"Sold. Every last one of 'em sold. Way things are going these days, if I were you I'd jump at this buy."

"In department stores, too, the goods are running low, and they're not being restocked. Same thing has started happening in the supermarkets."

"Yeah, everything everywhere's being sold off."

"How is that possible?"

"Efficiency, my friend, efficiency. And if I were you, I wouldn't wait very long to make a decision on this fine vehicle, or you're gonna lose out."

"How much cash up front are you asking?"

"At Friendly's you don't need a down payment."

"Really? But if I wanted to buy it I'd have to take out a loan, and I don't think the banks would give me one just now. I'm, well, temporarily out of work. That's why I need the transportation: to get around so I can find another job."

"No problem. You deal directly with Friendly's so you don't need to get a loan, which means you don't have to pay crazy interest rates, either."

"No down payment! No loan! No interest! I've never heard of anything like this before."

"That figure on the windshield is the full price—no hidden costs."

"When would I have to start paying it off? And in what amounts? How long would I have?"

"Pay whatever you can manage, whenever you like."

"Are you serious?"

"Before the newspapers folded, these policies were printed in our last ad campaign."

"Terms like that are pretty difficult to turn down."

"Best Deal on Wheels! That's our motto."

"You've made a believer out of me. Where do I sign?"

"A handshake'll be fine. I can see you're a man we can trust."

"What? I think I'm pretty honest, but this is a very strange way to do business."

"Why do you think we've sold all our cars and trucks except one, young man?"

"I see."

"When the customer is satisfied, Friendly's sales increase. When the customer is not satisfied, Friendly's sales decrease."

"You'll need my name and address."

"We know who you are. We know where you live. All you need to do is start the engine and drive away."

"That's all?"

"Start the engine, and drive away."

"Say, this is really a great way to buy something."

"The only way."

"Where's the nearest gas station?"

"Five miles down the road."

Err-err-err-Vroom!

"Well, I'll see you around. And thanks. Thanks for everything."

"It's our pleasure to serve you...."

After the vehicle rolled away over the pavement, the friendly salesman said to no one in particular, "So long, sucker. The gasoline is all sold out, too."